MISFITS ANONYMOUS

MISFITS ANONYMOUS

DOROTHY COLLINS

AUTHOR OF NO TIME FOR DADDY'S GIRL

In Memory of my late daughter Bonnie
She inspired me to publish the novels I wrote.
Thank you to my family for their support.
and
Thank you to Terry Unger in appreciation
of her encouragement
and words of wisdom

Animals do not demand anything.
All you have to do is love them.

Chapter One

*T*he day started like any typical day except for one difference. Matt was late for his time with his dog. The dog was miffed, and Matt was scowling. A bad start to what was supposed to be a companionable outing.

Matt took off down the path only to be pulled up by Suzette. Yes, Suzette. The dog was his brother's idea of a joke saddling him with a White Pekingese named Suzette. He could have given him a Great Dane or Springer Spaniel, not Donny. Despite her looks and name, Matt had grown fond of Suzette, except for this morning. She would not budge until Matt apologized. A dog with demands. I think not. Matt started pulling, but Suzette must have been glued to the ground because there was no moving her.

Coming towards them was another dog and its owner, a petite blonde with a Chihuahua, named Oscar. Now Oscar may be miniature in stature, but he was as large as a Labrador in his mind. He went past Suzette with his nose and tail in the air and a growl from his lips. The noise of a massive dog.

Suzette became detached from the ground and hid behind Matt. Matt was still mad at her for her previous behavior of making him grovel or trying.

"Looks good on you, Suzette," Matt announced with a sneer at her cowering.

The petite blonde apologized for her dog's ferocious attitude. "He is just protecting me. Come, Oscar." She smiled sweetly and took off, her dog prancing down the path.

Suzette wasn't going to be outdone by this male chauvinist, now leaping down the path dragging Matt with her. They passed the Chihuahua at a gallop. Matt was now the one to apologize. He felt ridiculous chasing after a half-pint dog all six feet two inches of him. But when Suzette finally got motivated, Matt wasn't about to stop her. He liked a good jog in the morning, which ended all too soon when Suzette suddenly stopped. Matt nearly went ass over teakettle.

"Now what? You think Oscar has an attitude. Well, believe me, Suzette, you are the one with an attitude." Matt roared, hoping to humiliate her. No way, Suzette was here to stay.

Dog number two was heading towards them. Now here is a dog, thought Matt. It was a Mastiff. Sensing Matt's approval of the Mastiff, Suzette nipped at the dog in passing. Suzette is no shrinking violet and had surprised Matt at her reaction to Oscar.

Again, Matt apologized, now to a leggy redhead with a figure to match. Bruno, as the redhead called him, was crouching on the ground. He couldn't believe what his eyes were seeing. Suzette was now prancing along. Matt's silly grin was quite evident.

Along the path came dog number three. No one can relate to dogs like a dog owner, and this one needed relating to because it was so ugly, Matt noted as the dog passed him. The dog's ancestry was questionable. The charming strawberry blonde owner was calling him 'Handsome.'

Handsome, was that ever a misnomer.

Suzette latched onto Handsome and started prancing by his side. Matt tried to drag her back, but no, she wasn't having any of that. How could Matt walk beside this blonde female he didn't even know nor wanted to know? But Suzette was not letting up.

The blonde did her best to ignore Matt, but Handsome wasn't ignoring Suzette. By Handsome's reaction, he was looking for a permanent relationship.

Matt chirped. "Good morning." He had to be amiable as their steps were in sync.

The surprising answer, "not really." The strawberry blonde thought. *Why didn't this bozo get lost?*

Usually, dog owners are friendly to other dog owners under these circumstances, thought Matt.

They were coming to a fork in the path. Suzette always went to the right on the shorter route and less exercise being a creature of habit.

Not today, she went to the left, and Suzette gave a cute yip toward Handsome, inviting him that way too. Matt usually wanted this path for the added distance but not this morning. Not when he was doing double time beside a reluctant female that could call 'rape' at any moment.

Matt stopped. Who is the boss here, anyway? His arm nearly yanked out of its socket. He was propelled forward into the woman who was doing her best to ignore him. The blonde being unprepared for this added weight, fell face down with her leashed wrist and Suzette's lead under her

Matt landed spread eagle on top of her. Matt was hampered by circling dogs that had jumped over them and held the now twisted leashes taut, further hindered by Suzette's leash under the blonde so that he couldn't roll off her immediately.

The young woman had gone down with a whoosh. The breath knocked out of her. Aided by his six feet, two inches of pure masculine brawn, she was flattened and unable to move.

Recovering her breath, she demanded, "get off me, Oaf."

"I would, but I'm kind of tied up here." He was trying to untangle the dogs, hindered by both licking his face. You have never been loved until two tongues, both canine, lather you and one of these tongues is massive.

The leggy redhead's appearance added to the plight because her haughty "really!" expressed her fury and disproval of his behavior.

The woman on the bottom yelled, "help me. I'm being attacked."

Matt thought, *Humm, she is being attacked. What about him and her dog's massive tongue? He was the one under attack.*

Before Matt could roll off the blonde as he had freed himself enough to do so, the redhead changed her perception of the situation. She started hitting Matt over the head with her purse, which caused him to sink away from the blows and grind his masculine body more deeply into the female under him.

"Pervert! Pervert!" was the redhead's lament.

Matt certainly felt like the underdog here, and no pun intended. He hadn't created this situation. It was Suzette aided by Handsome.

This sweet young thing pinned under him was yelling, "help me. Help me."

The redhead was still pounding him with her purse. "Pervert! Pervert!"

If he wasn't in the middle of the situation, he would think it was funny in more ways than one. But he was in the middle, and that purse felt like it contained a week's supply of canned dog food. So, he would be black and blue for weeks, heck for months.

How was he going to repair the situation? He couldn't think while this redhead she-devil was raining blows of such magnitude. She must be one of those bodybuilding females in bathing suits you see on television, flexing their muscles like men. Oh, where was I? Oh yes, how can I recover the situation? *Wham! Wham!* This has got to stop. Matt threw up his arm, grabbing the purse on the upswing. His arm nearly dismembered. Thanks to the dogs' movements, he was still tied up on the ground. The handbag was on the downswing, but he could deflect it.

"Hey! I am not having fun here. I need help."

The leggy redhead was knocked off balance by his deflection of the purse. She fell on top of him, squirming. On any other occasion, he might appreciate that, but not under these circumstances.

Just then, two male joggers put in their appearance. Now, what is a man supposed to do? When tied by the twisted leads over him, one woman under him, and one squirming on top, but yell. "Rape! Rape! Help me?" in his best masculine voice. Would the guys at the office believe this?

Not wanting to be put off stride, the two joggers were jogging in place, looking the situation over.

Jogger #1 said, "should we leave him to his fate, Tony?"

Jogger #2 said, "no way, let's spoil his fun, Ray."

Fun? Where is this guy coming from? He obviously isn't in the middle of this fiasco.

"Let's join in the fun." Jogger #2 adds in a lustful voice. He grabbed the redhead, but her dog tried to bite him. But, he still managed to lift her off the pack. Suzette and Handsome watched the proceedings with great interest. Front row seats to a comedy of errors.

The redhead didn't take kindly to her jogger captor and pelted him. Ray was laughing.

Now Tony yelled, "help."

I know how he feels that purse had such a big wham to it, and her arm moved like a jackhammer.

Not to be outdone in this situation, along comes a husband and wife with two dogs. The dogs both decide to get in on the fun, dived in tangling the leads more, barking up a storm to the wife's, "really! What is going on here, Albert?" in a shriek of disgust. The husband, a man who enjoyed jokes immensely, took in the situation and arrived at a funny scenario, stood there and laughed.

Just what the occasion needed, laughter. Albert wasn't the one on the ground tied to a squirming angry female and two dogs barking in his ear.

At last, the joggers made some headway. Tony had the offending purse on the ground. An angry female clamped immobile in his arms. Ray was trying to untangle the leads, which were under the two people on the path.

The angry female underneath Matt had the leash on her wrist trapped beneath her. So, the jogger removed the lead from Handsome instead. Handsome had a front-row seat, and he wasn't about to leave until the comedy was over.

The laughing husband gagster finally straightened, got his dogs under control, and handed them to his wife, who had stopped shrieking. He then helped Ray remove the restraining leashes while yelling his name and phone number. It turned out he was a lawyer and thought that someone here must want to sue for damages.

Matt realized that he was almost free, and the poor female crushed under him must be feeling quite squashed and bruised under his solid bodyweight. On the other hand, she might be memorizing that moron's name and phone number.

Jogger #1 finally pulled Matt up. Matt turned and pulled the girl up off the ground. She had been innocent in all of this other than her calls for help. As soon as she gained her footing, she shook off his hands.

"Are you hurt?" Matt asked in concern.

"Hurt! Hurt!" she flung at him in a frustrated, strangled voice. "I will never be the same."

Matt thought that was poignant in that this was supposed to have been a quiet walk through the woods. Although this had all played out in a matter of minutes, it felt like hours since he left home, and he lived two blocks away.

"Well, I'm inclined to agree with you," Matt replied lamely.

The redhead, having had enough of the jogger's hands of steel, demanded to be released. The grinning jogger was rather enjoying having the attractive female plastered against him. In an overly innocent voice, he inquired, "are you okay? I didn't hurt you, did I?"

The redhead pulled back with a glare and didn't deem to reply. So, jogger #1 handed her the offending purse, and she grabbed her dog's lead and took off immediately.

Now the lawyer was trying to hand out his cards, much to everyone's annoyance. Especially the two from the ground trying to recover their dignity and dogs.

Parting company, no one exchanged names. The joggers took off, still laughing. The wife dragged the lawyer idiot away, leaving the original two. Now, both were having a glaring match.

"You are such an oaf. Do you know that?" she said through gritted teeth. She was so angry.

"Well, I didn't exactly arrange for this to happen. Give me a break, lady. After all, I was the one taking the beating from that ferocious redhead and her ten-ton purse that you called into the mishap. Just as I was about to roll off of you, like the proper gentleman that I am," Matt said, puffing it out indignantly.

"Hah, gentleman, you don't know the meaning of the word." Pushing hair out of her eyes.

"Do so, it means . . ."

She cut him off. "Well, you certainly aren't one in my books, that is."

He looked around. "You have books?"

She broke out laughing, unable to retain her anger at his latest comment. "You know what I mean."

"Now that you have calmed down, I apologize. I didn't mean to hurt you or your dignity. Will you let me apologize by taking you out to dinner? Show? Walk? A crawl?"

Once again, pushing her hair out of her eyes and laughing. "No, thanks. I think I will quit while I'm ahead. At least I can still walk."

Matt, the perfect gentleman, commented, "good. I'll walk with you to make sure you don't run into any more mishaps."

"I think not."

"Which way are you going?" ignoring her comment.

"That way, I am completing the circuit." Her hand pointed to the left.

"Suzette, would you like to go back or complete the circuit?"

Suzette took off after Handsome, the decision made. Catching up to the blonde, he tried once again. "I am truly sorry about that fiasco back there."

She promptly ignored him.

"Fine, don't accept my apology, but don't say I didn't try. Suzette, are you enjoying your walk?"

Suzette woofed in a pleasant reply, and Handsome followed suit. They were happy to be together even if their owners weren't.

Matt felt ridiculous. Would this ever end? What had started as an 'oh hum' walk had turned into anything but. It was time he finished it. He stopped, ordered Suzette to halt, and reversed direction. Neither Suzette nor Handsome were pleased. Both emitted plaintive noises of sad parting. Matt and Handsome's owner ignored the sounds, and each went their own way.

When Matt got back to the house, Suzette disappeared with an air of disdain. Matt didn't see her for hours. He should kill his brother for saddling him with such a feminine dog with an attitude.

Chapter Two

Matt and Suzette now took their walks on the Riverside path that took them far from their usual walk. He had to drive to this path. It wasn't that he was afraid to go back to the disaster scene. But he figured it was best to let some time elapse before incurring any contact with the blonde dog owner. He was sure she felt rather disdainful towards him.

It wasn't as if he wasn't male enough to handle it, but he did like the Riverside path too. Yeah, keep telling yourself that, and then you will believe it. You know you found the blonde attractive.

*****

Monday, he was back in the office viewing the weekly reports when the intercom engaged. "Mr. Hadden, there is a young lady to see you regarding the McDonell account. She doesn't have an appointment. She is hoping that you could spare her some time. She does look like it is important to her, sir."

"Yes, I think I could fit her in. Please direct her to my office." Matt put aside the reports.

He hadn't looked up yet when he heard a shrill screech. "It's you."

Matt looked up, and there she stood in a suit, which he noticed was very becoming to her appearance. It was the young lady from the wood's fiasco. Matt stood up. *What could he say? Welcome to my lair.* No, that wouldn't do and settled for. "Yes, it's me. Good morning, Miss . . ." He stuck out his hand, reaching across the desk to her.

"Err, Diane Mackenzie." She barely touched his hand, then pulled back her hand in her astonishment. She didn't know what to do or say. Gone was her crisp, businesslike manner.

"Well, Diane Mackenzie, what can I do for you?" Waving her to a seat so she could sit down and give her a chance to recover.

"I didn't know you were Matt Hadden," Diane mumbled lamely as she awkwardly sat down. She was not the usual efficient person she liked to portray.

"Well, I didn't know you were Diane Mackenzie either. So, can we get down to business?" He continued in a businesslike behavior to save the situation. After all, he now realized that he might have to deal with this woman on more than one occasion if she handled the McDonell account.

Diane reached down into her briefcase to give herself time to recover her business persona. She couldn't believe that jerk from the woods was Mr. Hadden. Her fingers clumsily sought the prepared outline she had on the McDonell account.

Will she ever find what she is looking for soon? Obviously, she is reluctant to speak to me. How can I ease the situation?

Just then, her head popped up. She gave a half-smile and preceded like nothing occurred when she came into the office.

"Mr. Hadden, this is an outline of the method I will use to handle this account for you. My company can put its time and effort into completing this plan within the three months allotted. We are willing to obligate our staff to this commitment too." Diane hesitated, but he didn't respond.

"The outline shows that we can provide the tools and the know-how required for a smooth time-wise effort on our part. The cost is reasonable. The plan is feasible, and our method guarantees success, as shown by our past performances in this area of expertise."

Diane stood up to place the paper on his desk, but he made no effort to reach for it. He was just staring at her. Was he assessing the outline, or was he just watching her? She sat down again with an awkward bump as she almost missed the chair. She had miscalculated the distance it was back from the desk. She blushed in embarrassment. Why did he just sit there? Why does he just stare? Can I work with this jerk?

Matt, known for his hard-headed CEO no-nonsense manner, just sat there like a bump on a log watching her.

"Miss Mackenzie, what is the purpose or goal of your company? Is it to find yourselves amongst the top ten companies? Or is it to strive to be the best advertising company comparable to Howell & Davis?"

Diane was certainly not expecting that question. What about her outline? He hadn't even looked at it.

Now, why in the world would I ask her a question like that? Why don't I just stick to the outline? She is going to think I am ridiculing her.

"Mr. Hadden, my company is one of the top ten now, right behind Howell & Davis. But the point here is the outline. Will it be workable for your client? Do you want a different method, or is our method acceptable?"

Matt glanced down at the outline. It was neat and precise.

"No, it is not acceptable, Miss Mackenzie . . ." he paused.

Diane's face fell, but she quickly regained her composure. What does this man want? He wouldn't know a good plan if it stared him in the face, which it is.

"It is perfect." Matt finished with a smile.

Diane, not listening to his continued comment, said, "Mr. Hadden, this is definitely a workable plan. My company prides itself on its success. But if it is not to your satisfaction, I am sure we could work it out."

"Over dinner at eight?" he offered.

"Certainly not." *I don't go out with business associates.*

"Miss Mackenzie, you weren't listening. I repeat, I said it was perfect." His smile was more extensive. He had dimples in his cheeks.

Diane caught her breath at this handsome man. She had never noticed that before. Her anger at him stopped her from seeing him as a man that fateful day.

Matt stood up, knowing he had a 10:30 board meeting. However, he would much rather gaze at Miss Mackenzie.

"Thank you for coming in, but I am afraid I have a board meeting. I need to be there in five minutes. Leave the outline, and I will present it to them, along with the other applicants."

Diane rose to her feet, grabbing her briefcase, forgetting it was open in her haste. The papers fluttered everywhere as well as a calculator and pens.

Matt kept a straight face with some difficulty. "What do you do for an encore?"

Diane wanted to hit him, but she went down on her knees to recover her papers instead. *This was terrible. I cannot work with this man. I am an idiot around him. Why?*

"Nothing," she boomed.

Matt felt that his last comment, which failed as humor by her, was wrong of him. So, he bent down to help pick up some of the fallen papers surrounding his feet. He had only succeeded in making her mad again. Matt stood up and waited while she rose to her feet. He stuck out his hand with the papers. A picture of a man was on the top, a muscleman in a T-shirt and shorts, a blond Adonis.

"Is this an advertising gimmick?" he questioned grinning.

Diane blushed again. It was the picture Laura was showing around the office. Laura must've put it in her briefcase as a joke. Diane grabbed for the papers and the image.

"No, it isn't." She did not enlarge on that statement. *Let him think what he wants.* She wasn't about to set him straight. It wasn't any of his business.

"Well, Miss Mackenzie, I can see now why you refused my offer for dinner."

Diane glared at him, clicked her briefcase closed, grasping the handle and headed for the door. She opened it with her head held high, saying. "Thank you for seeing me, Mr. Hadden," as if it was an afterthought and sailed out of the door. She was sure he was laughing at her.

Matt, however, was not laughing. That picture disturbed him. He had hoped to follow up on his request for dinner at a later date to get to know this pretty blonde.

He headed out the door for the boardroom.

"Miss Canning, will you see if I have any appointments for this afternoon and put them on my desk?"

Miss Canning wondered what had gone on in the office. Something definitely had happened in there. The look of hurt pride on the lady and his abstract message about his appointments was unusual.

The board members approved Miss MacKenzie's outline over three other competitors' submissions. He wondered why her proposal was late. Was she a feather brain? If that blond Adonis is any example, perhaps she was. However, he knew from her remarks her company had a good reputation in the marketplace. There has to be a reasonable explanation.

When he returned to his office, he spoke to Miss Canning, who insisted on formal names between them during business hours.

"Please get Miss Mackenzie on the phone. She left a card, didn't she?"

Miss Canning replied, "yes, she did. I will put the call through to you." She picked up the phone and dialed as he entered his office.

Diane was back at work, reprimanding Laura for the Adonis picture and said that it was her fault if she lost the account.

"I felt like a silly schoolgirl with her first crush or first date in my clumsiness. He sure is a handsome man." Secretly smiling at the thought. A man I could easily fall for maybe.

Laura laughed hysterically as Diane portrayed a picture of her on her knees with papers scattered everywhere, as Matt thrust a photograph at her with the comment. "Is this an advertising gimmick?" knowing full well, he probably thought that it was Diane's boyfriend.

"Quit laughing. I don't want to lose this account. I was looking forward to working on it because I have spent a lot of time in preparation. So much time that I was almost too late in submitting." But in the end, she broke out laughing too. "I can't believe he is the same guy I told you about from the woods."

"Doesn't sound like your relationship has improved." Laura had finally managed to recover from her laughter.

"No, it hasn't, from my perception at least. Maybe I should let you handle the account if we get accepted."

"Oh, no. You spent a lot of time on that outline. It is your baby," replied Laura with feeling.

"Do you think I can work to my potential when I am cringing inside each time I am near him? That doesn't make for a good business relationship."

"You have run into creeps like this before and handled it with great aplomb, yet this time you are holding back." Laura smiled encouragingly.

"Well, this is beyond creep because he is a fascinating, handsome man. Rather nice looking, but he acts like a jerk around me. So, I lose my professionalism, like dumping my briefcase incident. I looked like a bumbling schoolgirl out of her element. I just can't see him again. The memory of the woods keeps popping into my head every time I look at him."

"Well, Diane, I am just too booked up with the Steward and Jones accounts, or I would help you, but you'll have to bumble along. Sorry." Laura wondered if Matt acted like a jerk and Diane acted like a schoolgirl around each other, could there be a plausible reason? Laura smirked at the prospect.

Diane grumbled and went back to her office with a gloomy air. She needed to ignore the situation and regain her positive approach to her everyday life, which had disappeared in the woods one day, and she was innocent in the whole melee. Come to think of it, Handsome has been different since that day too. He seems to moon around the house as though he has lost his best friend.

*****

Matt was pleased with the Board's approval. So, what if he asserted a little more pressure than usual to have Diane's outline accepted. Why should he feel guilty? It was excellent. But he knew he wanted it approved because he wanted to see Diane again. He was intrigued by her. Diane's work was second consideration in his mind.

He remembered how cute she'd looked when she realized in horror who he was. She knew that the man she would have to impress was the very man who had humiliated her on the path in the woods. Her self-vision had deflated. She had come off as an untested rookie. Matt was sure she never projected that in any other of her business dealings. He imagined her portrayal as being very efficient. Matt chuckled to himself as the intercom rang.

"Yes?"

"Miss Mackenzie on line one for you."

"Miss Mackenzie, Matt Hadden here. I just called to let you know that the Board members accepted your proposal. They think your outline has the potential to get the account completed to both our satisfactions." Matt had on his best business CEO voice.

Diane pulled the phone away from her ear and raised a hand in a cheer.

"Miss Mackenzie, are you there?"

"Yes, I am here," putting the receiver back to her ear. "Thank you. I look forward to working with your company.

Who will be my contact there?" Diane had her fingers crossed. Let it be someone else that she could work with.

"As a special concession to you. I thought you would be more comfortable working with me. So, I have arranged to be your contact on the McDonell Account. I usually don't get involved in the dealings in these accounts, but I thought I would in your case."

Just great, that's all I need. He decides to concede for me.

"Miss Mackenzie, are you still there? Do we have a bad connection?" Matt knew full well that Diane didn't want to work with him personally. But he liked the idea just fine. Here was his chance to get to know her better.

"Thank you for your faith in my work. I am looking forward very much to be working with you. But you don't have to put yourself out on my account. I am willing to work through normal channels." Diane replied through clenched teeth.

"No, I think it will be best if I handle the account with you, as it is already arranged. The dates are being set up as we speak. Miss Canning will contact you as soon as she has the details worked out. She will phone you for verification of the dates and times. I do my best work over meals, don't you? Well, until we get together for our first meeting, I'll say goodbye. Have a good day, Miss Mackenzie." Matt put the phone down while Diane sputtered.

He sat back in his chair, wheeling around to look out the window. Matt saw the city below him, and he felt like he was on top of the world. He was looking forward to working with Diane. Putting his hands behind his head with his feet up, he recalled Diane and her scattered papers at his feet. She was cute when she was flustered. Oh yes, this was going to be an enjoyable experience.

The intercom buzzed again.

"Yes?"

"Miss Mackenzie again, sir."

"Miss Mackenzie, what can I do for you?" Matt said in all innocence.

"I can't work with you. I mean, I cannot work with you at mealtimes. I am on a special diet, and it would make me uncomfortable to watch you eat."

"Miss Mackenzie, I am sorry to hear that. Have you had the condition long?"

"Condition, what condition?"

"The condition that has you on the special diet, of course."

"Oh, that condition. Yes, ah, ah, for several years, since my teens."

"I am sorry to hear that. I will have my secretary change it to some evenings instead."

"I don't work evenings. That just won't do. Could I not work with another colleague that has more daytime available?" Diane asked hopefully.

"Miss Mackenzie, I do think it is best if we leave the arrangement as is. I will try to free part of my schedule if you give me a little leeway and work with mine. A few evenings wouldn't be so bad, and maybe we could make arrangements for meals that suit your dietary requirements occasionally." Matt was trying not to chuckle. He felt sure this was her way of avoiding him.

"But! But! I prefer to work with someone else. Someone as busy as you shouldn't need to be concerned with this account."

"As I said, Miss Mackenzie, it has already been arranged. Do you want the job or not?"

Diane was hemmed in, and she knew it. It was work with him or lose the account.

"Yes. I want the account. Yes. I will work with you. I will be waiting for Miss Canning to call me, and maybe we can figure out an agreeable working arrangement." Diane was resigned to do this regardless of her personal feelings.

"I am pleased that you have come to that decision. Miss Canning will be contacting you very soon. Good day, Miss Mackenzie."

"Goodbye." Diane slumped down in her seat. Why was he doing this? Why couldn't she treat this in her usual proficient manner?

Straightening her stature, Diane said, "I can do this and be my masterful self. So, Mr. Hadden will not recognize me as the same person that floundered on the consultation."

Laura came in. "Well, did you get things settled with Mr. Hadden? Was your outline accepted?"

"Yes, he set it up so that I am working with him personally. He even stressed how busy he was but was willing to change his schedule to accommodate our working together."

"So, why do you look so unhappy? You got the account, didn't you?"

"He wants to do our business over meals or evenings." Diane didn't look happy.

"Oh! Oh! Sounds like trouble. Are you going to do it?" Laura was looking at Diane appraisingly. Evenings and meals, oh, yes, that is interesting.

"Not if I can help it. Matt's secretary will be calling to verify the times and places. I am going to squash as many mealtimes and evenings as possible. I told him I don't do meals because of my condition. I am on a special diet."

"That is a good idea."

"No, that was a bad idea. Matt now wants to bring in special food to be served. He probably could arrange it too. He is likely to be one of those men who have the Maître'd in his pocket and will do anything to please him."

"But, Diane, you aren't on a special diet."

"I know, but I told him I was on a special diet since my teens."

"Diane, you are in trouble. What possible diet can you be on?"

"I don't know, but I have a feeling I had better come up with something speedily. Laura, help me with this. You are always dieting."

"Yes, but my diets are usually for losing weight, not conditions."

"Why did I lie? Why didn't I just say I preferred not to do meals and stick firmly to it? Laura, this man has me going around in circles like the dogs did that day we tangled in the woods with me pinned under him."

"Well, you have to make the best of it. This account is important to you. Your ideas are sensational and should overcome any of the downsides in this," Laura said, trying to make the best of the situation.

"Thanks for your vote of confidence. But I wish I could take you along to keep reminding me."

"I've got it," Laura said brightly.

"Got what?"

"Your special diet. Once, I got hold of a diet for Colic and thought it would work for me, you remember. Well, it is eating soy products mainly."

"But that diet isn't for Colic. It is for milk intolerance," said Diane.

"But he doesn't have to know that. Besides, you can make it sound an irregular cuisine and play it up drastically."

"Laura, Health Food Restaurants serve that stuff all the time." She knew it wouldn't work. "Besides, Colic isn't an adult condition." Diane shook her head.

"Well, I tried." Laura shrugged her shoulders.

Chapter Three

Matt went out to see Miss Canning.

"I want you to make up an appointment schedule for some office, business lunches, no dinners and some evenings. The list has to do with Miss MacKenzie. When you call her for verification, say that this is the best you can do with my busy schedule and stick with that. Can you do that for me?"

"Is there something about this Miss MacKenzie, that I should be aware of before doing this? You normally don't get involved in this part of the business."

"Well, maybe, I should give you an account of my fateful day in the woods with Miss MacKenzie." Matt proceeded to tell her about Suzette and Handsome's reaction to each other and how the two dogs tied them together in tangled leashes with Miss MacKenzie trapped under him. Neither could let go of the leads because they were under their bodies and over their wrists. The situation was heightened by other interfering people passing by.

"Suzette?"

"After all, I have told you, the only thing you picked up on is Suzette? Well, thanks to my brother's sick humor, I have a white Pekinese dog named Suzette."

"Not even a poodle."

"No, but he tried."

"Now, I understand. You want a close relationship with Miss MacKenzie."

"Well, it seems she has a blond Adonis courting her, but I thought it might be fun to work with her and not because she abruptly refused my apologies."

"Oh, she didn't fall for your charm as other females do. A situation of a comeuppance, I see."

"No, not at all, just that she is rather cute, and I would like a change in pace from my usual workload."

"Call it what you want. I think this girl has caught your interest whether you are willing to admit it or not. I will see what I can do, but I'm no cupid, nor do I want to be."

"Just do your best and find out her home address for the files."

"Files, huh, that is a new one."

"Miss Canning, where is your romantic heart hiding?"

Matt returned to his office with a big grin. Miss Canning was grinning as she started on the schedule. This was the first time she noticed Mr. Hadden let personal matters interfere with business. He always seemed to treat females with respect and had never got too close to them. Matt certainly was not the playboy type. As far as she could recall, he had never connected with any woman for a lengthy period of time.

When Miss Canning phoned Diane, she answered the call with some trepidation. The schedule was workable with her, the office arrangements were okay, but there were those business lunches and evenings. This was what she was afraid would happen.

"I told Mr. Hadden I don't do business lunches."

"Well, I am sorry, but if this project is to get done, Mr. Hadden has no choice." Miss Canning said in her most serious voice.

"But I am on a special diet."

"What diet? Maybe your business lunches could be at a specific restaurant."

Oh dear, what do I say now? I am boxed in.

"It is a diet for cholesterol and milk intolerance avoidance." Now that was dumb.

"My dear, what do you eat?"

Diane was franticly thinking. What? How did she get into this? The old saying goes, 'be careful of little white lies,' they will come back to haunt you.'

"Well, I am not allergic to all seafood, only certain seafood. No sauces am I allowed."

"How about Chinese Food?"

"I am allergic to peanut oil." Diane was digging herself in deeper and deeper. She would have to study up on the foods connected with cholesterol and milk intolerance and foods with peanut oil. Why had she ever started this falsehood?

Miss Canning was getting the message that this young lady didn't want any intimate lunches with Mr. Hadden. She probably didn't have any food allergies, but her only allergy was her potential boss. Miss Canning almost gave in. But she remembered Mr. Hadden's remark about 'where is your romantic heart hiding.'

"Miss MacKenzie, seafood with some limitations, is that right? Mr. Hadden frequents a perfect seafood restaurant over on Grenadier Place. You will like it. So, I will tell him you have okayed the business lunches, after all. Now, onto the evenings. Will that be a problem?"

"Oh, yes. I go out to special classes, and I exercise at the gym. I meet with friends for a book club. My evenings are full." *More little white lies. Why do I keep doing this?*

"Every night?"

"Oh, let me see, all except Saturday."

"Fine, Mr. Hadden doesn't mind working Saturday nights. I'll put you down for every second Saturday. Now, we may have to change that to every Saturday when it gets closer to the deadline. I will be sending you a copy of the schedule to verify the dates. Can I have your home address?"

"Just send it to my office." Diane gave her the office address.

"Thank you. I have all the correct times you have agreed to. It will be arriving within a few days. Mr. Hadden is anxious to get started."

I bet he is. Diane was feeling uncomfortable with these arrangements. Why would a CEO change his routine for her?

"Thank you, Miss MacKenzie. It has been a pleasure talking to you."

"Thank you, Miss Canning. I can't wait to get started either." *Like heck, I can't wait. I could delay forever, except the project wouldn't get done.*

Miss Canning rang off. She went into Matt's office.

"It is all verified. I made the office appointments with some business lunches and Saturday evenings."

"Saturday evening? That is a surprise."

"Yes, it appears she is busy every night of the week."

"Business lunches? I thought she was on a special diet. She okayed them?" Matt couldn't believe his luck after her call back with excuses.

"Yes, we came to an agreement that she could eat some seafood and plain vegetables. When I asked for her address, she requested the schedule be sent to her office." Miss Canning wasn't about to tell Mr. Hadden her inner belief that Miss MacKenzie had no dietary problems, only her contact with him.

After Miss Canning left, he studied the schedule. He would be seeing Diane three times a week plus every second Saturday. This arrangement should prove interesting.

Saturday would be at his place, but not right away. They would meet at the office for a couple of weeks. He didn't want to rush her in any way. If he played his cards right, Miss MacKenzie would be leaving Mr. Blond Adonis behind. No, their meeting together is supposed to be strictly a business venture. He wasn't looking to give up his bachelorhood, definitely not. But this girl was capturing his curiosity. I think Suzette and I will be back to our usual walking routine starting this weekend.

On Saturday, at about the usual walking time, Matt took extra time to shave. Usually, he showered and shaved after Suzette's walk. When he nicked his chin, he cursed and grabbed for the toilet paper to staunch the flow of blood.

Matt looked at himself in the mirror after removing the remaining lather. He was not handsome. But maybe a better term is good-looking or better than average. Yet, perhaps, classed as relatively handsome with blue eyes, clear skin and a tiny scar on the forehead. Why am I doing this? Usually, I just made sure my hair is tidy and my five o'clock shadow isn't too evident.

He brushed the towel over his face and went into the bedroom to dress in shorts and a classy golf shirt.

"I can't believe that I am acting this way. Diane might not even be there when I walk Suzette. This is ridiculous." He shook his head, sailing out of the bedroom. Suzette headed for the car as they went through the garage.

"Not today, Suzette. We are doing the dog path through the woods." The garage door opened at his request. He snapped the leash on Suzette's collar and headed down the street towards the woods. Suzette was eagerly trotting along.

They hit the woods in good time. Suzette had not done her usual sniffing along the way. The path was clear, and they started out at a quick pace. Suzette, almost running in her eagerness to be back on her favorite trail.

They passed a dog owner with a Cocker Spaniel, greeting them with a typical good morning with hardly a sniff between the dogs. They rounded the next curve in the path. There was the leggy redhead from that fateful day. Matt kept walking. Suzette was almost in a full run. Matt picked up the pace to bypass the redhead.

She spotted him. "Not you again."

Matt mumbled, "good morning." He was glad he was traveling so fast. He was well ahead quickly.

Suzette started barking, and an answering bark came from ahead. Suzette was in a dead run. Matt was jogging to keep up. When around the next bend, he spied Miss MacKenzie and Handsome. Handsome was going in circles around his owner in his excitement. Miss MacKenzie was reprimanding her dog for his behavior. Handsome unwound himself, heading up the path towards Suzette.

Miss MacKenzie was yelling, "not that way."

Handsome met Suzette halfway. They rubbed noses and barked with tails wagging furiously.

"Good morning, Miss MacKenzie. Are you well this morning? You do seem to be a bit troubled. Is there a problem?"

"Not that shooting my dog wouldn't cure," she said sweetly while dragging on the lead to no avail. Handsome was too busy rubbing noses with the eager Suzette.

"Are you going in the opposite direction to us this morning?" He knew full well the answer was no.

"Not really. Handsome seems to be having a problem with direction this morning." Still trying to get Handsome's attention, pulling sharply on the lead.

"Perhaps, if Suzette and I walk with you, Handsome would behave better." Matt offered helpfully.

"That's all right if you prefer to jog. Don't let us stop you," spouted Diane.

"Come, Suzette, let's continue our walk. Good day, Miss MacKenzie. See you on Monday. They took off down the path. Matt was quite sure Handsome would follow, although Diane held him firmly in place.

"See you Monday," Diane replied politely.

Matt and Suzette went about fifteen yards ahead when Diane let Handsome loose from her restraining grip. He took off like a shot, dragging Diane along. Diane was now jogging to keep up with Handsome, who was not responding to her yells to stop. She quickly caught up with Matt and Suzette.

"I didn't realize you like jogging, Miss MacKenzie." Matt fell into step with her. The two were jogging side by side. The dogs were running at a joyful gait. Happy to be together once again.

Thank heavens we don't have to talk while jogging. Diane was happy about that.

She is a game wee thing at five feet six or seven. Matt was checking her out of the corner of his eye.

Diane finally grabbed her side, calling Handsome to halt. Matt quickly restrained Suzette and stopped.

"Are you all right, Miss MacKenzie?"

Between dragged in breaths, she gasped, "yes, just a stitch in my side, that is all."

Handsome and Suzette were circling them again. Matt did his best to dissuade the dogs by letting go of the lead. Then grabbed Suzette as she circled by him again.

Diane was still holding her leash, so they were still getting tangled, and Suzette joined in circling again. Plastering Matt and Diane's bodies together. But at least they were standing this time. Matt was squeezed against Diane tightly, not allowing him to bend over. Suzette and Handsome were sitting there observing their handiwork with smug looks. Diane struggled to get away from contact with Matt. She was only pulling the leads tighter.

Matt was yelling, "hold still, or we will both fall over."

Diane was shrieking, "you, oaf, you have done it again."

Matt couldn't stop Diane from moving. He couldn't undo the leads while she kept trying to pull away from him. Matt was worried that they would fall over.

The two joggers from last time put in an appearance. They both started laughing. They looked at each other with smirks on their faces. "Do we leave them, or do we help them?" asked Jogger #1. Jogger #2 replied, "leave them," and started to jog away.

Jogger #1 responded, "no, we can't do that." He proceeded to help Matt.

Matt was still yelling at Diane to quit moving, and she stopped.

"You idiot, you did it again," spouted Diane.

When they were apart, Matt thanked the jogger.

Jogger #1 imparted, "man, you've got it bad to tangle with her." Then the two joggers took off.

Diane was still fuming. "How could you do that to me again? Do you realize how humiliating that is?"

"Me? What about your dog? He started it. He was just as involved as Suzette?"

"Well, you're a man. You should have better control over your dog."

"Just like a woman, put all the blame on the man. Come, Suzette." Matt tried dragging Suzette away. Handsome was trying to come with them. Matt came back.

"Look, I'm sorry that happened again. Can we call a truce? After all, we are going to have to work together."

Diane glared at him stubbornly.

"Please, Miss Mackenzie, a truce. We can walk side by side, and then maybe the dogs will be happy and behave."

"Oh, all right. But only to the end of the path. Then you go your way, and I go mine."

"That's fair enough." They fell into step together. Suzette and Handsome pranced along without further mishap. Matt tried to strike up a conversation, but Diane was only giving minimal answers.

At last, the path circuit was complete. Matt was getting ready to peel off to the left when Diane did the same.

"You live this way?" Matt was surprised.

"Yes, I live on Mason Street."

"Well, I live the next block over on Sussex Place. I guess we can't part at the end of the path, after all," remarked Matt.

They continued on their way until Handsome turned the corner at the first side street. Suzette promptly followed him.

"No, Suzette, we are going home," corrected Matt firmly. Suzette was not about to be parted from Handsome, now that they had found each other again. Both dogs started barking.

"Quick, start running before they tangle us again." Matt realized what the woofs were all about. Fortunately, Diane was planning her escape by taking off and did so at a full sprint. Much to the surprise of the two dogs.

Handsome followed at a fast run while Suzette pulled at her leash. Matt stood firm, stopping Suzette from following. He stood watching Diane flee from him like a graceful gazelle. Suzette was giving a moaning woof, letting Handsome know she missed being with him. They stood there like two lost souls. Matt's eyes never left Diane until she turned into a house about three-quarters of a block away.

"Come, Suzette, let's go home. Now that we know where she lives, we will see them again. You can count on it."

Chapter Four

Monday morning, Matt put all his reports in his briefcase, meaning to go over them later at home. He wanted his desk clear for when Diane came. He wanted to give her his undivided attention without any distractions.

The intercom buzzed.

"Yes, Miss Canning?"

"Miss Mackenzie is here. Shall I send her right in?"

"Yes, please send her in."

Matt rubbed his hands together. This was a great day. He stood up as Miss Canning opened the door and gave him a wink. Matt was surprised and smiled in return. Miss Mackenzie floated through the doorway, and the door closed quietly behind her. She glanced back at the closed door with some trepidation.

"Good morning, Miss Mackenzie. Did you have a good weekend?"

"Good morning, Mr. Hadden. My weekend was fine." Diane spoke in a sweet voice as though nothing had happened between them on Saturday.

"Well, shall we get down to work?" he quickly whipped a chair over beside him behind the desk.

Diane's veneer of briskness slipped a little. "I can't sit there. I thought we would be doing this in a room with a big table to lay out the plans that I brought with me." Indicating the four tubes she was carrying in a strap for easy handling.

"No, I have cleared my desk for this express purpose. Come sit down,"

Diane looked at him, not sure of herself. He appeared to be quite businesslike. She had admonished herself in front of the mirror that morning to be professional at all costs.

Matt held her chair invitingly. She walked around the huge mahogany desk with feet that felt like cement. *This is not a good idea. Why don't I just run?*

"Mr. Hadden, I usually work in a boardroom or a small conference room." Diane was trying to keep her voice from revealing her uneasiness.

"Well, for today, we will use my desk and see how it works. Then we can seek somewhere else if it doesn't suit." Matt enjoyed her discomfort only because it let him know that their trail incidents had affected her, which pleased him. So, this might work after all.

"Miss Mackenzie, are you comfortable? Can I get my secretary to get you anything before we start? Coffee, juice, or plain water?"

"Water, please." Diane would not look at him, keeping her eyes on the four tubes. She had placed them on the desk and was removing the strap.

Matt buzzed his secretary for water for them both. Then he pulled his chair closer to her. She glanced at him quickly, only to have the four tubes scatter in all directions when they had escaped the restraining strap. She made a motion to grab at the fleeing tubes, throwing her body sideways. Her breast knocked against Matt's arm. Diane went as red as the trim on her ecru blouse with tiny red flowers that showed at the neck, under her black suit.

She jumped back as though she had been stung. Matt grabbed for the wayward tubes, giving her time to recuperate. It was not his intention to embarrass her.

"Miss Mackenzie, which tube would you like me to open first?" Displaying the four tubes held in place by his masculine hands.

"Tube marked A would be first." The red was receding from her face seeing that the incident had not affected him.

She reached down beside her and opened her briefcase to retrieve a small pointer and pen. When she straightened, Matt's arm was in front of her, and she shrunk her body away from contact. He was anchoring the plan with a weight at each end.

She immediately started pointing at different aspects of the plan and its many sketches in her speedy manner. In her tension, her hand was whizzing back and forth while Matt listened dutifully. Finally, he moved his hand to point out a few things himself, and their hands brushed occasionally. Diane flinched each time like she was receiving electric shocks.

Both worked on each plan in order. Diane and Matt were only interrupted when Miss Canning brought the water, which Diane drank right away as though the office heat was unbearable. Matt could see that his close proximity was disquieting to her. He wasn't sure now that he was wise moving the chairs side by side, disrupting her professionalism.

They had been working steadily for a couple of hours when he asked, "will there be more plans at the next meeting? If so, I will make arrangements for a small conference room or continue here."

She replied, "no, our next appointment is a business lunch. So, I will have only some papers. I have most of the data in my head."

"That's good because I realize that using my desk isn't practical. Sorry about that. I will make other arrangements next time we meet in the office." Matt was trying to relieve her mind about their close proximity, to have no dread of their next meeting. He realized this young lady was brilliant and knew her plans inside out. Her ideas were clear and precise and well thought out. The McDonell's should be pleased with his choice of an individual to handle their advertising account.

After the plans were back in their respective tubes and anchored with the strap, they both stood up. Matt held out his hand, which she grasped firmly in relief that this meeting was over. She stepped back, and her foot went into her open briefcase, still sitting on the floor. She shrieked in surprise and threw herself forward to catch the edge of the desk. The briefcase flipped, putting her off balance.

Matt caught her in his arms, clamping around her like steel bands.

"We will have to quit meeting this way," Matt said with some humor.

Diane was struggling for release to recover the offending briefcase and herself. Why was she such a klutz around him? She never was that way usually.

"I have to get going now." The now-closed briefcase was in her hand as she reached for the strap on the tubes.

"Thank you for coming, Miss Mackenzie. I think that this was a very productive morning, don't you?"

"Well, I guess we did cover a lot of ground. Goodbye until our next meeting." Diane was edging toward the door.

When Matt inquired, "how is Handsome?"

"Oh, fine, I guess."

"You sound kind of puzzled."

"Well, he seems to moon around a lot. Also, he seems to be off his food. So, I don't know what is the matter with him," she said in all innocence.

Matt thought Handsome's hormones were raging for Suzette, which was good. So that made two of them. "That's too bad. Suzette doesn't seem to be her usual self either," Trying to give Diane a hint which she didn't pick up on, surprising for such an intelligent woman. Or was her intelligence keeping her from reacting?

"I think I will have to take him to the vet." She felt she had to say something as she headed for the door.

"I would hold off on that temporarily."

"Thank you for your advice. Well, I have to get back to the office. I'd better make my departure."

When they next met, it was for lunch at Zaidi's, known for its seafood. Matt, who enjoyed seafood, went there quite often. He had Miss Canning arrange a private room that he knew was available for small parties. The arrangement was that Diane would meet him there.

Matt arrived early.

When she entered, Matt stood up to receive her. Diane was looking around with some nervousness. *Why were there no other diners?*

"Good afternoon, Miss Mackenzie. Did you have any problem finding the place?" Matt's politeness flared as though he didn't realize she was looking around doubtfully.

"No, I have been here before. I mean in the main dining room, but not in here," Diane responded anxiously. "There are no other diners?"

"That is right. I thought we could work more comfortably here minus any other distractions." The waiter arrived as Matt finally managed to get her seated.

"I was going to preorder, but with your special diet, I wasn't sure what you could have." Then looking at the waiter, he asked for a bottle of Sauvignon Blanc.

Diane was perusing the menu. The food she liked best all came with a wine sauce, but that supposedly wasn't on her diet.

Matt knew what he wanted, so he dispensed with the menu to sit gazing at her. She was more proficient looking, with her hair tied back with clips and another black suit with a pink blouse with tiny pleats running down under her jacket.

She was studying the menu like it was essential to read every word. Finally, she settled for a Dover Sole sprinkled with almonds and baby potatoes with vegetables.

"Is there something that meets your requirements, Miss Mackenzie?"

Diane gave Matt her choice of food for the luncheon. It wasn't really what she wanted, but she had come up with this idiotic diet. The idea had backfired because here she was dining privately with him.

"Fine, I am glad you found something that suits you. Now, Miss Mackenzie, we will wait until after we order before we start working. In the meantime, how is Handsome, any improvement?"

"No, I came home yesterday, and he was sitting staring at his leash and moaning. Do you know something I could do?" Diane was grateful for a subject that wasn't personal. Even though she knew Handsome's problem was missing Suzette. But letting him know that could cause remarks she didn't want at the moment.

"You know Suzette is not her usual self either. Perhaps we should put them together while we are at work. I could deliver her each morning and then drive you to work." Matt's heart beat faster.

Diane looked at him in horror, as this was what she was trying to avoid.

"Put the two dogs together? No, they would probably tear the place apart. No, that definitely isn't an option." *No way. You will never get near my place, Mr. Hadden.*

"Maybe if we walk them together before work, that might help." Matt was only too willing to be accommodating.

"No, that wouldn't work either. We take our long walk after dinner. Otherwise, Handsome has a pet door." That was an inane comment. The two times they met on the path was in the morning.

"Well, we could always walk them together at night," said Matt, ever the helpful one.

"I never know what time that will be. I don't stick to a rigid time frame." Diane replied so quickly she almost choked on the words.

The waiter came with the Sauvignon Blanc. Matt waited until he was through the usual ritual, and they had ordered.

Diane hoped the conversation would go on to other business matters. She was not about to let this man in her private life. She did not get personally involved with business acquaintances.

"Miss Mackenzie, do you want to start now?"

"Start? Start what?" Diane was so deep in thought her mind wasn't able to function. "Oh, yes, business." Diane straightened in her chair as though that changed her way of thinking into efficiency mode.

She settled into an easy chatter, going over her advertisement plan's significant points. She continued in a steady voice, explaining and clarifying the project. Her voice never seemed to rise or fall but just nattered on, knowing her topic so well.

Matt observed her facial expression with some amusement. Her lips were shaped in a cute inviting bow. Her eyes seem to be concentrating on his shoulder, or was it something past his shoulder? He almost wanted to turn around and look. A strand of hair had come loose from the clip and was falling in a curl near her ear. Her ear was perfectly formed and ready for some attention, which he would love to give. Matt came out of his reverie when Diana asked him.

"Do you agree with the length of the current program, or do you think we should change it to be statelier?"

"Statelier?" Matt wondered what in the world she was talking about. How could he recover this without letting her know his mind had been elsewhere? "I have decided to let you have full range on that part of the project," saved. That sounds like a reasonable answer.

What in the world was he saying? Assuredly, he has some thoughts on the matter. The presentation was becoming more complex than she imagined. She did want his input on phase three, at least, as she was undecided there.

"Mr. Hadden, I thought the purpose of these meetings was to exchange ideas?"

"Yes, well, I think your ideas are just fine." He wasn't about to admit he preferred gazing at her, only vaguely listening to her and her account ideas in the last few minutes, although he did take in a lot automatically.

"What about phase three?" Diane hoped to force him to discuss her problem area without letting him know that she was unsure about it.

"Phase three? Maybe you could go over that again so that I can provide a clear evaluation of this phase." Good recovery, Matt.

Diane once again started in on phase three, but because this was indecisive in her plan, which she hadn't been able to overcome yet, her voice changed.

Matt noticed the change in her diction and paid close attention to what she was saying.

"No, Miss Mackenzie, it should be shorter in length and broader in perspective. Can you perhaps change it to be a different symbol then embellish briefly?"

Diane smiled. That was the answer for phase three that she needed to get past the block caused by her dread of their upcoming luncheon meeting. He had succeeded in giving her what she had hoped for to make it successful.

She is so pretty when she smiles. I would like to see that smile more often at my dinner table. Matt smiled as their food arrived.

Once the waiter left, Matt remarked, "Miss Mackenzie, now that we have the business part of our meeting over with, we should dispense with any more of that dialog. Instead, let's enjoy our meal with some other social conversation. Tell me about yourself?"

"Me? You don't want to know about me personally. Is this a requirement in handling the McDonell account?" Diane was avoiding his question.

"No, but I would like to know something about your background. I think we should get to know each other better, don't you?"

Do I say no and be very formal in my dealings with him, or will that jeopardize our working relationship?

Diane took her time by chewing as though she couldn't talk with her mouth full.

"I went to university near where I lived. I grew up with two loving parents, not the single parent, which often happens these days. I enjoy my work. I work with a good partner." Diane hesitated, trying to think of something else to say without saying anything actually personal.

Matt picked up on the partner. "Partner, who would that be? Would I know them?"

"Laura Anderson is my partner. She is also my friend. We went through university together. We have been in business together for ten years. Her parents gave her the money to start a business right away after university. I was able to buy a full partnership in the company eventually. Although, I worked with her from its inception." Diane was glad to find a subject that was not too personal.

Laura certainly wasn't the Adonis. Matt was glad of that. Now how do I get Mr. Adonis into the conversation?

Diane had continued. "We worked hard to get our company in the top ten, as second to the best. Laura has as much drive as I have. Is there anything else you would like to know about our company?" Diane stopped. She had run out of ideas.

"May I propose a toast, Miss Mackenzie?" Matt lifted his glass and held it out towards her. "To a very close relationship that will be as productive as you and your partner, Laura."

Diane raised her glass and touched his with a bit of tinkle of crystal. As she lifted the glass to her lips, she was watching him, watching her lips with some concentration. Her tongue came out, just the tip. Matt almost melted inside. He could get used to that sweet face across from him permanently. He didn't want to break the moment, but he couldn't keep staring at her.

"Well, Miss Mackenzie, our evening appointment is for next Saturday. Will it be your place or mine?"

"Neither," Diane responded quickly. "My office will do fine. I can arrange with the nightguard to have you admitted."

"No, that is not sensible when we live so close to each other. Oddly, we haven't bumped into each other when you live nearby. You have a choice, my place or yours."

"I don't bring business into my home environment, and I don't think you should either," Diane replied hopefully.

"Yes, but Miss Mackenzie, why would you want to drive? What is it, ten miles to your office? Why would you want to drive there at night and disturb the night watchman? You could be at my place in five minutes without driving."

"Mr. Hadden, I don't go to strange men's apartments or homes."

"Condo," Matt supplied. "But, Miss Mackenzie, how can you say we are strangers when the dogs tied us together on two occasions in the most intimate way? That definitely removes the stranger problem."

"Mr. Hadden, I still feel this is improper."

"Fine, then the decision is made. The next meeting is going to be at your place. We will take Suzette and Handsome for a walk first. Then we will go back to your place. You did say you walked Handsome at night, didn't you?" Matt knew he was putting her on the spot, but this meeting was prearranged and wouldn't happen if he didn't.

"Well, I guess that will be all right." Diane couldn't think of any way to get out of it. Driving to the office was ridiculous when they lived a block apart.

"Besides, then we will have Suzette and Handsome as chaperons," said Matt positively as though that solved all their problems.

Two dogs that seemed to moon over each other won't be much of a chaperone. They will probably tie us together again was Diane's take on the situation.

"I have to get back to the office, so it is set at my place at 6:00 pm with you bringing Suzette." Diane was gathering her things for a hasty retreat.

Matt stood up and put out his hand, wanting to touch her. "Thank you for such a rewarding business luncheon."

Diane put her hand in his. He grasped her hand in a caressing manner. She was afraid Matt would raise it to his lips. His hand was signaling that he would like to do so. She finally managed to retract her hand. Diane turned and quickly escaped.

Matt stood there, watching her retreating figure. Things had progressed much better than he had hoped, considering their dramatic meetings on the path in the woods.

Chapter Five

*T*he week passed quickly, too quickly for Diane. She spent Saturday cleaning the house, which was delayed due to Handsome dragging his walk. She should have ignored his asking for a walk that early. After all, they were supposed to be going with Matt and Suzette tonight.

She went from room to room, shining floors even. That was not customary for her usual cleaning. The bedroom she left for the last, Matt wouldn't go in there. So, everything she picked up in the living room, den, and kitchen ended up in the bedroom stacked in the corner. Where had all this stuff come from? She must've had a proper place for it formerly. She looked at the clock. "Oh, no. Six o'clock, and I still haven't finished, nor have I had my dinner, although Handsome got fed at his insistence," said Diane to the room at large.

The doorbell rang, Handsome barked at the door. Diane looked in the mirror in horror. What could she do? She couldn't pretend she wasn't home. She quickly whipped off her top and pants, almost falling over while trying to reach into the closet. She grabbed the closest outfit, which happened to be a lavender pantsuit. It didn't require a blouse. She put it on as fast as she could while the doorbell pealed for the third time. She leaped for the bathroom, dragging the band out of her hair. She grabbed her brush, whipping it through her shoulder-length tresses, falling in a cloud of curls. No time now to tie it back, lipstick next, coating her lips. She seized a pair of socks. She should have put on pantyhose, but the socks would have to do.

The doorbell pealed for the fifth time, aided by heavy knocking.

Diane put one sock on, took three steps, then put the other sock on, and continued her way to the door. Handsome was barking loudly to the accompaniment of the knocking. She stopped, flipped back her hair, and opened the door as Matt's hand was coming up for another knock.

"You are here. Where have you been?" Matt questioned, concerned. Was she trying to avoid him? He had thought maybe she was hurt.

"I was stuck . . . I was coming . . . I was in the shower," Diane finished lamely.

"I began to wonder if you were hurt and lying here needing help?" Matt looked very concerned. "Or whether you were avoiding me." He added out loud by accident when he meant that to be a quiet thought.

Handsome and Suzette were rubbing noses and dancing around.

Diane said sweetly, "why would I wish to avoid you?"

"You took a long time to answer the door. But now that I can get a good look at you, it was well worth the wait. You look charming." Matt flashed a big smile, which implied you didn't have to do that for me, but I am glad you did. "Are you ready to go?"

"Yes, as soon as I get Handsome's leash and my shoes on."

Handsome wouldn't need a lead as long as Suzette was around, but he didn't make that comment.

Diane came back quickly, slightly out of breath, mainly from her girlish response to this man and the evening ahead. She bent over to put on her shoes when Handsome brushed against her leg, knocking her off balance as her other leg was suspended in the air with her shoe half on. Diane fell forward against Matt, his arms prepared to receive her as he watched the result of Handsome's maneuver. Her arms were thrown wide, so he drew her fast against his chest. Her head tipped up, and it was only natural that Matt should kiss her when she looked so appealing. She was kissing him back with enthusiasm. Realization set in. Diane was shocked at herself. She brought her hands forward against his arms, trying to pry herself away from him.

Matt let her go and said, "that was nice. Maybe sometime we can exchange that greeting again. What do you think?" Matt inquired teasingly.

"Certainly not." She reached up to push her hair back from her face in annoyance.

Matt chuckled. She certainly was pretty when irritated.

He said innocently, "well, shall we go?"

Fortunately, she had both shoes on now, so she was ready to leave. She bent down to put Handsome's leash on with a decisive click. Her anger was still there. But was she angry at him or herself for participating in the kiss?

"Yes, I am ready." The two dogs were leaping around in glee. Diane tried to avoid body contact with Matt as the dog pulled her out the door.

Everything went smoothly until they were on the last curve in the path. Then the unexpected happened. Diane was looking at Matt when she tripped on a root of a tree. She went down and Matt tried to stop her fall. Handsome and Suzette decided to get in on the action as he bent over to reach for Diane. The two dogs circled them, and in his bent position and the tightening leads, pulled him off his feet and onto Diane. Matt tried to roll free, but the dogs had pulled the leashes tight. Matt splayed out on top of Diane with his arms anchored to his side by the taut lead.

Diane was yelling for him to get off. The two dogs circled a tree and came to his side, tightening the leashes. Handsome and Suzette were licking Matt's face.

Enter the two joggers. They stopped, not believing their eyes. They looked at each other, shrugged their shoulders. "He must want her badly," said jogger #1.

"Let's leave him to his fate," said jogger #2. They both went running off.

Diane was yelling out for them to help her.

Enter the husband-and-wife team. The wife said, "there is that disgusting couple again, Albert."

Albert said, "let's leave them this time." They continued walking down the path.

The two dogs unwound themselves from the tree. Matt managed to roll off Diane. She rolled over onto her knees, reprimanding herself for being clumsy in tripping.

Matt was asking her to unwind the dogs.

Enter the redhead and Bruno. "Don't you two ever do anything but roll around on the ground?" But her dog proceeded between Matt and Handsome. Suzette jumped over Matt in jealousy as she had enough leash room, biting at Bruno. The redhead started whacking Matt. Diane came to Matt's aid and gave the redhead a dressing down in blunt language.

The redhead extracted her dog and took off, threatening them both saying, she intended to sue them. The lawyer ran back and handed the redhead his card.

Matt broke out laughing. Diane finally saw the humor in the incident. She laughed as she tried to unwind the dogs, unsuccessfully because she laughed so hard. The dogs finally cooperated and unraveled themselves.

Matt still sat on the ground, admiring Diane's gaiety. He put in, "I can't believe this happened again. No one will deem it could happen for the third time. Obviously, these people think we are staging this by design."

Diane finally pulled herself together, offering her hand to Matt. The temptation was to pull her down, but he respected her too much to prolong the mishap. He jumped to his feet and gave her a heartfelt thanks. They continued on their way home with the two dogs trotting along, acting innocently in the whole affair.

Matt apologized for messing up Diane's outfit. She accepted his apology this time.

When they got to Diane's place, she made them a drink while the two dogs curled up beside each other on the rug before the unlit fireplace.

They spent a productive night discussing business. Matt left early to let the situation end in harmony.

A week went by. Matt had to admit he was smitten with Diane. His bachelor days were coming to an end. The more often he worked with Diane, the more he wanted a relationship. His days and nights were becoming an obsession with Diane. However, he felt she did not reciprocate his feelings. He met her only once this week at the office, and she was courteous but kept her distance.

*****

Suzette wanted Handsome in her life again. Matt could tell she was mooning because she wasn't her usual playful self. He and Suzette changed their route to Riverside run instead of the woods to avoid further mishaps with Diane. He wasn't sure that was the right decision as he did want to see her in high hopes that their relationship could progress.

Matt tried going out with Barbara, a girl he saw off and on for a year. Barbara was beautiful, and she had the intelligence to go with it. She dressed in a stylish, chic manner. Her smile lit up her face so much that he quickly returned the smile.

He knew Barbara had hopes that their relationship would be more permanent. But she was also aware that Matt was a confirmed bachelor, despite her wishes otherwise. Barbara accepted that. She had hoped that one day as their relationship advanced, it would tell him it was time to settle down. Matt knew she just wasn't for him. The chemistry was not there between them like it was with Diane. Going out with Barbara only confirmed his feelings for Diane were here to stay.

Matt had a full life. He was busy almost nightly. He had a group of male friends who kept fit by meeting at the gym and playing racquetball or jumping for basketball hoops. Other times, they met for a beer at a local pub.

But now, since meeting Diane, it wasn't fulfilling anymore. He found himself lost in his thoughts about her, even when he was with the guys.

He couldn't figure out why this woman was changing his life. He had never dwelled on one woman, always content with his bachelorhood. Now, he was obsessing over Diane. Night and day, she would filter into his mind. Matt knew, at last, he was truly hooked.

He saw her the following week at their business lunch, which ended up being very little business. This time Diane had enticed him into talking about himself. He didn't usually open up to women. Matt was a very private man and kept it that way, except at this luncheon with Diane.

He spilled his inner feelings and his past like water flowing in a rippling stream, cascading over the rough events in his life. These were things he never shared with anyone. "I was an only child with parents that loved to travel and be together. My father's occupation gave them the perfect opportunity. They sent me off to private school and in the summer months to Aunt Edie, then on to Aunt Alice, and I also spent some time with my grandparents. My parents made me feel like a cast-off shoe in the closet but never worn, just moved around. I didn't feel like I fit in anywhere, even when I was with my aunts or grandparents. They would consent to take me for a week or so if they weren't too busy, that is."

"Perhaps that is why I haven't married. I guess I felt that if I didn't get involved emotionally, I wouldn't get hurt. So that was why my bachelorhood has been so successful."

He continued, "I have had women in my life, but no meaningful relationships. I have male friends, but I only meet with them away from my home. I am invited to parties as I supposedly have a pleasing personality and humor. At these parties, the hostess always tries to pair me off with this girl or that one. But so far, none have amounted to anything, although some I dated more than once. My friends all kid me about being a confirmed bachelor."

Diane responded, "That is quite a life you had. I would share my story, but I have an appointment that I can't put off." She stood up to leave and kept apologizing.

Matt stood up as he glanced at his watch. He was amazed at the passing of time since they arrived there. Matt leaned over for a quick kiss. Diane, not expecting it, turned, reaching for her purse. The kiss landed on her cheek. Diane smiled and walked away in haste for her next appointment. His eyes followed her.

Matt deliberated while waiting for the bill. His friends would be amazed that he was obsessing about Diane. Even though Matt never contacted her except at their scheduled appointments. But that wasn't because he didn't want to. It was just that they were still on Miss Mackenzie and Mr. Hadden's protocol when they were together.

Matt decided that their next Saturday night, Diane would meet at his place. It would be on first-name bases for sure was his intent. It was unusual to be so formal when they were together so often, particularly after those three mishaps in the woods, which they had laughed over today. He had to find out if she would ever respond to him as a person.

Apparently, Handsome is lovesick for Suzette, which Diane finally admitted today. Matt mentioned that Suzette and he had been jogging on the Riverside trail. But kept to himself that his intent was to run off some of his frustrations. He knew that something had to change soon.

*****

Diane and Laura were at lunch. They were at the restaurant near the office where Diane was bingeing on a cream sauce fish dinner and cheesecake smothered in berries and whipped cream.

The McDonell account was going well. It was due to be presented at a board meeting with the McDonell's attending. Diane felt Matt was starting to keep her at a distance. He had canceled a couple of business meetings. Diane was getting depressed about Matt, especially after their last luncheon when she thought they were getting closer in their relationship. His open talk about his growing up gave her a sense of hope until this latest distancing tactic.

"Laura, I have never worked so closely with a man before and still be on a formal name basis. Doesn't he like me?"

"Sure, he does. He's just a confirmed bachelor. That is his way of keeping you at a distance."

"Distance. He doesn't even walk Suzette in the woods anymore. Handsome and I do the circuit twice in high hopes. Handsome is wanting Suzette as much as I want Matt. When we get near the end of the path, Handsome starts to droop. By the time we have completed the second circuit, his head is practically dragging on the ground."

"Diane, have you thought of phoning him with a business problem then branching off into something personal?"

"Oh, yes. I have picked up the phone so often, but I chicken out. I have even gone as far as to hear Matt's voice, but then I hang up. He gave me his home phone number in case I needed to call if I was otherwise occupied and couldn't make the next day's appointment."

"You do care for Matt, don't you? When is your next scheduled business meeting?"

"This Saturday night, we haven't finalized where yet my place or his. When we last met, he said he wasn't sure. But he would let me know on the Thursday before, at the latest, and today is Thursday." Diane's face looked woeful.

"Diane, what are you doing sitting here? We should be back at the office." Laura gathered her purse to get money to pay the bill. Diane followed suit, except that she did it without enthusiasm. *Do I really want to be there waiting for his call? Do I want to be that available?* The truth was yes, but she was still reluctant to return to hear his 'Miss Mackenzie' once again.

What if she just started calling him Matt as though it was a slip of the tongue? Would he pick up the ball and start calling her Diane? Could she invite Suzette over to see Handsome? Would that be too forward?

When Laura and Diane got back to the office, Colleen called to Diane. "Your phone has been ringing, but when I said you weren't here, he hung up without leaving a message. Then I let it go through to your voicemail. But it still rings, so he evidently isn't leaving a voicemail either. Who is he, do you know?"

Laura said, "quick, get to your office and check your voicemail. He might've left you a message after all."

Diane dragged her feet. Why was she doing this to herself? Although, her heart was racing in anticipation of his call. Will it still be Miss Mackenzie?

She entered her office. She listened to her voicemail messages. Three were from other clients, and five were from Matt. Each started as Miss Mackenzie and ended with I'll call you back.

Diane stared at the phone but not really seeing it, just waiting.

She was sad that she was still Miss MacKenzie. Things were not progressing. Why did she feel this way? Until now, she had never wanted just one person in her life. She had worked very hard on her career. Maybe too much, avoiding dates in favor of doing an outline for a client. She did have male friends who took her out occasionally. But her career always came first.

Diane did have a group of friends that would phone her at random and leave messages. Stating where the group would be meeting that night, either at their favorite pub or a cafe. It was a group of men and women that were good friends but not paired off in any way. But such good friends she drew from them for an escort when she attended parties if she didn't already have a date. Diane thought the impromptu companion was the perfect solution. Her career life was her main focus.

She also had her book club friends. Then, there were friends at the gym, which she attended three times a week. She used her lunch hour, taking either an early lunch or a late one so that the gym wouldn't be too busy. These days she usually brown-bagged her lunch to eat on the run.

But right now, all she wanted was for Matt to recognize her as a woman. What could she do to change his attitude from Miss Mackenzie to Diane? The last time they met for lunch, he freely spoke about his life, and so did she, to a degree. But it was still Miss Mackenzie when they parted.

She was ready to scream. What was wrong with her? Maybe she should put it out for comment to her male friends when she went out to the bistro or pub night. Perhaps, they could shed some light on the situation if enough males showed up. It varied from time to time, depending on who was free. No, maybe, she shouldn't expose herself in that way. Diane was usually not that open with people. But how would she find out if she didn't ask for help?

Diane was seesawing back and forth with that idea when the phone rang. She sat and stared at it like it was a monster that had her mesmerized. It should go to her voicemail after five rings, but this time it didn't. That was unusual. I wonder why it keeps ringing.

Diane picked it up quite breathless as though she had run for the phone. When in actuality, it was an inner fear that the inevitable Miss Mackenzie would sound in her ear.

Right on cue, Matt's voice said, "Miss Mackenzie, is that you at last? I have been trying to connect with you for the past two hours." He paused. He wanted to let her speak. To hear her voice, now that he finally was talking to her.

"Oh, hello, Mr. Hadden," said Diane as though she hadn't expected his call. "I have been out on a business appointment." Just a little white lie because she and Laura had discussed some business matters at lunch, but not much. They tried to keep business back at the office. No business talk was a requirement by Laura when at a restaurant.

"Well, I'm glad I finally reached you. We were supposed to be meeting at my place this time. But I have a dinner that I have to attend that night."

Diane's heart fell. She wouldn't see him after all.

Matt continued, "I wonder if you would attend the dinner with me as my dinner partner. It is a dinner for a colleague who is transferring to the coast. A group of us are giving him a send off. It will be at the Hilton Hotel downtown. Will you come with me?"

Diane's heart perked up.

"Yes, I think I can manage that," trying to sound off-hand, as though she had some doubt. When her heart was saying 'yes, yes.' Would he have to address her as Diane now?

"Good. I will pick you up at your place at 7:15. Will that suit you?"

"Oh, yes. I can be ready then," trying not to sound too eager but not succeeding.

"Well, see you then, Miss Mackenzie." The phone went dead before she could reply. Darn, there is that dreaded Miss Mackenzie. Would things ever change, or was she fooling herself?

Chapter Six

Matt hung up because he intended to pass her off as his fiancée. But he thought that was a subject best handled in person. The reason was an old flame might be there, and his pride was motivating him to take some measures against her at the party.

He and Norma had been an item several years ago, but she ran off with a billionaire instead. He had to confess she had been the only other woman he contemplated a more potential relationship with. But her disappearance made him realize he was relieved.

Saturday night, he arrived at Diane's place fifteen minutes ahead of time. Matt hated to admit that he was anxious to see her. When she invited him in, she looked gorgeous.

"You look lovely tonight, Diane."

She had changed a few times before she made her final decision about what to wear. His admiring gaze seemed to say she had made the right choice.

Diane asked, "would you like a drink?"

He politely refused. Matt hesitated. Should he broach the subject now?

"Diane, I have an unusual request for you tonight." He paused.

He finally called me Diane. Wow, for that, she was willing to say yes to anything he had to say.

"Diane, will you pose as my fiancée for tonight?"

Anything but that. "I don't know why you would want me to do that. We barely know each other."

"No, I only mean as a pretense," he implored.

"Why ever for?"

"There is a lady that might be at the party that is my ex-girlfriend that I would rather avoid. I wondered if you would help me out?"

"I don't think I could pose as your true love. The intimate relationship we would have to portray is probably beyond me. We have never even been on a date. I just wouldn't feel right responding to you with the intimacy required."

"Diane, you just have to let me put my arm around your shoulders or hold your hand occasionally. Is that so difficult?"

"Well, that doesn't sound too difficult. Maybe I could carry it off."

Matt drew out an engagement ring and reached for her left hand. Diane was so shocked that she accepted the ring he slipped on her finger without protest.

"Where did you get the ring?" enquired Diane in a paralyzed voice.

"It is on loan from a jewelry salesman friend of mine." Matt's comment was off-hand like it was perfectly natural to have friends that loan you a diamond ring.

Diane looked at it with awe. It was a gorgeous setting and sparkled brightly in the overhead lighting. Matt lifted her face with his fingers. He leaned in to place a kiss on her lips. She was so surprised, her lips sealed with his. When he lifted his head, she had her eyes closed and her lips poised like they wanted more.

Her eyes sprung open, and she looked at him accusingly. "You said an arm or a hand, nothing about kissing."

Matt stood back with his hands up in all innocence as though he didn't know that could happen. He quickly said, "it is time to go. Are you ready? Do you have a coat?"

Diane went to the hall closet to reach for her evening jacket. She splurged one-day last spring, seeing it in the window of her favorite dress store.

Matt's eyes lit up with admiration. She was the picture of elegance. This pretense was going to work out much better than he thought.

He ushered her out to his Cadillac and held the door open for her. Diane slid in with a grace that pleased her. She usually was quite awkward getting into cars on the passenger side for some unknown reason.

The powerful vehicle zoomed through the night, arriving at the Hilton Hotel. Diane prepared to descend as the door opened by the doorman. Matt left the car for the valet and escorted her inside.

A sign directed them to their private party in the Empress Room.

Matt spotted Norma as soon as he entered the room. She was looking towards the door watching for the arrivals. Matt quickly turned to Diane and helped her off with her evening jacket, intimately caressing her shoulders. Diane was tingling inside. He handed her coat to the coat check girl, slipping the ticket in his pocket.

His steps carried him back to Diane as he heard a voice call his name.

"Matt, it is you. I didn't know whether you would be here or not?" Norma was suggestively running her hand up his arm as she stepped to his side.

Matt shook her off courteously as he sidestepped to bring his arm snugly around Diane.

"Norma, I would like you to meet my fiancée, Diane Mackenzie. Diane, this is Norma Foster. Oh, no, you are married. What is your last name now?" Matt had pulled Diane up against his body like they were inseparable.

"Belmont and I are divorced now. We split up six months ago," she said invitingly, as though she had been expecting them to take up from where they left off. She was certainly ignoring Diane. Norma moved in on him again, rubbing her hand up and down his chest like he was her sole possession.

Matt brought his arm up to thwart her efforts, saying, "Diane, there is June and Dave. Please excuse us, Norma. I want to introduce Diane to them."

Matt guided Diane away towards a couple standing a few feet away. She was not unhappy to be leaving that cloying woman behind. No wonder he needed her to pose as his fiancée. They stood talking to June and Dave for a few minutes.

Matt guided her around the room, introducing her as his fiancée to some surprised looks or raised eyebrows. His friends certainly had not expected him to show up with such an elegant woman on his arm and as a fiancée no less. They didn't even know he was courting anyone.

Some couples were dancing to a trio of strings with piano accompaniment. Matt pulled Diane into his arms, guiding her into the cluster of dancers. He pulled Diane close as if this was perfectly natural and murmured in her ear.

"Darling, you are carrying this off splendidly." Matt kissed her temple lightly, playing the loving fiancé. Diane was trembling inside. She didn't react in a negative way in case Norma was observing them. Diane wouldn't give her the satisfaction of knowing that this was a sham. Norma was a rude clinging woman. How could Matt ever have been involved with her?

Matt was a smooth dancer, relaxing Diane, so she leaned into him. He tightened his embrace. She spied Norma as one of the dancers observing them, so she turned her head, brushing his chin with her lips. Then calmly looked back at Norma. Norma's expression had turned to fury.

Matt not realizing what Diane was up to, gently guided her head around to his and kissed her lips, wanting more after her light kiss. Diane melted against him in surrender to his lingering kiss.

"Hmm. That was nice. I could do more of that, but I don't think we should overdo it."

Just then, one of his colleagues bumped him on the back and said. "this is a party, not a bedroom. You'd better cool it, don't you think?" to Larry's loud laugh.

Diane's face turned deep red, pulling back from Matt. He was sorry that Larry had embarrassed her. He was such a jackass.

Matt whispered, "I am sorry, Diane," as the music came to an end. Matt guided her off the dance floor, not even acknowledging Larry's remark.

"Shall we get some refreshments?" He hoped she would ignore the comment thrown their way on the dance floor. Matt didn't regret the kiss, only the embarrassment caused by Larry.

"Yes, please." Anything to get through the moment until she could recover from blushing.

Matt was walking beside her with his hand on her back for guidance. There was a large table with delectable goodies from Hors d'oeuvre to hot dishes.

Diane wasn't hungry, taking a minimal amount on her plate, but she accepted some seafood offered by a server. Suddenly the thought hit her. She was supposed to be on a special diet where Matt was concerned. She was thankful she wasn't hungry. She might have filled her plate with things she had said she was restricted from, distracted by her mortification. She must confess to him someday about her special diet if their relationship continued.

Matt found a quiet corner with chairs to partake of their repast. He was sorry he had kissed her so passionately, setting her up to ridicule. But then Matt wasn't sorry that he had kissed her because the effect warmed his heart.

"Diane, I am sorry I put you in an embarrassing position. You know that wasn't my intent in the least." Matt reached over and picked up her hand, bringing it to his lips, putting a soft kiss in her palm. "It just happened." He ended. Then he let go of her hand, not wanting to embarrass her more.

Diane put her hand into her lap, closing it gently as though to capture his kiss inside.

"I understand. I know that wasn't your intention. I did not take offense that you kissed me. After all, we were just playing the part of an engaged couple."

Matt was not happy to hear Diane's interpretation of the kiss. That was not acting on his part at all. He had wanted to kiss Diane for a long time. Matt thought he better drop the subject until they were alone. Even though they were in a quiet corner sitting eating, they were still amongst a multitude of people. Matt looked away from her only to find Norma barreling down on them. There was no way they could avoid her.

"Matt, darling, we haven't danced yet. You know how well we dance together. Come, you must have one dance at least for old time's sake, or is your fiancée too jealous to let you dance with an old flame?"

Turning to Diane, Norma said, "it is all right for you to have Matt in your clutches because he was unaware that I am available. But that will change now that he knows Belmont is gone, and I am a widow now. A rich widow, I might add. Belmont died after we divorced, but because he didn't change his Will. I inherited everything minus a few stipends to some immediate staff." Her voice sounded like she didn't think the staff deserved it. Norma turned back to Matt, dismissing Diane completely. She reached for Matt, caressing his arm from shoulder to hand in a possessive way.

"Come, darling, for old time's sake." Her voice sounded so cloying.

"I'm sorry, Norma. I am sitting this dance out with Diane. We sat here for some privacy to enjoy a private conversation which you have interrupted." *Rather rudely.* "We would like to continue." Matt turned to Diane, dismissing Norma.

Norma, who was now grasping Matt's hand with her claw-like hand, closed it firmly around his and squeezed. "I think not. You can have a conversation later. It is your duty to comply when a lady asks you to dance," she said sweetly, having difficulty keeping the nastiness out of her voice.

Matt disengaged Norma's hand and reached for Diane. "Please, darling, will you dance the next dance as we seem to have lost our privacy."

Diane sat there, looking from one to the other. *How could Matt ever have fallen in love with this shallow woman? No wonder he wanted me to help him out by posing as his fiancée. But maybe Matt is just saying that so as not to embarrass me further. Perhaps he is sorry he had to be polite to me under the circumstances and really wants Norma now that she is free.*

Matt continued. "Shall we dance, darling?" he was invitingly looking at her, imploring her to come with him. So, there would be no further confrontation with Norma.

Diane arose with a swift motion wanting to escape. But knowing that wasn't possible. Matt dropped his arm around her back, escorting her towards the dance floor.

Norma stood there, fuming.

While they were dancing, Matt apologized once again. "Maybe coming tonight wasn't such a good idea. All I have succeeded in doing is to put you in the path of ridicule and embarrassment. I had no idea Norma would act so callously. Do you wish to leave? We have been here long enough. Our appearance was expected, but we can leave here at any time. We will just go and congratulate Tim on his promotion to the coast. Tim and his wife, Audrey, are a lovely couple. I know them quite well, so I wanted and needed to come to say farewell. We won't wait for the speeches.

Diane had a feeling of gratitude for Matt's understanding of her situation. It had become an embarrassment. She wanted to escape. "Yes, I think I would like to leave. It has been a very different type of gathering than I am used to," she said kindly.

Matt led them to Tim and Audrey. He congratulated them with best wishes for happiness in the couple's future. In return, Tim and Audrey wished them well in their upcoming marriage. "We would like to return for the wedding."

Matt smoothed over that, saying they hadn't decided on a date yet. Matt and Diane finally made their escape without further notice or ado from others. When they were safely in the car, there was a silence neither seemed to want to break.

When they arrived at Diane's place, she quickly said, "don't bother walking me to the door." She stuck out her hand, warding him off, shaking his hand, thanking him for asking her to partner him this evening. Then she quickly left the car, making her escape.

Matt sat there, watching her fleeing figure to her house. A refuge from the blundering evening that had ended in chaos. The evening had not gone at all as he envisioned. It had been a disaster and a setback in their relationship. He was disappointed and afraid it would be a long time before she would be willing to accept him into her life as more than a friend. This was not the end to the evening he had hoped for at all. Matt slowly guided the car home.

Diane stood with her back to the door, half expecting him to come and make a further overture of apology. But she heard the car drive off instead. Diane let out her breath. She hadn't realized that she had been holding it. Only to look down at her hand to see his ring glistening on her finger. In her quick exit, she forgot the ring's removal.

The warm feeling that had crept into her body when Matt had placed the ring on her finger receded. That feeling of gladness to be somehow a part of him. Now, as she watched the sparkling facets of the diamond glittering in the light from the crystal chandelier, she felt used.

How could Matt have loved such a dreadful woman? Was he a different man with Norma than he revealed with her? Diane couldn't believe that she could like a man that would love a woman of that nature. Had Norma been different when they were together?

It was a new experience for Diane to be part of a love triangle. How could she face him and not show her feelings that she was dishonored?

She continued staring at the ring perched on her finger, secretly wishing the ring was placed there for real.

Chapter Seven

Matt arranged the next scheduled meeting in the conference room down the hall from his office through Miss Canning.

Diane was directed there upon her arrival. She placed the briefcase on the conference table. She kept fiddling with the papers from her briefcase. She was dreading this meeting since the fateful night of the 'Norma fiasco.'

Matt finally came rushing in, full of apologies for keeping her waiting. Then they got down to business, discussing different aspects of the advertising project they worked on as though Saturday night had no significance to their relationship.

Then as soon as they finished, he excused himself with a comment that he had another urgent appointment. "Miss Canning will speak to you about our next appointment because we need to change it."

Matt sailed out of the room, not letting her make any comment, one way or the other. She stared with her mouth open in shock. When Miss Canning arrived, Diane blinked her eyes, bringing herself back into focus.

"Miss Mackenzie, Mr. Hadden asked me to arrange your next appointment here again. It will be the following day after your scheduled luncheon meeting, which we will need to cancel. Will that date be all right with you? Mr. Davies will be sitting in with you as Mr. Hadden is very busy and might be away. Is that date all right with you?" Miss Canning repeated.

"Yes aah . . . that should be okay unless something has changed in my absence from the office. I will let you know for sure, Miss Canning." Diane was overwhelmed with the change in Matt's manner and that Mr. Davies would replace him in the next meeting. Was this Matt's way of getting out of last Saturday night's situation? Or was this his way of distancing her to be with Norma again?

Diane finished packing her briefcase, standing ready to leave. Miss Canning watched her walk down the hall towards the elevator. Diane was not walking with her usual swinging gait. Miss Canning was going to give Mr. Hadden a piece of her mind.

Diane pushed the button for the elevator with her left hand. Her eyes picked up the shining facets of the ring. Oh dear, she had meant to return it today. But his quick business manner was discouraging so that she forgot. Maybe she should go back and give it to Miss Canning. But she felt she couldn't embarrass Matt or herself in that way. The elevator pinged. Diane entered when the doors opened to receive her.

When she got back to the office, Laura was waiting for her, ready to pounce on her for information. "What happened? What did he say when you gave him back his ring? Did he tell you to keep it and tell you that you were truly engaged?"

"No, Laura. I forgot all about the ring when we were together. He was all business today and left almost before the meeting was officially over. Matt was so different. I wonder if he has made up with Norma in the meantime?" Diane looked so downcast.

"Matt never showed me any personal attention until the party. But then he was only acting a part. Now, he has made it abundantly clear that his interest in me is strictly for my business capabilities. Norma is probably back in his life. He passed me off to Mr. Davies for our next meeting, which changed from a luncheon to the office. Oh, Laura, I had such high hopes when Matt placed that ring on my finger. In my optimism for some strange reason, I wished it to be real, and now all my dreams are dashed." Diane's shoulders slumped.

"Diane, he wouldn't have gone back to Norma surely, the way you described her. No way Matt could fall for her again. That just isn't possible."

"Why else would he pass me off to someone else?"

"Not for that reason, that's for sure. Matt's purpose may be perfectly natural as he must have duties that he has been putting aside to do the McDonell account with you."

"I don't know what I'll do now. I look forward to our meetings, and Handsome is mooning over Suzette still."

"Diane, Handsome is a dog." Laura wasn't an animal lover.

"I know he is a dog. But he still has feelings. He still has a heart. Handsome sulks every time I take him walking now if we don't meet up with Suzette."

"Well, it sounds like there are going to be two people sulking in your home from now on," said Laura sympathetically.

Diane left Laura to creep into her office to nurture her broken heart.

*****

Matt quickly left the office, heading to his car. His thoughts occupied as he drove toward his next meeting. Seeing Diane again after their Saturday night party disaster was uncomfortable with the way his friends humiliated her.

Matt came up with the ring and fiancée to get Diane's attention, not because of Norma. He had known long ago the error in his judgment of having a fondness for Norma. She had actually done him a favor by running off with her billionaire. If only he had told Diane how he felt about Norma that night on the way to the party.

And that loud mouth Larry had spoilt the moment of their first kiss. He hadn't planned that kiss. It came so naturally when she had grazed his chin with her lips. A moment that could have and should have been meaningful. Instead, it was a source of humiliation for Diane, innocent in the kiss.

After Matt had left her that night at her place, he had decided the only thing he could do under the circumstances was to back off for a while. She truly had not wanted his attention from the beginning. He had forced the issue by taking over Reg Davies' job, who generally handled the McDonell account. His reasoning was to get her exclusive attention and have her in his life. Diane had just set off a spark of interest for him with those mishaps in the woods.

She never at any time in their relationship gave the impression that she was interested in him. So, he was setting her free. But despite that, Matt had one pouty dog encased in his condo, mooning over Handsome. Not to mention that he would be joining Suzette because he would not see Diane anytime soon.

Matt was surprised that she had stayed as long as she had, without insisting they leave the party Saturday night. He had exposed her to Norma's maliciousness not once but twice that evening.

Also, he remembered his insistence on luncheon meetings when she said she didn't do lunch because of her odd diet. But for business's sake, she had gone along with holding meetings in his private office and the Saturday nights at her place. Diane was a nice lady to accept his unusual timetable.

He felt a cad after putting her through the unusual locations, especially after the woods three episodes. But Matt did grin at the memory of the antics of Suzette and Handsome. The chances of that predicament happening not just once but three times with the same two joggers, the redhead and the lawyer couple. What were the odds that could ever happen?

Matt's face straightened, knowing how hard it would be to remove Diane from his life. At last, he looked at his watch and noted the passage of time. Matt pulled into the parking space across from Bill's office. His meeting was with Bill Lindstrom, a stock deal with Western Alliances. Matt again looked at his watch. He had been driving aimlessly around for half an hour. He would have to apologize for being late. He rushed across the street, through the traffic wending its way along the busy roadway.

Bill greeted him upon his arrival and waved off his apology. Then they got down to business. The passing of an hour allowed his personal idiosyncrasies to be temporarily forgotten.

*****

Suzette and Matt were doing their daily run at Riverside trail when he noticed Suzette did not respond in her usual peppy trot.

"Are you missing Handsome the way I'm missing Diane?" Three weeks had passed since he had left her abruptly in his office. "Do you think it is time to go to the woods for a walk tomorrow being Saturday?"

Suzette yipped and wagged her tail.

The next day they both set off with high expectations. Suzette had picked up the scent almost immediately as she dragged Matt along. So, he picked up his pace, jogging towards Diane. But each corner they turned in the dense woods, she was never in sight.

They came to the fork in the path. Matt let Suzette decide. It was the left fork they took with her leaping ahead. Matt jogged behind her. He kept his eyes focused as far forward as the visibility allowed.

Suzette started yelping. Around the next bend, there was Handsome in a fast run, coming towards them with Diane in tow. With wagging tails, the dogs kissed and licked each other lovingly. Matt and Diane just stood there as if they both had turned into statues. They looked their fill. Matt broke the silence.

"Hello, Diane, how are you?" *I missed you very much.* "Are things working out well between you and Mr. Davies?" *You look beautiful but tired.*

"Hello, Matt, I am fine. How are you?" *I missed you, and I am glad to see you.* "Yes, Mr. Davies and I are right on schedule." *Matt, you look as handsome as ever. What do you think about me?*

"Yes, I am fine. That's good that things are fine for you, Diane." *What can I say to bridge the gap between us?*

Suzette and Handsome had decided it was time. They wound themselves around their masters, drawing the leashes tighter, causing the distance between them to dissipate.

Matt was yelling, "no, Suzette."

Diane was yelling, "no, Handsome."

Both were flailing their arms in protest. But the dogs were faster than their masters had been able to react in their preoccupation with each other. When their bodies were sealed together from shoulder to toes, they broke out laughing.

To Matt's. "I don't believe this." Diane was saying, "not again."

She had her left hand splayed out on Matt's chest. He looked down and noted his engagement ring still encircling her finger. This surprised him. He had expected her to dispose of it promptly after that Saturday night of humiliation. But instead, he placed his hand over hers. It felt natural.

When the sound of two joggers' voices penetrated, "not again? I don't believe this," said one jogger. The other jogger said, "this guy has it bad. Hey, why don't you two get married so you can quit getting tied up this way?" The two joggers took off in gales of laughter.

Matt decided he had better disengage the leashes before someone else put them up to more ridicule. But, because of their proximity, it was challenging to do this without more body contact than Diane needed, Matt was sure. He wouldn't look at her but just concentrated on untying their restraints. Suzette and Handsome were no help. They were very proud of their handiwork.

A big Doberman came pelting down upon them. He was in full stride, and as he whipped by, his leg caught in one of the leashes—the fast movement flipping Matt down on his back with Diane on top. Suzette joined in, kissing Matt, and Handsome joined in too.

Diane turned a bright red. She wanted to be close to this man, but not this close so soon.

Enter, owner of the Doberman from around the bend. "Here, Rover, where are you?" She came to an abrupt stop, looking down.

"Well, I find this disgusting," she said. Then it must've dawned on her that her dog might have been responsible in some way. "Oh, dear. Did Rover cause this?"

Matt quickly said, between licks, "yes, to a degree."

"Oh, dear, let me help." And her efforts with the leads only glued Diane more firmly against him. Matt quickly let go of the leashes, but they were still under them. His face took on added color as Diane's breasts pressed against his chest.

"Look, lady, will you just undo the dogs? Then, we may have more success," said Matt hopefully. The body plastered against him fit perfectly. He had wondered how he would ever get close to Diane again. But he wasn't sure this was quite the way to succeed tactfully.

With the lady's help, Matt and Diane were free from each other. Then amid their thanks and explanations that they knew each other, the lady took off yelling, "here, Rover."

Matt wondered how best to handle it now. The bland way could be best. "Can I take you for a drink?"

Diane laughed, "okay, we don't seem to be able to control our dogs. I think because they want to be together.

They are forcing us together by tying us up." The two dogs now released were sedately walking side by side in all innocence.

They took the dogs home first. Diane changed her outfit to a more casual one.

Seated at the restaurant table, Matt looked at Diane, drinking in her beauty. It wasn't so much physical beauty, but the beauty that seems to come from within that he appreciated.

The waitress came, and Matt ordered iced tea for them both. Diane waved her acceptance with a cute bob of her head. At that moment, Matt knew with certainty that he was love-struck. His bachelor days were numbered, as he previously thought.

They sat in the restaurant for a long time talking about the weather, the world problems, the local news, and themselves, most importantly themselves. This was the first time there was no business between them, only a conversation as friends. Matt was just about to request a proper date when a voice said.

"Hello, Matt." It was Norma.

Matt was watching Diane's face. So, when Norma's voice pierced the air, he saw Diane's face change like a shutter on a camera. His hopes smashed, and Norma's next words sealed it further.

"I have been looking all over the place for you. I finally saw your car and figured you were here. I wanted to tell you that Saturday night will be fine for me, after all." She bent down and gave Matt an open-mouth kiss. Then turning, she walked sedately out of the restaurant.

Matt spurted, "Diane, I have . . ."

Diane had slipped his ring off her finger and plunked it on the table.

"Here is your ring. Thanks, but no thanks for the drink." She stood up and stormed out of the restaurant before Matt could defend himself.

Matt had wanted to say he had no date with Norma and never intended on one, but he hadn't gotten the words out fast enough. She had removed the ring and made her speech instead and walked off.

Did he go after her? Would she believe him? When he saw the ring on her finger earlier, he had such high hopes. He picked up the ring with great sadness. Maybe if she was still nearby, he could explain about Norma.

He stood up to pay for the drinks. When he got outside, Diane was nowhere in sight. A taxi had probably picked her up. Why would there be a taxi available without asking today of all days?

When Norma pulled her little stunt, he was so flabbergasted. He had been too slow to react. It must've looked to Diane that it was real. He knew Norma was getting back at him for his brush-off on Saturday night. She must've been in the area and seen them through the window. It was not because she spotted his car because Norma had no idea what type of car he was driving now.

Matt couldn't believe the way he was feeling. From the top of the world to the most bottomless pit in two minutes. How could that have happened? Why didn't he respond to Norma by saying that she was lying? Now Diane would never believe him. Well, Norma had succeeded in humiliating him and with grave consequences.

Chapter Eight

Diane got into the taxi that had dropped off a customer in the area. She told the driver to take a long route to her place in case Matt had gone there.

She almost believed Matt had an interest in her. The conversation at the restaurant made her think that until Norma showed up. Why did she not realize that a man's first love came foremost in a man's life?

The taxi driver knew she was upset. He was willing to bet a man was involved. So, he took her home via the park. He drove around ever so slowly, letting her get her emotions under control.

He liked watching the carefree people in the park. It helped to relax him. When he got a miserable customer, he drove here to renew himself. He loved watching the older people happily feeding the birds.

Diane finally pulled herself together and looked around, seeing the park. She asked, "what are we doing here?"

The taxi driver looked at her and replied, "I knew you were upset about something, and I was giving you time to think it through without running up the meter. I come here when I get angry, and it relaxes me. So, I thought it might do the same for you. Do you want to talk about it? Your problem, that is?"

"No, I don't think so. I know I looked upset when I got in. But there is no reason to be upset. I hardly know the guy, and we haven't even had a date yet. So, why should I be upset about someone I don't truly know?" She straightened up and looked around. "Yes, it is relaxing watching these lighthearted people. Oh, look at that darling wee girl running to her mother, isn't she sweet?" Diane said, too brightly.

The driver knew she was putting on a brave face. So, he continued just cruising at a snail's pace. Finally, Diane said, "that is enough. Can you take me home now? I appreciate your concern. I am glad you brought me here rather than driving aimlessly around and pushing up the meter cost. Thank you for your interest, but I'm all right now. She gave him her address, and the taxi took her home.

She looked anxiously around as they turned the corner. But Matt's car was nowhere in sight.

*****

A couple of months passed, and Diane buried herself in her work once more. The McDonell account was a thing of the past. She had taken up with her friends again, going to the bistro or pubs wherever the message indicated the location for that night's gathering.

Meanwhile, Matt was delving into work or attending the sports program at Saint Andrews Orphanage. He was deeply involved now. It had all started when he had lost Diane. He stopped in to see his friend, Danny, whose vocation was a priest.

Matt had driven around aimlessly after Diane left the restaurant that fateful day. But he came upon a church and remembered his friend Danny was the priest there. Matt parked the car in the parking lot and went inside. He hadn't been inside a church since he was a choirboy in his early teens.

He walked to the first pew and sat down. He stared at the altar, which was very ornate with sculptured angels and a cross in the center. Someone was playing the organ. Matt sat there, letting the hopelessness of his situation flow over him.

A voice said, "I don't believe it. Matt Hadden, what are you doing here?"

Matt looked up from his reverie. Father O'Malley, who was actually Danny O'Malley to him, was standing there. Matt gave a half-smile.

"Caught. Would you believe me if I said I was looking for you?"

"Me? Why did you want to see me?" his amazement showed openly. They hadn't seen each other since their university days. "Come, we will go to my office."

Matt stood up and followed him.

When they were seated inside his office, Father O'Malley went into his role as a listener. "Well, Matt, I know you didn't stop here to discuss our university capers. So, what's bothering you?"

Matt grinned. "You always did understand me even back then. Do you miss the freedom you always wanted?"

"Freedom is what you make of it. I am free to do what I like best, and that is working with children. I spend all my leisure time working or being with the children at Saint Andrews Orphanage. A pet project of mine. Now tell me, my friend, what brings you here today?" He sat there, waiting patiently.

He knew it was a long time since his friend Matt had been in a church. They had been fraternity brothers and roommates at university. Although he hadn't decided the direction of his life at that point, he was leaning towards serving God even then. They had talked for many hours about religion. So, he knew Matt's life had been void of his faith since his teens.

Matt hesitated. *Why am I here? Diane and I have never had a close friendship, let alone a personal relationship, only a business one. Why am I so upset?*

Matt began to talk to Father O'Malley, telling him about Diane and their dog antics in the woods. Then how they had met in business, and how he tricked her into luncheon meetings and Saturday nights at her place. He told Danny about the Saturday night party that turned out to be so humiliating for Diane. Then the latest event in the restaurant with Norma. He explained that his hopes for a future with Diane ended there.

Matt ended, saying, "I was on my way to find a liquor store wanting to get drunk when I noticed the church. I felt inspired to come seeking you instead."

"Well, I am better than a drunk any day, particularly the day after. You must be lovesick, my friend. You truly want this girl, but it doesn't seem to be working. I love the dog antics. Really, did it happen three times?" he chuckled.

"Yes, it did. I think our dogs are so much in love that they keep tying us up in hopes that we will fall in love or become close friends."

"Dogs are smarter than humans by the sounds of that. Handsome, is he truly as ugly a dog as you say?" Father O'Malley was enjoying his friend's conversation.

"Yes, but a heart of gold. Somehow, he grows on you. I don't even think of his ugliness anymore. He is just 'Handsome.'

"Well, to get back to your problem. Won't Diane let you explain?"

"Norma was pretty convincing. I was so dumbfounded. I even let her kiss me without stopping her, open mouth too," he added.

"Open mouth, that is bad. I am surprised you let Norma do that. You weren't one for public displays."

"Yeah, well, I was horrified for Diane's sake. She was stunned."

"Maybe you should let it die there."

"But I want this girl in my life. I can honestly say I have never felt that way before."

"The famous bachelor is willing to go into wedlock. I don't believe this." Father O'Malley chuckled once again.

"Well, believe me, and it's hopeless."

"Give it time. Then approach Diane again. When you tell her Norma is out of the picture, you will succeed. Or perhaps you could start walking in the woods again and let Suzette and Handsome help things along." This time he broke out in a roar of laughter.

Matt cuffed him playfully on the jaw. "Now, tell me about your pet project?" inquired Matt.

Father O'Malley settled down to tell Matt about our society's misfits that end up in orphanages. "Not that they are truly misfits. It is that they have been dealt a blow through their parents' abandonment or necessity. They are all God's children. They never had the advantages of you and me."

He continued. "They are my pets. I spend as much time as I can with them. I try to make them believe in themselves. But I sometimes don't succeed. It doesn't matter that they don't get adopted, I tell them. They can still go out into the world when they are old enough and conquer it."

Matt sat, thinking. "Danny, what if you started a sports program with these kids? Where they excel at something, then it would give them some self-esteem."

"We don't have the funds to run such a program, nor to hire someone to start one."

"But I do. I could supply you with the funds for equipment. I will even appoint myself to run it. What do you think of that?"

"Well, my friend, I think you better be careful what you offer. Don't be too hasty. Come and meet the children first."

"Where do we go?" Matt stood up. He felt like a different man from the one that had entered the church or the one that had left the restaurant driving aimlessly. Talking out his woes with his friend had done that.

Father O'Malley said he would be staying longer than Matt, so they rode in separate cars. Father O'Malley stopped his car outside the orphanage.

The orphanage door flew open, and a bunch of flying bodies came barreling down the walkway. Father barely removed himself from his vehicle when the children raced up and clung to every available space on his body. Matt stood back, observing his friend's laughter at the children's exuberance. Matt chuckled at the sight of the spontaneous feelings the kids were showing.

Matt looked up at the house. It was an extra-large brick building that was probably used initially for a business venture. It looked immense and imposing, with a veranda extended across the front, which appeared added on sometime later.

But what drew Matt's attention were three children that stood apart on the veranda. The looks on their faces were entirely different from the gleeful children around Father O'Malley.

The first boy was of foreign extraction, his stature quite belligerent. The lad near him looking lost was of Native Indian descent. The third child was a little girl shyly peeking around the veranda post. She was holding on to it quite firmly.

Danny loudly proclaimed to Matt. "Come meet the children," who were still leaping and laughing all around him. Matt walked over to him. The children were all eyeing Matt warily. Matt didn't know whether it was his height or that he was a stranger. Father O'Malley was five feet ten to Matt's six feet two inches. Some backed up and hid behind Father O'Malley.

"Matt, I want you to meet my children that are very special to me. Children, this is my friend, Matt Hadden. But I'm sure he wouldn't mind if you call him Matt." There was a course of HI's, some loud, some quiet.

Matt gave them a big 'HI.' Then he looked towards the veranda at the children still poised there. Father O'Malley followed the direction of Matt's eyes.

"Come meet our latest recruits. They have only been here a short time and haven't quite settled into living here yet."

Matt followed behind as Father O'Malley and his entourage walked to the veranda.

"Hello, Benito. How are you today?" The boy swiftly turned and walked into the house without answering.

"Hello, Running Deer. How are you today?" The boy didn't answer. He just stood there.

"Hello, Princess. How is my little darling? Come out to meet Matt."

The little girl peeked around the pole again then came forward with a stiff gait. Matt looked down. Her spindly legs were in braces. She dipped her head, and her eyes went to the ground.

"Princess, Matt wants to see your pretty face. Don't you, Matt?"

The child lifted her eyes then raised her head, stealing a glance at Matt. Then quickly dropped her head again.

"Well, shall we all go in?" Father O'Malley picked up the little girl and crossed the veranda. A nun with a serene smile was framed in the doorway.

"Good afternoon, Father O'Malley. The children are happy to see you as usual."

"Good afternoon, Sister Ruth. Yes, it is always a pleasure to be received so warmly. Sister Ruth, I would like you to meet my good friend, Matt Hadden. Matt, this is Sister Ruth."

Matt didn't know whether to shake hands, so he just said, "hello."

"Good to meet you, Mr. Hadden. The children like to have new visitors."

She turned and led them into the house, which was more like an institution with a big foyer. They walked forward. There seemed to be many rooms around an open area that looked like an assembly hall. The floor was in black and white large tiles, which gave the appearance of a giant checkerboard.

Sister Ruth went to the far side and clapped her hands once. The children quickly ran into the center and formed four rows of seven facing Father O'Malley except for the three children from the veranda. Four older girls stood facing the children, with their backs to Father O'Malley and Matt.

At a signal from these girls, they began to sing. The song was 'Danny Boy.'

It filled Matt's heart to hear those sweet young voices paying tribute to his friend. He looked at Danny, who was still holding the little girl. Matt was sure Danny had tears in his eyes.

When the song ended, the silence was deafening. Then Matt started clapping, and some of the children joined in. He wanted to give Danny time to recover his voice.

"Thank you, my children," said Father O'Malley with a rich Irish brogue. He bent over to put the little girl down. She walked with her unusual gait to one of the teenagers, placing her hand in the girl's as though these two had formed a special bond.

The other two boys were standing off to the side but apart. Obviously, neither fit in yet.

Sister Ruth thanked the children and instructed the older children to take them out to the play area. The squealing kids ran as though released from captivity.

Sister Ruth came forward to offer the two men tea. "Mother Anthony is waiting for you in the study."

The two men walked over to a room at the back of the checkered floor. Father O'Malley knocked. A voice said, "come in."

"Hello, Mother Anthony. That was a nice surprise the children had for me today."

Mother Anthony stood and came around the desk, holding her hand out to Father O'Malley. He grasped it warmly.

"The children wanted to do something special for you."

"Well, that was certainly special. Now, I would like you to meet my friend, Matt Hadden. Matt, this is Mother Anthony."

Mother Anthony held out her hand to Matt. He shook it briefly, saying, "pleased to meet you."

"Mother Anthony, I have brought Matt here today because he has offered not only to provide the funds but his services in starting a sports program for the children."

Mother Anthony looked back to Matt with a warm smile.

"Mr. Hadden, that is very generous of you. Not only the funds but your personal guidance too. That is wonderful."

"In my teens, I was a counselor at a sports camp. So, I am looking forward to providing a sports program for the children. When do you want me to start?" Matt inquired positively.

"Oh, ho. You better grab him quick, Mother. Such enthusiasm shouldn't be allowed to wane." Father O'Malley said with a chuckle.

Matt offered, "If you can supply the ages. I can supply the equipment. The sooner, the better. When I know their ages, I can set out some games or training accordingly."

"Sister Ruth can provide you with a list of names and ages. Can't you, Sister Ruth?"

Sister Ruth had just entered with a large tea tray.

"Yes, I will get one assembled right away." Sister Ruth set the tray on the table before a couch. There were also two matching chairs. She bowed her head to them, murmuring, "I will get right on the list." She left the room quickly.

Mother Anthony was directing the men to sit. She served the tea then settled back to exchange some talk with Father O'Malley about the children. Eventually, the three newest children came into the conversation.

Chapter Nine

"I have noticed Benito and Running Deer have not settled in yet," commented Father O'Malley.

Mother Anthony replied, "it will take a while yet. They are still feeling like misfits because they are different from the other children. At least that is what they think in their minds, I am sure."

"I was hoping they would have settled in more by now. What about Princess? Has she accepted a name yet?"

"No, she just keeps shaking her head, no, when we call her by a name. We have tried several. Normally, Mr. Hadden, when children come to us without names or backgrounds, we assign them a name. But this little girl keeps rejecting the names firmly. So, evidently, she wants her own name. But as she never speaks, we don't know what it is. The one boy accepted the name Benito that we gave him. The other boy we named Jason but Running Deer prefers his original name." Mother Anthony ended.

"Have you tried getting the little girl to pick out letters?" Matt inquired. "Her mother may have written her name for her."

"That is a good suggestion. If only it will work. Our understanding is that they died in an accident, and she was abandoned. A relative brought her to us but said they had no idea what her name was because they were unfamiliar with the family being a distant cousin of the mother and living elsewhere. I felt she wanted to get rid of the child as quickly as possible. If she knew any facts, she wasn't willing to supply us with them."

Matt's heart pulsated. How could anyone abandon such a pretty child? Matt looked at Father O'Malley, noticing that his lips puckered at the child's predicament.

"Well, you can only do your best for all three. Time will have to be the healer of these three anonymous misfits. Let's hope they don't stay that way too long." Father O'Malley was concerned about these three children. He hoped that they would soon accept their new lodgings and mix in with the other children.

"We are working on that, Father."

Danny turned to Matt. "When can we meet to clarify details?"

"Once I have the list, I will put things in place as quickly as possible. Then I will give you a call. Perhaps if I had both your numbers, I could call both of you."

"Sister Ruth can add that information to the list that she is compiling," supplied Mother Anthony.

Matt stood. "Thank you for the tea. I will leave now." He said goodbye.

Mother Anthony directed him to Sister Ruth's office, two doors down.

Matt left them to talk, proceeding to Sister Ruth's office for the list she compiled. She added the telephone numbers that Matt requested.

"I notice the youngest is four."

"Yes, any children under four get adopted as soon as they come here. People don't seem to want older children. Although we have placed a few four or five-year-old occasionally." Sister Ruth smiled to lessen the seriousness of her statement.

Matt thanked her and smiled. These orphans were a new experience for him. His family had never been overly affectionate, but he had always felt they cared.

When he got into university, his parents started traveling more and eventually settled in Florida. He went to see them rarely. Sometimes Christmas or Thanksgiving and maybe for a birthday. Now that they lived in another state, his parents seem to be closer to him when he visited. But it seemed that he always left thinking about his childhood, being palmed off to relations for the summer so they could travel.

Matt felt the need to help these less fortunate children.

The fate of heartbreak seeing Diane walk away and his anger towards Norma drew him into that church. He and Diane had seemed to be successfully creating a new relationship until Norma's possessive act built on lies caused Diane to leave. It wasn't religion that had drawn him into the church but despondency.

When Father O'Malley had taken him to meet these children, he felt that he had changed inside. He was no longer depressed but hopeful about being allowed to help these unfortunate children. Maybe Diane was not meant to be his.

The list held 36 names, 16 girls and the rest were boys. The oldest was 16. He could see activities taking in 4 to 6 and 7 and up in his mind's eye. He spent the next day looking at sports equipment. His primary goal was baseball for the seven and up and softball for the 4 to 6. He did not intend to separate the boys and girls.

Another game could be soccer, so he bought soccer equipment. He wondered if they had the space outback required for these games? Matt bought basketballs, volleyballs, equipment. His purchases gave him a feeling of accomplishing something worthwhile.

Matt was looking forward to being back with his friend Danny. They had formed a good relationship through many nights of sitting theorizing on life and worldly problems. He wondered why they had not kept in touch. Surely, even though Danny had chosen the church, they still could have been friends.

After leaving the sporting goods store, he wondered if he had gone overboard in his buying. He felt everything would be useful in the years ahead. He would have to call Sister Ruth to see where this could be stored together. Otherwise, he would provide a shed big enough to house it all.

During his lifetime, he had always liked sports. His family had sent him to sports summer camps in his early teens. He had even been a counselor at a sports camp for two years. So, he felt in his element with this new project. Now for Princess, what could he do for her? She wouldn't be able to run bases. Maybe if he got an electric cart, she could. Would she be able to handle such a cart? He would have to talk to Danny.

His next stop was to purchase indoor games such as monopoly, checkers, chess, and backgammon. Cards for fish and old maid, if they were allowed to play cards. Oh, well, they could give them back, and he would replace them with other games for rainy days.

Everything was set for a week Tuesday for the activities to begin, as arranged with Danny. Matt had rented a big canopy tent to cover the tables and chairs he supplied for a picnic lunch. During which time, he intended to promote his games to the children. Matt knew that some wouldn't want to participate. He could have them as a bat or water girl or boy. But he would do his best to have all share in the activities.

Matt found out that there were five nuns besides Mother Anthony and Sister Ruth. He planned to get them involved if Mother Anthony would allow it.

He had been in contact with Sister Ruth and many times with Danny. He felt that this project would be a success. Now, he just had to convince the children. The numbers had changed because two more children had arrived, and a baby. Sister Ruth had informed him of this during their last phone call. The girl was three, and the boy was eight. Matt knew that the baby would be out of his jurisdiction.

Tuesday morning, Matt showed up at 11:30 with Danny. He said it would be easier for the children if Matt called him Father O'Malley or Father. Matt, who would always think of him as Danny, would feel strange calling him Father. However, for the kid's sake, he would call him Father.

The door opened, and the children spilled out. Some even ran to Matt, although the majority ran to Father O'Malley. Matt whipped a couple of the younger ones up under each arm and proceeded up the walkway. Princess peeked out from behind her usual post, and two kids stood near Benito and Running Deer.

Matt assumed that these were the two new ones. The girl looked like she wanted to join the others in their enthusiasm, but the boy held her back. These two were obviously brother and sister.

Matt put down the two scallywags he was carrying. They soon headed off to join the group around Father O'Malley.

Matt stuck out his hand but not to any particular child to see if there would be a response. Benito turned away, ignoring him. Running Deer took a step forward but came no closer. The new little girl advanced, but her brother pulled her back. Princess put one finger in his palm but did not move from behind the post.

Matt's big hand held still for a moment to see if Princess would withdraw her finger, but she just wiggled the finger. That was all he was waiting for as his hand engulfed her finger and closed around her hand. He slowly drew her towards him. Princess slid one foot only inches than the other, during which Matt had a firmer grip now and was bringing his hand back towards him. The girl was following his lead. Matt quickly caught her as her feet reached the edge of the veranda.

Danny watched this byplay and was amazed at Matt's gentleness and the child's response. Princess had never gone near strangers, not even some of the nuns.

Matt lifted her high into his arms. He climbed the three stairs and put his hand out to the other little girl in passing. She grasped his hand, although her brother tried to jerk her away.

Sister Ruth stood in the doorway. She was pleased to see that the children were taking a liking to Matt and responding visibly. Sister Ruth had wondered about putting her charges in his hands. According to Father O'Malley, she knew he was a powerful man in the business world. She had pondered if he was doing this for personal glory. But now she could see he was a personable man who cares about children. The two little girls were responding to his open manner. Despite the fact, they were both very timid.

"Do we have a name yet, Sister Ruth?" hugging Princess closer.

"We took your advice. Princess moved the blocks around each day for six days in her room. The outcome was that her name is Lily."

"Lily, that's a pretty name." Princess smiled. She would be called Lily from now on. He smiled down at the little girl with the brother in tow.

"What is your name, sweetheart?" Matt prompted.

The boy said, "her name is Glenda, and mine is Martin. We are leaving here as soon as my mother comes back to get us." He stuck out his chin decisively.

"That's good. Please to meet you, Glenda and Martin. My name is Matt." Matt noticed; Sister Ruth was shaking her head. Matt assumed that meant that their mother wouldn't be arriving.

The orphanage was a whole new concept for Matt. The lives of these children were so different than he had experienced. No wonder Danny looked so happy in his calling to have these children to fend for when he came.

They all eventually went inside. The children ran to their places before Sister Ruth could clap her hands. They sang.

Good morning to you
Good morning to you
We are happy this morning
And we hope you are too

Matt felt they were singing for him this time. He clapped and said thank you, and Lily clapped too. He put her down, and she walked over to the same girl as the last time.

Father O'Malley came up beside Matt. "Well, what do you think now?"

Matt replied, "overwhelmed." He turned to Sister Ruth. "Sister Ruth, did the caterers arrive? Has the tent been set up?"

"The tent, tables, and chairs did. But the caterers should be here any minute, or at least that is what they indicated when they called to confirm the meal with me.

Matt and Danny headed outside to see if everything was in place. There was a head table, but Matt intended to sit with the children. The caterers appeared from around the corner of the building carrying big trays. Some were covered with linen, while others were metal-covered.

There were hot dogs and sandwiches with various salads and ice cream with cake for dessert for this occasion. Also provided for their afternoon break were a big apple, orange, or pear along with juice or milk to accompany their meal.

Matt trailed Lily, following the energetic children to the picnic tables. The older children spread out amongst the tables. Matt sat beside Lily with Martin and his sister, Glenda, on his other side. When Martin realized that Matt would be sitting with them, he quickly switched with Glenda. Martin seemed to want to maintain some distance from adults.

Father O'Malley followed Matt's lead, picking a seat between Benito and Running Deer, which meant a couple of the girls got to sit at the head table.

The caterers had disbursed themselves amongst the tables, serving food like they were serving steaks at a formal dinner. The children accepted their haughty manner, and a polite "thank you" could be heard.

Lily was stealing looks at Matt but put her head down shyly when he looked at her. He wondered how she would make out with her meal. So, Matt started talking to the two boys across from him. He asked them questions about baseball and soccer to find out how much they knew, which he discovered wasn't much.

Glenda dropped her juice on Matt's pant leg. Matt quickly rescued it and saved some, putting it back on the table. Glenda started to cry. Matt dropped a kiss on her cheek, causing an 'ooh' in amazement. Her brother, Martin, loudly spoke a comment about her clumsiness, drawing Matt's stern look.

One of the caterers came to sponge him down. But Matt waved him away as though it was nothing. Lily was staring at him openly now. The spilling of the juice must have made her decide Matt was all right after all because he didn't get mad. He ate a hot dog along with the children, and it tasted like ambrosia. He couldn't recall the last time he had one. He drank milk along with the little ones around him. Occasionally, he would daub a chin or cheek with his napkin so quickly that they didn't get a chance to draw away.

The ice cream and cake were a huge success. After the dessert had vanished, at Mother Anthony's request Matt stood up to accept their thanks. Everyone clapped, including the caterers. The caterers had jokingly gotten into being with these jovial children. They soon were enjoying themselves, as their clapping indicated.

Matt moved to the side of the tent, where everyone could see him.

"This luncheon marks the send off for a new project that Saint Andrews will be embarking upon today. I have arranged for sports equipment for this facility. It is for all ages and both boys and girls. Some games will be geared to ages 4 – 6 while the others will play together regardless of age.”

“Sports can be serious or plain fun. That, my friends, is why I would like to see this categorized as just fun. Today you will be learning about the game of baseball and soccer. Some may excel in one area over the other and some in both.” He paused, looking around to see the pleasure appearing.

“The main purpose is to have fun, so poor sportsmanship doesn’t belong here. For the less enthusiastic, please participate anyway. If you get good enough as a team, we may challenge other schools or institutions. But that is not a priority. I want four of the older children to be responsible for the equipment, getting it out each day, and putting it away. Please, see me after if you want to take on that responsibility.” He paused, giving a big grin in response to the hands waving in the air.

“The first lesson will be instructions on how to play the game and the rules of the game. Father O’Malley, do you want the soccer group or baseball?”

“Baseball, I think that was my game at one time.”

“Fine with me. Now, I will take the 4 – 6 group and talk about soccer over there.” He pointed to the west side of the tent. “Father O’Malley, you have the rest over on the east side of the tent. Anyone knowing something about baseball or soccer, come forward and make yourself known to Father O’Malley or myself. Are there any questions?”

The girl sitting beside Lily asked, “how will Lily play?”

“Good question. Lily is going to be the instructor’s helper. I am working on getting a motorized cart for her so she can join in more. While she is waiting, she will be bat girl for baseball or ball girl for soccer.”

“Any more questions?” he paused, “no, well, let’s get started. Walk in an orderly fashion to the area assigned to you now.”

When the lesson was over, Matt spent some time with Lily. He was bound and determined to make friends with this little girl. She accepted that Matt was not going to ignore her in her shyness. He insisted on being her friend.

The days flew by. Then it was Saturday. Matt went back for another sports day experience. Only this time when he arrived, Lily put her whole hand in his when he held it out to her. Then Matt pulled her towards him slowly. He lifted her and carried her into the assembly hall for their morning song.

When released after assembly, Matt divided them into teams. The little ones started by kicking a soccer ball to each other, controlling it by passing it from foot to foot. Then kicking the ball across to the person opposite. The ball was larger than they imagined, so it took a while for the children to get used to kicking between their own two feet. When they kicked it across to the other team member, they weren't giving it a powerful enough kick. So, Matt tried holding the ball in place, saying, "kick with all your might." That went a little better.

Then they switched groups, and Father O'Malley instructed the little kids in baseball, and Matt worked with the older children on the concept of soccer. They handled the footwork better, just needing more work at kicking the ball harder to give it direction.

Matt was pleased with the response of the children to their training.

Chapter Ten

While Matt was devoting his time to the children, Diane was lonely for the sight of him. How could he just come into her life then disappear? They had seemed to be getting along companionably that day at the cafe. Maybe he had a reasonable explanation for Norma's action if she hadn't walked out before he could speak. Then she remembered she had slammed the ring down and left before he could finish his clarification.

She walked Handsome at various times but to no avail. She even walked past his condo, but she never saw him.

Laura wanted to call his office to consult with him about an account she was handling on a pretense to mention Diane.

"Don't you think he will figure out your sudden interest in him since he knows you are my partner? Matt would know right away that there was a purpose behind your consulting him. Besides, you probably wouldn't get him in person anyway." Diane cautioned her.

"Do you know why he stopped seeing you? Could the reason be that he is seeing Norma now?"

"I walked out before he had a chance to explain. He probably thought there wasn't any point after that."

"You could always just phone him and ask him how Suzette is?"

"He would see through that right away. Besides, what about Norma? I couldn't ask if he is seeing her again."

"Well, then I guess it is truly over, and you will have to get on with your life. Why don't you come to the party on Saturday night? I know there will be available men there because Susan always has a string of them lined up for her parties."

When Saturday night came, Diane dressed with care. But she didn't feel joyful. Laura intended to pick her up, or she might have changed her mind.

The night started with Diane's introduction to several nice men. But none that Diane felt she could relate to. Then finally, Andrew, a blond bodybuilder type, was similar to the picture Laura had once shoved in her briefcase, and he showed interest in her.

Andrew was enamored with Diane right away and glued himself to her side all evening. Hopefully, he asked to take her home from the party. Diane was hesitant at first. But thought she would accept because the timing was right to leave. Laura had been relieved because she wanted to stay longer. Laura had met a fascinating couple and wanted to prolong their conversation.

Diane was still doubtful, but Laura all but pushed her out the door. During the uneventful trip home, Andrew was very gentlemanly and polite. Diane granted him that. When they pulled up at a red light, she looked past Andrew to meet Matt's eyes in the car beside them.

Matt gave her a nod, noticing the blond Adonis was with her. Well, that settled that, he thought. She was still seeing her Adonis.

Diane acknowledged the nod. She knew he was looking at her escort and would believe that they were going together. Well, let him. He hasn't made any effort to see me.

*****

Matt was now extremely involved with Father O'Malley in the orphanage activities. He was spending Tuesday afternoons and all day Saturday there.

Lily had crept into his heart. Finally, he had managed to get her a special electric cart made for her so she could play baseball.

She stood to hit the ball. When she did, then someone ran to first base for her. Then she would take over in her cart and do the rest herself. The other children were helpful. They tried not to get her out, but sometimes they had no choice. But being able to participate at last had changed Lily. She was no longer as timid and talked more freely.

When Matt first came, she would always be behind the post. But now, it was a game rather than shy. Matt would pretend. "Where is my Lily?" he would ask the other children.

The children would answer. "Lily is hiding."

Matt would lean forward and peek around the post and say, "there is my Lily." Lily would laugh her beguiling child laugh and race towards Matt. He would sweep her up into his arms and hug her, and Lily would give him a smacking kiss. Glenda would run forward sometimes and leap on him. He would accept her loud kiss too.

Matt was finding the children more friendly, accepting him at last. Running Deer had become an All-Star baseball player. That seemed to give him a purpose for his existence, so he now fit in. He was fairly talkative now, too.

Benito was their soccer star, but he still had a chip on his shoulder. He stood apart when soccer was over. Matt tried getting him involved with teaching the little kids soccer. But Benito was too rough for them. So, he put him in charge of the soccer equipment instead.

If Glenda's brother left her alone, Glenda was willing to participate in everything. Matt realized the only time there were difficulties was when Martin applied pressure on her hand or arm. Martin still expected his mother to return. No matter how many times the Sisters told him otherwise.

As a special treat, if Matt noticed someone was trying their best, no matter how they succeeded. He would reward them with a trip to the local ice cream parlor. He would take four at a time. The rule was that if they went twice, they could pass their next reward to someone else that they personally felt warranted it. The awards worked out fine. A popular event each time Matt came to the orphanage.

He was very popular with the children, almost as much as Danny. Father O'Malley was their 'Father,' and no one could take his place.

When Benito had excelled past his two trips to the ice cream parlor, he passed his reward to Father O'Malley. Father accepted it graciously and went to eat in the ice cream parlor with the other award winners.

On this particular day, one of them was Lily. Lily was now more outgoing and talking since she had her cart, which helped her fit in.

Father O'Malley watched Matt with Lily. He knew Matt was obsessed with this little girl. At first, he wanted these two to meet to encourage Lily to be more outgoing, but now he wasn't sure it would end the way he would like. One day, Matt will walk away from Lily and the orphanage, leaving her devastated. This little girl was going to feel it more than any other child at the orphanage.

Matt wiped her mouth, rimmed with ice cream. He was doing it playfully, pretending he had wiped away her nose too. Father O'Malley watched with sadness in his heart. He would have to speak to Matt about getting so attached to Lily.

After everyone finished, they headed back to the orphanage. Father O'Malley asked Matt to follow him to the church. "I want to speak to you about something."

When they were in his office, he sat studying Matt. They still had that special bond between them that they had developed in university.

"What's up, Danny? Why do you want to speak to me?" Matt was curious about why his friend was studying him.

"Matt, I have really appreciated what you have done for the children. You have gone beyond the help I expected of you in the beginning. Do you intend to stick with this for the long-term?" Father O'Malley stapled his hands in front of him with the tips of two fingers touching. As though praying for guidance in what he had to say to his friend.

"Why do you ask? Is there some problem I am not aware of?" Matt straightened in his chair. His friend was earnest. Too solemn, he felt.

"Matt, I don't know how to say this any other way than the way it is. I appreciate all you have done for the orphanage. But you must realize, as difficult as it is, that you can't single out one child over the others. It just isn't wise."

Matt immediately knew what was coming next.

"When do you plan on leaving us?"

Matt looked at him for a minute before answering.

"I wasn't planning on leaving. I was enjoying my time here. Should I be leaving? Should I find someone else?"

"You're missing the point. Someday you will leave, and then you will leave the children behind. Any child that has become attached to you will be heartbroken."

"Meaning Lily?" Matt decided to speak clearly.

"Yes, also Running Deer and Glenda. They all feel that they are special to you, particularly Lily. When you leave, do you realize how much it will hurt them? That is why I never get close to any particular child but treat them all equally."

Matt sat, looking at his friend, realizing Danny knew he had a special spot in his heart for Lily. Her quiet, shy ways, her laughter when she hid her shyness and joined in. Her sweet way of walking, making her braced legs walk faster to get to him. He would hold his breath, expecting her to fall, but she never did. The joy and happiness she expressed about the electric cart, allowing her to keep up with the other children. Her hiding behind the veranda post-game. The way she walked her fingers up his palm, so he could engulf her hand, to draw her forward. The way she fell into his arms with a smacking kiss.

In his heart, Matt knew he wanted Lily. Yes, she was special to him.

Matt had never really thought about children for himself. This is because he was a confirmed bachelor at present.

Diane hadn't worked out at all. They had never gotten close. If they had, maybe children would have entered the equation, but not now. Instead, Diane had her blond Adonis. She was still seeing him, as he recalled, seeing them together one night last week.

Father O'Malley watched his friend, knowing that Matt's thoughts would be turbulent. He sat, contemplating Matt's final reaction to his warning. Would he find a replacement and stop coming? Father knew Lily was why Matt raced to the orphanage. What would happen to her when Matt quit coming? She was just starting to fit in, at long last. Matt's leaving could be a real setback for her.

"Danny, I want to adopt Lily." Matt stopped. He was surprised at what he had said.

"Adopt? Matt, have you thought this through? That is not a decision to make on the spur of the moment. This wasn't what I was trying to warn you about." He paused for effect.

"Matt, you're a bachelor. How can you look after Lily? She needs special care because of her legs. That was why they abandoned her in the first place. Her mother's distant cousin didn't want her because of her affliction."

"Danny, I can't walk away and never see her again. Yes, she has become embedded in my heart. I look forward each time to seeing her, Running Deer and Glenda also, but particularly Lily. I can't imagine not seeing her. It gets harder and harder to leave her behind when I go home."

"Matt, that is what I mean. You can't take these children into your heart in a special way. They are not yours to take. God saw fit to bring you to me that day you walked into my church. The opportunity to give meaning to these children was wonderful. But I didn't intend for you to become involved with one particular child but to share yourself with them all."

"Danny, I repeat, I want to adopt Lily."

"Matt, haven't you heard what I have been saying? You have no prospects of marriage. You are a bachelor, working every day. How can you look after Lily?"

"I don't know, but I want to adopt her, that I know for sure. So, I intend to start proceedings right away."

"Matt, please, I beg you, give this more thought. Promise me you will do nothing about this for three weeks, at least. Then we will discuss it again. Will you do that?"

Matt sat, contemplating. Now, he knew this was the right thing to do. The adoption of Lily. Danny had just brought it out in the open.

"Okay, Danny, three weeks. I just realized that this has been in the back of my mind for a while now."

"Good. Now, my friend, I have a meeting to attend. It might be wise to look for someone to help you run the games since you could use a helper now."

Matt knew he was making an effort to tell him that he had gotten too close. That it was time to move on before the children or he got hurt.

Matt did find a young man who worked at the gym. Mike said he liked children and was looking for a part-time job. Matt would pay his wages, of course. He arranged to meet him at the orphanage the following Tuesday afternoon. Sister Ruth was surprised to see the young man since she did not know about Father O'Malley's talk with Matt. Matt introduced him as Mike Snyder.

"I hope this doesn't mean that you're leaving us, Mr. Hadden?"

"No, just recruiting more help. The children could do with more individual attention. So, we can break the classes down to include basketball and maybe instruct them in volleyball."

"That sounds interesting. How are the children doing? They appear to be enjoying the sports."

"Yes, they are progressing nicely." Matt looked around. "Where is Lily?"

"Lily was taken out by Father O'Malley. A church congregation couple wanted to meet her. I hope it works out for her." Sister Ruth knew Matt had a special feeling for Lily. She had been a bit worried about it, should he decide to leave them. However, this latest couple might be interested in taking her.

Matt made the decision then to go ahead and make the arrangements to adopt Lily. The thought of someone else having her was too much for him.

He got Mike started with the children, teaching them the fundamentals of basketball until he got back from seeing Mother Anthony. Matt asked Sister Ruth to arrange the meeting.

Mother Anthony asked him to sit down.

"I suppose you want to discuss the children's sports program. How are they doing? What I see when I look out the window is very favorable."

"The children are doing fine. Better than I hoped. Some are real naturals." Matt paused. *Here goes!*

"Mother Anthony, the reason I wanted to talk to you is I want to adopt Lily."

"Mr. Hadden, are you aware Father O'Malley is introducing her to a family from the church as we speak?"

"Yes, I am. Father O'Malley and I already talked about the adoption of Lily. He advised against it. He made me promise to wait three weeks, but I can't. I want Lily in my life. I have become very attached to her. So, when I heard Lily wasn't here, I felt I had to go ahead with my request."

"Mr. Hadden, Father O'Malley mentioned that you were interested in Lily. I had no idea you wish to adopt her. What about the three weeks?"

"I can't take the chance that someone else might want Lily."

"But, Mr. Hadden, Father O'Malley is against you adopting her. Why?"

"Because I am a bachelor, and he feels I wouldn't be able to give her the attention she needs."

"Mr. Hadden, we recommend that couples adopt, and the wife be willing to stay home. You go out to work daily. What about Lily then?"

"I will do more work through the computer at home. And I will take her with me to the office, if necessary, or hire a housekeeper or nanny. I will do whatever it takes," said Matt anxiously.

"Mr. Hadden, I appreciate that you want this child despite her disability. But we don't feel a single parent is the proper way to provide for the child. If you had a wife, things would be different. Then I am sure Father O'Malley would be more accepting. But the fact is, you do not have a wife. I get the impression from Father O'Malley that it is out of the question."

"But I am getting engaged, and my fiancée and I will arrange to wed soon," Matt said in desperation.

"Well, in that case, that would make a difference. Could you bring in your soon-to-be fiancée so that I can meet her?"

Oh, gee, what now? Matt stood up. "Thank you for seeing me. I will bring my wife-to-be in soon."

"Thank you, Mr. Hadden, for your generosity and devotion to the children. I look forward to meeting your fiancée. Bring her in as soon as you can, and we can start on the paperwork. I am pleased that you have decided on Lily. She thinks you are special too."

Matt left the room, not feeling exactly jubilant. He would have to come up with a reason why his wife-to-be couldn't come right away to meet Mother Anthony. So, they could start the necessary paperwork. *Please, don't let this couple take her away from me.* He knew deep down why

Father O'Malley was doing this. Taking Lily out of his realm, so he wouldn't attempt to adopt her. But he also knew it was impossible without a wife.

Matt spent the afternoon going through the motions of being there for the children. But somehow, it wasn't the same without Lily.

Chapter Eleven

Matt was now obsessed with giving Lily a real chance at life. He would inquire into doctors that could improve her legs. It was irrelevant to him if there was no leg solution because what he wanted most was this little girl in his life.

On the way home, his car automatically went to Diane's house. He could see that Diane was in her backyard playing with Handsome. He stopped the car and sat there watching her. Since Diane had walked out of his life, the orphanage children and Lily satisfied only part of the emptiness that was still in Matt's heart. He wanted both Diane and Lily.

Diane happened to look towards the street. She saw Matt's car sitting there. She came out of the gate and walked over to the car.

"To what do I owe this visit? Do you want to see me?"

Matt opened the door and got out. "Hello, Diane. I thought I would stop by to see if you were home and find out how you and Handsome are doing? Suzette misses Handsome a great deal.

Diane looked at him for a moment. What could she reply? *I am miserable without you. I walk by your place in hopes of seeing you. I can't sleep from thinking of you.*

"Fine. We are both fine." Diane settled on this comment.

"That is good."

"How have you been, Matt?"

"Fine, just fine."

"I don't see you around the neighborhood at all," said Diane meaningfully.

"No, I have been busy. Suzette and I run the Riverside trail now. We like to jog rather than walk." *Why don't I come out and say I miss you so much, Diane? Why can't I say that I need to be around you?*

"Do you still go out with your blond Adonis?"

Why did he ask that? "No, I'm not seeing anyone in particular right now. But I am busy with the job most of the time," said Diane lamely.

"That is good." Matt smiled, but his mind was busy. *Are you happy? Don't you miss me even if things were rather turbulent?*

"Do you want to come in for a coffee?" she looked at him expectantly.

"No, thank you. I just stopped to say hi." Matt's eyes were devouring her.

Handsome picked that moment to make his presence known by putting his head back and howling.

"I think Handsome wants to see you." Diane started to walk toward the backyard, hoping Matt would follow, which he did. She opened the gate, Handsome shot out, leaping on Matt. When he bent down to pat him, Handsome tried to give his face a big slurp.

"Handsome evidently missed you. Are you sure you won't come in for a drink?"

"Well, maybe, I have time after all." Matt consulted his watch. It felt good just walking beside her through the gate and into the house.

"How is Norma?" *Why did I ask that?* She frowned.

"I am not seeing Norma. I never intended to see her. That was just Norma's crude way of making a point for blatantly ignoring her at the party."

Diane's heart lurched. "Oh. I didn't know."

After she had served iced tea in the backyard, Diane sat across from him, studying his face. "No, new girlfriend?"

"Yes, I have a new little lady in my life."

Diane's heart fell into her stomach.

He continued. "She is the light of my life. She has the cutest smile. She wants to be held."

Diane was cringing inside. "That is wonderful. Who is she? Someone I might know?"

"I doubt it. Lily is only four years old."

Diane was amazed. "Four? How did you meet her?"

"I met an old friend of mine, Father O'Malley. He got me involved in Saint Andrews Orphanage. Lily is one of the children. She is adorable."

"What do you do there?"

"I run a sports program for the kids. I enjoy my time with them very much."

"Sounds wonderful. This Lily is one of the orphans?"

"Yes, that is right. Would you like to meet Lily sometime?"

Diane liked children and wanted some of her own someday. "Yes, I think I would like that."

"Would Saturday be too soon?"

"No, I think I can arrange that. What sports do you teach them?"

"Baseball, soccer, basketball, and good sportsmanship while having fun." Matt ended with a grin.

"I was good at baseball when I was in school. So, I look forward to seeing them play." Diane was pleasantly surprised at Matt's visit.

Matt stood up, thanking her for the drink. Then he quickly left before she could change her mind.

Matt called Friday to let her know that he would pick her up at nine in the morning and to dress casually. Diane inquired about Suzette. The call ended with a cheery, "see you Saturday, Diane."

*****

Saturday arrived. The day was sunny and bright. Matt was to have his two favorite girls in his life today. He had phoned Sister Ruth to make sure Lily would be there.

106

Sister Ruth replied, "sadly, the couple was taken aback by Lily's legs."

Matt was sad for Lily's disappointment, but that meant happiness for him. She was still available. Should he prepare Diane? Would she feel the same as he? Lily's legs were just not a problem to him. It was the child herself that mattered.

Diane was waiting outside when Matt arrived. He opened the car door, and she settled in comfortably as though it was a daily occurrence. Diane was utterly relaxed, ready to enjoy every moment of their time together today.

Most of their conversation was about the children. She could hear his love for Lily in his voice.

When they drove up to the orphanage, the children came tumbling out the door, yelling an enthusiastic hello. Diane stood back to watch the joy on Matt's face. It transformed him into a very caring man. So handsome with a happy glow of pleasure.

Diane noticed that there were some children on the veranda. One was peeking out from behind the post. As Matt and his entourage approached the porch, he said, "I want to introduce this beautiful lady who has come to visit today. Her name is Diane. I will tell you their names. The one tugging at my arm is Running Deer. Hello, Running Deer."

Matt looked at another boy. "Good morning, Benito." Benito didn't turn away this time. Instead, he just stared at Diane.

"Good morning, Glenda and Martin. These two are brother and sister."

Glenda said a cheery Hi, and Martin dragged her away.

Matt put out his hand. He didn't say anything, just stood waiting. Finally, a little hand appeared after a longer time than usual. One finger went into his palm. Immediately, Matt knew it was because of Diane. Matt kept his hand out when the finger drew back out of sight.

The little hand appeared again, and this time she walked two fingers from his fingertip to his palm. Matt closed his fingers around them, engulfing her hand, and slowly pulled. Lily came gradually out from behind the post. All the children were watching. They knew this game, but it was being played out slower than usual because of Diane.

Diane knew something important was happening. She watched in expectation of what she didn't know.

Matt pulled Lily towards him, dragging her legs because she felt shy. The braces were making a clicking sound with her movements. She reached Matt and leaped into his arms.

"Diane, this is Lily. Now everyone, say hi to Diane. The children's voices rang out loud and clear with a few leaps thrown in. But Lily hid her face in Matt's neck. No smacking kiss today.

Sister Ruth appeared. "Come, children, let Matt and his lady friend inside. Hello, Matt."

"Hello, Sister Ruth, I would like you to meet Diane Mackenzie. Diane, this is Sister Ruth." The women exchanged greetings over the sound of the joyful children entering the facility. Matt and Diane proceeded up the steps to follow Sister Ruth.

Diane looked around with interest as the children lined up to sing a song for Matt. Sister Ruth clapped her hands. Then the children started singing, led by older children.

> *Good morning to you*
> *Good morning to you*
> *We are happy this morning*
> *To see you Matt and your lady too*

Matt had put Lily down to clap. She had gone to Renee as usual. Diane watched her walk away with a strange feeling for this little girl. She knew this child was Matt's little lady love.

Matt said, "thank you, everyone. I would like to introduce Diane to those who were not outside to greet us." He placed a hand on Diane's arm and drew her to his side.

He looked at her to get her reaction. She broke out into a wide smile. All the children were saying a big "hello."

"Thank you very much for the welcome and the lovely song. You have wonderful voices." Diane shone her wide smile on them. The children broke out laughing at her praise. These children who didn't have a family existence appreciated any recognition. Some of them were also in awe of this pretty lady who was Matt's friend.

Sister Ruth dismissed the children to the playfield, saying, "Mike is already waiting for you." The children took off with Running Deer dragging behind, waiting for Matt. Sister Ruth told him. "You go ahead, Running Deer. Matt will be out with you shortly." She turned to Matt. "You have made quite an impression on that boy. He has settled in at last. Glenda would settle in if Martin would only let her. But he won't, and Benito, of course, is our rebel. He rebels against everything." She paused and looked at Diane.

"It is nice to meet you, Miss Mackenzie. Mother Anthony is waiting for you both in the study. She wants to meet Miss Mackenzie." Matt should have expected this when he showed up with Diane. He wished now that he had mentioned to Diane that Mother Anthony might want to meet her. What could he say now to prepare her? The hall wasn't that long.

When Matt took Diane down the hall, he stopped to ask, "Isn't Lily adorable? I couldn't help but let that little one into my heart." He stood, waiting for her reply.

"Yes. Lily is a sweet little girl. I can understand your feelings."

Matt sighed in relief. "Mother Anthony is nice, so don't feel intimidated by her, okay? I should have anticipated this, but I had hoped you would get a few visits in with Lily before meeting Mother Anthony." He took Diane's hand, drawing her to the door and knocked.

A voice said to come in.

Mother Anthony was standing as they entered. She had been looking out of the window. She had noted that one of the older girls, Renee, had taken an interest in Mike Snyder.

"Come in, Mr. Hadden. I see you have someone with you today. Welcome."

"Mother Anthony, I want you to meet Diane Mackenzie. Diane, this is Mother Anthony."

"Well, it is certainly a pleasure to meet you, Miss Mackenzie. Mr. Hadden, you have an eye for beauty, I see." Matt grinned.

Diane uttered, "hello."

"Sit down, please, make yourself comfortable. I took the liberty of starting the papers for the adoption when I heard you were bringing your fiancée."

Diane's eyes zoomed to Matt as coloring rose in his cheeks. He avoided looking at Diane because he didn't expect to do adoption papers so soon, or he would have warned her.

"Thank you, Mother Anthony, that is good of you." He trailed off.

"Shall we get started? Your full name and address, Mr. Hadden."

Matt gave her the particulars she requested.

"Your full name and address, Miss Mackenzie. Of course, you are aware of the expected adoption responsibility, especially with Lily, who will need extra care. I feel you should have come a few times before this step. But Mr. Hadden was anxious to get started on the proceedings as soon as possible."

The interview progressed with information as to their background. Matt and Diane clearly answered questions regarding their likes and dislikes and their expectations for Lily's future. After the initial shock of the situation, Diane carried it off with the dignity it required. What was she agreeing to here, marriage and a readymade family? Matt had not even let on. How could she go through with this? She hid her feelings until the interview was over.

Mother Anthony put down her pen. Satisfied with the way the interview had progressed.

"When are you two getting married?" looking from Diane to Matt.

"In three months . . ." Matt started.

"In a year . . ." Diane replied at the same time. They both stopped.

Mother Anthony looked at them in wonder.

"Well, we mean three months," Matt countered. "We are speeding it up if there is a possibility of getting Lily that soon." He gave Diane a sick look but changed his expression when he looked back at Mother Anthony. "Is it possible to get Lily that soon?"

"I will put your application before the board and the church for approval. From your responses, I would say that the adoption will be feasible."

Matt turned to Diane, holding out his hand. "Diane, will you marry me in three months?" Matt's decision to ask before Mother Anthony held a lot of hope. Diane could say no. Then he would have to confess to Mother Anthony what he had done. He waited and waited. Diane was looking from Matt to Mother Anthony and back. She could admit that she knew nothing about the marriage or the adoption. But she hadn't let on during the interview, so how could she renege now?

Matt was dying inside. His dream of having Diane and Lily depended on Diane's answer to his proposal, which Mother Anthony only thought was a time change. When, in fact, it was a proposal of marriage.

Diane smiled and placed her hand in his.

"Yes, darling, we can be married in three months." Then turning, she smiled at Mother Anthony, who congratulated her on the decision to put the marriage forward.

Matt squeezed her fingers in gratitude. Diane and Lily were to be his. He was so thankful she hadn't let on that anything untoward had happened. He had only meant to introduce her to Lily today. It shocked him that Mother Anthony had filled out the application that fast. He had intended to broach the subject over a few dates before asking Diane to marry him. But things had changed upon entering Mother Anthony's office.

Mother Anthony stood, holding out her hands to them both. When they put their hands in hers, she brought them together, engulfed in hers. "Bless you. I can see you two are in love with each other. I feel that having Lily in your marriage will be a blessing for both of you."

They both thanked her, and Matt said, "we will await the approval of the application with hope in our hearts."

Diane proceeded Matt out of the study as Mother Anthony said, "go in peace." Matt thought, how appropriate that was. He closed the door and waited for Diane's comments as they walked down the hall. She was quiet. He took her arm and stopped her.

"Diane, I am sorry. I didn't know she was going to do that today. I thought I had time to discuss it with you during the next week or so. Today was only supposed to be to meet Lily."

Diane slowly turned and looked at him. Her mind was in such turmoil. The magnitude of what had happened in that office hadn't quite sunk in yet.

"Matt, this isn't the time to discuss things. Go to the children. I am sure they are waiting for you. I will come and watch."

Matt's heart sunk. Was she going to refuse later? Was she angry and unable to see what he was trying to achieve? The thought of having her back in his life was delightful. Why had he not told her that on the way here? Diane and Lily together would make his world perfect. Matt knew he was wrong, not telling her. But he had tried a few times in the backyard, but the words hadn't come out.

Matt gave her a pleading look before taking off down the hall. He had wanted her to meet Lily first before asking her to marry him. But Mother Anthony had forced the issue unknowingly. Diane had accepted, which surprised him when he asked her to marry him. She could have told Mother Anthony the truth, but she didn't. Maybe, she was too stunned, or perhaps, she didn't want to do it publicly. Either way, he would have to wait. As soon as he hit the play area, the children's greetings made him put the question out of his mind.

The magnitude of what had just happened in Mother Anthony's office filled Diane. Can this be happening? I wanted him in my life, but marriage, and with a child no less. At first sight, Diane had responded to Lily the way Matt had. She was adorable, especially the game she played with Matt.

Diane stood outside near the door watching the children. Matt was playing baseball with the little ones as their pitcher. She was amazed to see Lily batting, standing awkwardly, but firmly holding the bat. Another child stood nearby. Lily hit the ball, and it rolled towards third base. The boy standing near Lily took off for first base. The third baseman Running Deer, who was good at throwing the ball, picked it up and sent it to first. The first baseman caught the ball, but the runner had already reached the base. Matt yelled, "safe." Diane watched Lily. She walked over with her funny gait to a motorized cart and climbed on. Then she headed down to first base to replace the boy standing there. Matt waited for her to get into position.

Matt wound up to pitch to the next girl. Diane watched the children noting that they were quite animated in their participation. Matt looked younger as he stood there, waiting for the ball to come back to him. He wound up and pitched again. This time the girl hit the ball towards the shortstop, but the girl at shortstop missed it. Lily took off in her cart for second base. The batter ran to first. Diane saw how efficient Lily was with her cart. She knew Matt must have arranged that special cart for her.

Matt got two batters out. Then the next batter hit the ball toward second base. Diane held her breath, concerned that Lily on second would be struck. But Lily took off for third base, and the ball sailed past her, but the fielder caught it.

Matt yelled three out, and the teams changed places. Diane was curious as to Lily's position. Lily drove her cart off to the side. Then walked over to home plate. Matt was there waiting for Lily to put on her face mask and baseball glove. Lily became the catcher. Matt walked back to the pitching mound. He had given Lily words of encouragement as he seemed to do for all the players.

He knew Diane was watching but didn't look her way. He was proud that Lily had hit the ball like all the other children. He wanted Diane to see Lily at her best. Diane watched for a couple of pitches. Lily was successful in catching the ball after the batter had missed.

Diane wandered over to the older group, noting that a young man helped them. This must be Mike. She noticed one of the older girls eyed him rather boldly. The older group was playing baseball too. They were more serious. The girls were just as good as most of the boys. She noticed Benito seemed to excel at sports, as did Martin. These two were competitors, Diane soon realized. In contrast, the other children seemed to be in for the fun.

Diane was pleased to see the spontaneity between the children. She wondered if it was because they were all orphans and had formed a special bond with each other.

The girl who was eyeing Mike was the same girl Lily went to in the assembly hall. Mike tried to appear impartial, ignoring the admiring looks.

He spent a great deal of his time watching Benito and Martin, keeping them in check. Mike enjoyed being with the children. However, he didn't want to jeopardize his opportunity to come here by being the recipient of a young girl's attention.

The game was over. The cheers of the victors were loud. The equipment was quickly gathered up and put away. There were no arguments and no fuss. Everyone seemed to know their duties.

Soccer balls and nets soon appeared—the next game scheduled for after lunch. There was a massive jug of water, and several were drinking. Mike stood consuming water from a plastic cup. Renee was trying to strike up a conversation with him when he spied Diane.

Mike excused himself and walked over to her. Holding out his hand, he said, "my name is Mike Snyder. I take it you are Matt's girl?"

"Yes, I am Diane Mackenzie. I came with Matt. The kids looked like they enjoy each other and the game." Diane offered in comment.

"Yes, they do. I have to keep my eye on Benito. He doesn't seem to be a loner while playing against Martin. So, I encourage them to be competitive with each other. But I don't let it get out of hand," Mike said honestly.

"I could see that was happening. I also saw that you have an admirer." Mike blushed.

"Yes, Renee has decided to pay me extra attention. I am trying to keep her at a distance because I want this job. I enjoy sports with the kids. I am so glad Matt asked me to join him here. "Hello, Father O'Malley."

Diane turned. There was a young man about Matt's age heading towards them in clergy garb. This must be Matt's friend who got him started here at the orphanage.

"Hello, Mike, how is it going?"

"Fine, Father O'Malley. This young lady is Diane Mackenzie, Matt's friend. Diane, this is Father O'Malley."

Father O'Malley put both hands out and grabbed her hand. "I am pleased to meet you, Diane. I heard that you were here by both Mother Anthony and Sister Ruth."

Diane gave him a warm smile. But she felt he knew the true situation from the twinkle in his eyes.

"Pleased to meet you too, Father O'Malley. Matt has told me how you got him involved here." Looking down the field, Diane saw Matt was heading in their direction.

"I hear you and Matt started adoption proceedings. I hope that wasn't too hasty as you only met Lily for the first time today."

Before Diane could answer, Mike cut in. "Adopt Lily? You and Matt are going to adopt Lily? That is wonderful." He grasped her hand and shook it.

Matt caught up to them. Mike went over and punched him on the back. "Keeping secrets, eh? Congratulations on your wife-to-be and the adoption."

Matt knew right away that Father O'Malley had talked to Mother Anthony and Sister Ruth. He didn't know which one to look at first, Diane or Father O'Malley. He settled for Diane.

"Diane, have you met Father O'Malley?" Matt was trying to avoid Danny's usual outspoken comments.

"Yes, Mike introduced me."

Matt noticed her smile seemed forced. "Well, Father, what do you think of my girl?" he put his arm around Diane, hoping she wouldn't shrug it off.

"May I add my congratulations to Mike's for your upcoming marriage and adoption. However, I wish you would have consulted with me first on the adoption. After all, you are supposed to be my best friend." Danny said, looking meaningfully at Matt.

He continued, "you didn't answer my question, Diane, about being rather hasty in the adoption." But he never removed his eyes from Matt, letting him know that he surmised what had happened here today.

Diane cleared her throat. "Lily is such a cute little girl. I know I will just love her." She replied evasively. She felt Father O'Malley knew this was all a surprise to her, but she didn't want to lie to him.

Matt came to her aid. "Mother Anthony had the paperwork started when we arrived. Apparently, Sister Ruth told her I was bringing Diane today."

Father O'Malley was definitely not pleased. He knew that Matt hadn't seen Diane in a long while. He also knew how much Matt wanted to adopt Lily.

Every once in a while, Danny had made a point to inquire if Matt saw Diane at all. The last time they spoke, Matt had mentioned the blond Adonis. How did these two suddenly appear at the orphanage engaged and starting adoption proceedings?

Danny decided not to force the issue at this time but said, "Matt, I wonder if you could drop by the church tomorrow afternoon?" Matt knew it wasn't a question but an order. "Alone," Father added, then looked at Diane.

"Nice to meet you, Diane. Mike, I want to speak to you for a few minutes if you don't mind.

The school bell rang for lunch, and the children filed into the building.

Matt led Diane away as Father O'Malley walked in the opposite direction with Mike.

Chapter Twelve

"**M**ike, it has come to my attention that Renee is sending special looks your way." Father O'Malley stopped and turned to look into Mike's face.

"Yes, I am aware of Renee, but I don't encourage her. I know how important this job is to me. I love being with the children. I wouldn't do anything to jeopardize my chances to work here. Honestly, Father O'Malley, I want you to know that I have never encouraged her in any way."

"All right, Mike. I believe you. I will have Mother Anthony talk with her. How are Benito and Martin fitting in any better?"

"As long as I let them compete, things go along fine. I watch that it doesn't get out of hand. They could easily end up in a fight." Mike liked Father O'Malley. He wanted to do an excellent job for him.

"Keep up the good work. I am pleased Matt brought you to join us." Father O'Malley turned and watched Matt walk with Diane. Matt was doing the talking. Diane's body language was hard to read.

Mike followed Father O'Malley's eyes to the couple. "They make a wonderful couple, don't they? Isn't it wonderful about Lily?"

Father O'Malley gave a reserved "yes" to both questions. But he did not elaborate. "Are you coming in for lunch?" putting his arm around Mike to direct him inside.

Danny doubted Matt would make lunch today. He felt that he had some tall explaining to do to Diane. He gave the couple another cursory look of apprehension.

Matt talked to Diane in a concerned voice. "Diane, I know you are aware that Father O'Malley knew nothing about our supposed marriage. So, that means you are wondering when I planned this?" He paused, but Diane did not respond.

"Diane, what do you think of Lily?" He thought he would try a different tactic.

"She is adorable. But, Matt, that doesn't change the fact that you got me here under false pretenses."

"Diane, honest, I didn't know Mother Anthony intended to process the papers today."

"Matt, she must have known about me before today. Tell me the truth, was it before the day in the backyard?" Diane watched him closely.

Matt couldn't lie. "Yes, she knew before I came to the backyard. But I do love you. I want to marry you. You are important to me, and not just because I want to adopt Lily. I wanted to tell you that day when I came to your place, and now I wished I had."

Diane replied, "I believe you want to marry me. But I doubt the love. How could you tell Mother Anthony that we were engaged when we don't even see each other socially?"

"Not because I didn't want to see you. After all, you were still going out with the blond Adonis."

"Blond Adonis? Is that what you thought?" Diane was amazed.

"Yes, well, you were. You carry his picture around in your briefcase, and I saw you and the blond Adonis in his car one night."

Diane decided to ignore that issue.

"Just when were you going to tell me about the marriage and adoption?"

"Sometime this week after you met Lily. I swear my only intention today was to have you meet Lily. I intended to ask you out on a few dates and discuss the possibility of marriage and adoption during those occasions. Mother Anthony knew I was anxious that Lily wouldn't get adopted by someone else. Perhaps that was why she went ahead and started the adoption papers."

Diane noticed Sister Ruth was waving to them. "Matt, Sister Ruth is calling us."

Matt turned, looking to the doorway and waved. "They want us to come in for lunch. The children like me to eat with them. They are probably waiting for us. Can we discuss this after?"

Diane said, "yes," not wanting to delay the meal any longer.

They were ushered to their seats to find that Glenda was on Diane's right and Lily on her left, with Matt between Lily and Running Deer. It was apparent that the children had arranged it that way, saving a seat for Diane and him. They looked at each other then sat down. Father O'Malley said the grace, and the meal began.

Father O'Malley sat between Mike and Benito when Renee slipped into the chair beside Mike. Mother Anthony noted this move and gave Father O'Malley a look. He returned an answering nod, letting her know that he had spoken to Mike, and all was well.

Mike was finding it difficult because Renee kept rubbing his leg beneath the table. He gave Father O'Malley a pleading look. Father asked Benito to change places with Renee for dessert so he could talk to Mike. Benito was cooperative for a change because Mike was his hero. He let Benito play in competition with Martin. Otherwise, Benito didn't acknowledge any of the other children. He was firm about never fitting in. Father O'Malley kept trying.

Dessert time came. Renee changed places begrudgingly. Father O'Malley received a smile of reward from Mother Anthony

Renee took the opportunity to comment to Father O'Malley that Lily looked very happy sitting between Diane and Matt. "Do you think they will adopt Lily?"

Father O'Malley wasn't happy about this question but answered it for Renee. "We will have to see if that comes about."

Diane couldn't help but respond to Lily and Glenda. They were both adorable. She also realized why Matt was so committed to Lily. She was like him. Matt was a joyful person, with his pleasure coming from small rewards rather than big ones. Lily also was happy with little rewards. The fact that she could sit beside Matt was the gift she wanted most. To Lily, Matt was special. Even when he talked to Running Deer, she sat watching him.

Diane tried to get her attention, and with Matt's direction, she succeeded. Diane knew Lily was a bright child in talking to her. Diane realized that Lily's only drawback in life was her legs. She knew that if there was a possibility of changing that Matt would do so.

Lily spoke, "Matt is going to be my father soon. Renee overheard Sister Ruth and Mother Anthony talking. Does that mean you will be my mother?"

Diane was at a loss for words. "Lily, I don't think you should count on it just yet. That has to be approval by the board and the church."

"But Matt will make it happen. I know he will as he made my cart happen. Are you going to be my mother?" Lily looked at Diane intently.

"I can't say. There is more to be settled first."

"Don't you want to be my mother?"

Diane's heart stopped. What could she say now?

"Yes, I would like to be your mother. It just may not be possible, that is all." Diane was evasive but still left her with some hope.

Matt overheard the last and looked at Diane searchingly over Lily's head. He would have his work cut out for him to convince her, and he had Father O'Malley to contend with also.

Diane did not give Matt any sign that she intended to make it easy for him.

It was too grave a matter to take lightly. Not only would she be taking Matt for a husband, but she would also be taking Lily, who needed special care. Diane had not had much experience with small children or babies. She had been too busy with her career. Her friends were mostly career girls, so they didn't have children.

Diane turned to Glenda and started talking to her.

Glenda said, "my brother believes that my mother will come and get us. That is why he tries to stop me from making friends with anyone. Do you want to be my friend?" Glenda smiled up into Diane's eyes.

"Of course, I would like to be your friend. But I don't know how often I will come here. So, it may be difficult."

Glenda patted her arm. "That's okay because Martin probably won't let me have you for a friend anyway." Diane's heart went out to this little girl. How can you prefer only one? Diane wanted to adopt them all. They all had their charm and sad story.

Even Running Deer was trying so hard to win Matt's attention. How can he only look at Lily and not see the others? Diane wasn't sure it was a good idea for her to come again. Emotionally, she could lose a bit of herself each time she came unless she came every week as Matt did. Besides, what if she wanted children? Would Matt want them too? Was she doing the right thing in marrying him?

Matt bent over Lily and whispered in Diane's ear.

"A penny for your thoughts. I hope they include me."

Diane smiled at him. "A penny for what I am thinking isn't nearly enough."

"I was afraid of that. Come, it is time for round two of the sports activities. Lily and Running Deer, we will see you outside."

They both shouted "yes" excitedly as they joined the younger ones heading outside. The older ones started cleaning off the tables. Matt and Diane headed for the door.

Matt's afternoon was playing soccer with ages seven and up as the little ones were learning basketball. The net had been lowered considerably for them.

Lily did not participate in basketball. She only watched for stray balls at the soccer field and recovered them with her cart. Diane felt some of the children sent them out of bounds on purpose to give Lily something to chase.

The afternoon ended all too soon. Diane said goodbye to Mother Anthony, Father O'Malley, and Sister Ruth, as all three came to say goodbye and wish them luck on the approval of the adoption application. Although Father O'Malley gave Matt another hard look, saying that he would see him tomorrow.

Diane waved to the children grouped on the veranda as they drove away. Her heart went out to them all.

"What do you think? Aren't they the nicest bunch of kids?" Matt inquired.

"Yes, they are special. I can see why you come here each week. How long have you been coming?"

"Since the day you walked out on me. I was upset that you left that way and I wouldn't see you again. I drove around aimlessly, thinking I would pick up some liquor to get drunk in frustration of losing you. I ended up in church instead and met with Danny. Father O'Malley to you. Danny and I go way back to our university days. He was my roommate. After we left university, he decided to devote his life to the church. He has his own church here along with the responsibility of the Saint Andrews Orphanage."

"But you had Norma back in your life. Why did you want to get drunk?"

"Norma pulled that stunt to get back at me for thwarting her attempts to drag me back into her clutches. Before I could explain that, you walked out. Hence the wish to get drunk as I had lost you."

"Well, I'm glad you found the church and Father O'Malley. He is super nice, and so are all the children."

"Diane, I wanted you to meet Lily without knowing that I wanted to adopt her. So, you would see what a wonderful child she is. The fact that she wears braces on her legs doesn't enter into the picture for wanting her. I fell for her the first day I met her. Diane, are you still angry with me?"

"Matt, you must admit that it was hard for me to hear that you intended to adopt Lily before you came seeking me. The knowledge that you had used me to get into Mother Anthony's good graces to adopt Lily is upsetting."

"I know, Diane, and I don't blame you for being angry. But I do want you in my life, and I do want Lily too. When I heard another couple had met Lily, it forced my hand to act sooner than I intended."

"Another couple met Lily?"

"Yes, Father O'Malley introduced her to a couple from his church last week. I overreacted before discovering that they were taken aback by Lily's legs. Diane, are you sorry you agreed to marry me?"

"Matt, I disapprove of your tactics, putting me on the spot with Mother Anthony." She glanced at him, enjoying looking at him.

"Diane, you won't back out on my proposal, will you?"

She knew he had left the balance of the question in the air, which was, 'and have me lose out on the adoption of Lily.'

Diane had hoped this particular question would not come up quite so soon. They had reached her house, so she delayed answering. She invited him inside. Diane went to make the coffee while Matt played with Handsome.

She reviewed the morning's experiences along with her feelings on the adoption and marriage proposal. How did she really feel? Yes, she wanted Matt in her life. But she hadn't thought past that point. Did she want to give up her career? Lily would require full-time care. Lily was part of the marriage proposal. Would he have proposed if Lily hadn't been in the picture? Did he want me, or was it just the means to get the child?

Diane automatically started making dinner without asking Matt to stay. She was so deep in thought that her hands were moving robotically. She had put some small steaks under the broiler and some vegetables to steam. She opened the microwave to make baked potatoes and intended finishing them under the broiler.

Matt finally walked into the kitchen. He had been giving her time to digest the day's events. Now that she had time to think about it, he was afraid that she would refuse his proposal forced upon her in front of Mother Anthony.

"I see you are making dinner."

"Yes, you will stay, won't you?" Diane was still without a firm decision.

Matt walked over to the cupboard, taking out dishes to set the table. He worked silently, dreading the conversation that would include her final decision. They moved around the kitchen, so naturally. Anyone looking on would think they had been together for a long time, rather than being a first-time meal in her home. Both were deep in thought.

Matt opened a bottle of red wine that he found in the cupboard. Matt left it to breathe while he set the table. When all was ready, Matt poured some wine, and when they were both seated, he proposed a toast to her.

"Diane, I missed you dearly. My life was empty without you. I am so glad you accepted my marriage proposal." He raised his glass and reached out to touch hers.

She did not respond with her glass.

"Matt, I accepted your proposal because I didn't know what else to do. But I am adding a provision."

"A provision?" Matt wasn't sure he liked that.

"Yes, the provision is, I will marry you. I will accept Lily as part of the marriage. But it will be in name only." She paused for effect, then went on. "I will have to give up my career, which I fought for extensively. Plus, we haven't been seeing each other socially. We are almost strangers. So, I hardly think we should jump into an intimate marriage."

Matt was not happy with her provision. He digested the information. Matt sat there, staring at her with his mind whirling. He considered the statement, and he cleared his throat. "Diane, isn't that a bit drastic?"

"The ending of my career or the marriage in name only?"

"Diane, you wouldn't have to end your career completely. I would share in Lily's care. Couldn't you handle some of your work here in your home? Perhaps we could even get a nanny or a housekeeper?" he was avoiding the intimacy clause for the moment.

"Matt, I suppose we could work something out. But I need some reassurance of your commitment to Lily."

"I can do some of my work from home. We could spell each other out if you want to spend more time in the office? When we have meetings and such, we can make sure the other will be home." Matt was willing to offer her anything at this point. Besides, he had already decided on this route before, when he had intended to adopt Lily alone without Diane.

They both started eating while their minds were busy hashing out possible problems. Neither tasting the food and just going through the motions.

Matt finally said, "Diane, I want you as a proper wife. But if this is the only way you will marry me, I will accept your provision. I was a bit underhanded mentioning you to Mother Anthony ahead of time, and it resulted in the proposal and adoption without your prior knowledge. But I want it on record that I am not happy about marriage in name only."

Diane was relieved Matt had agreed to her hasty provisional demand.

They busily tidied the kitchen. When finished, Matt took the towel from Diane, placing it on the counter.

He took her in his arms. "We didn't seal our proposal and your acceptance with a kiss."

His lips came down slowly, capturing hers with light kisses, and his arms tightened around her. His mouth sealed over hers in expectation. The kiss deepened at her overwhelming response. Diane was breathless as Matt pulled away.

Matt kissed her lightly on the tip of her nose. "I had better leave before this becomes more them platonic. Suzette will be waiting for her dinner. I will bring the ring tomorrow night when we celebrate at the restaurant, Avian Rose. You can go tomorrow night, can't you?"

"Yes, but the ring, I am not sure I am ready for that."

Matt wanted the ring on her finger. So, what if it wasn't a real marriage but in name only? It didn't matter. He just wanted her in his life in marriage.

He had paid the jeweler for the ring after they had played the fiancée charade, and she had kept it on her finger. His intention at that time was to make her his fiancée for real.

He didn't force the issue now, but he meant to have that ring on her finger someday soon somehow.

Chapter Thirteen

Diane went to work on Monday with the reality that she was getting married in three months. She was to be a wife, but significantly, the mother of a four-year-old daughter. The glow was because she was to be married to Matt.

Laura and Colleen noticed right away. "Diane, why the radiance? What have you not told us?"

"Why do you think there is a what?" Playing innocent. Diane broke into a grin.

"Because your face is lit up like a Christmas tree, and it isn't Christmas. Tell us. It's Matt, isn't it?" Laura was prodding her.

"How do you feel about me cutting down my hours in the office?"

"Diane, I knew it. It is Matt, isn't it?"

Diane smiled coyly. "A certain person is to be married in three months and will also be a mother," she said intriguingly.

Laura jumped on that message quickly. "Married and a mother? Who? How?"

"Matt proposed. We filled out adoption papers to adopt a four-year-old girl named Lily."

Colleen leaped in. "Diane, you haven't even been seeing Matt. How did this happen?"

"Matt took me to Saint Andrews Orphanage. There is an adorable little girl that Matt and I have decided to adopt. Lily is as pretty as her name."

Laura was concerned. "Diane, isn't this rather sudden? Did Matt force you into this? He did, didn't he? Boy, he is a fast worker. Here you have been mooning over him, and now you are getting married. Well, I would never have guessed that as a possibility."

Diane tried to cover up the shock of the sudden proposal by saying, "Laura, you said I was mooning over Matt. So, when he came back into my life, I was ready for the commitment."

"But, Diane, why the adoption? Isn't it too soon to know if you can't have children of your own? Do you want a child this soon?"

"Matt took me to the orphanage, as I said. I fell in love with this little sweetheart named Lily." Diane figured, saying this would alleviate more questions about how all this had happened.

"But, Diane, why not wait until you can have your own children? Why adopt?"

"If you saw Lily, you would understand. There are two others, a girl and a boy, that I would like to adopt. The girl's name is Glenda, and the boy's name is Running Deer."

Laura stared at her in horror. Had her friend gone mad? She thought she better hold her tongue until her friend had time to think about what she was saying. What had come over her?

Diane started laughing at Laura's horrified expression. She headed for her office to think about Matt and his proposal instead of work.

She was surprised that Matt had agreed so readily to a marriage of convenience only. Down deep, she didn't want that type of arrangement. She had thought Matt would have talked her out of it immediately. He must have a guilty conscience over telling Mother Anthony about her being his fiancée when they did not see each other socially until last night. Their dinner at the Avian Rose was pleasurable. As if by consent, both evaded the situation and had an enjoyable dinner.

Then her mind went in a different direction. Perhaps, she could suggest a change to their adoption agreement to include Running Deer. She had observed how Running Deer looked at Matt, his hero. The boy would be devastated if Matt chose Lily only.

Diane called Matt's office. When he came on the line, Diane asked if they could meet for lunch at the Winchester Restaurant?

Matt agreed readily. But he felt there was some underlying motive behind her request. Was she changing her mind? Would she have more conditions in their marriage? Stipulations that would impede them from ever being close.

Matt arrived at the Winchester. Diane was sitting there looking demure. He bent over to kiss her on the cheek, and she showed no objection in front of the Maître'd. He sat down. They asked each other about their morning, making small talk. Diane had preordered wine and was sipping some to bolster her courage. Matt was surprised to see this, as the Maître'd filled his glass.

Their waiter arrived immediately. Diane picked up her menu to peruse this as though she had never seen it before. She had arrived early and had studied the menu thoroughly to put in time while she anxiously waited. Was she making the right decision? Maybe she should not have arranged this luncheon?

Matt asked, "do you know what you want, or have you already ordered?" He was a little disturbed at the wine she had preordered. Would she be independent like this after they were married? Was she setting a precedent by ordering before he got there? He wasn't late. She must have been extra early.

Diane colored faintly. "no, I haven't ordered." Looking at the waiter, she said, "I will have the Avocado Salad." Then she smiled sweetly at Matt.

Matt quickly ordered, "Asparagus Soup followed by Wellington Grilled Steak, thank you," handing the menu to the waiter. Matt gave his full attention to Diane. What was she up to now? He knew it had to be something. She was drinking her wine in gulps rather than sips. Naturally, Matt poured her more wine. He picked up his glass.

"To what do I owe the honor of being invited to lunch with you?" He raised his glass to her and drank some, waiting for her reaction.

Diane's color heightened. She took another gulp of her wine.

She was definitely up to something. Matt reached over to pause her hand. "Diane, this isn't a drinking lunch. What is going on here?"

Diane quickly lowered her glass to the table. "Matt, I invited you to . . . to ask how Suzette is? She had rushed to that answer because her reason for inviting him didn't seem right now. She saw that he looked so self-sufficient, and her suggestion to change their agreement might appear to be a criticism of him. Two children, what in the world had she been thinking? No, she wasn't thinking clearly. She had gotten carried away while talking to Laura.

Matt's mouth fell open. "Suzette?" That couldn't be why she arranged to meet him. There had to be more. What does she want, or better still, what did she not want now? More provisions? If this kept up, they would need a prenuptial agreement on behavior.

Diane rushed out with, "Yes, how is Suzette? Handsome misses her." She trailed off inanely.

"Diane, I hardly think Suzette is the reason you have been downing your wine like water."

"You noticed." She picked up her glass and took another gulp.

"I noticed you are acting strangely. Now out with it, what is bothering you. What are you proposing now? More stipulations?" Matt asked, dreading the answer.

"No, nothing like that. But we will have separate bedrooms," Diane ended

"Diane, marriages of convenience usually have separate bedrooms," *which I don't want.*

"Good," Diane agreed.

"Is this what is bothering you?"

Diane picked up her wine again in preparation for needing more spiritual support. *How do I get out of this now? He knows I'm up to something.*

Before she could take another drink, the waiter arrived with their soup and salad. Diane put down the wine glass and picked up her fork. She delved into the avocado salad to fill her mouth as though she hadn't eaten in months.

What is going on here? How do I get her to tell me? Whatever it is, she has changed her mind.

Matt picked up his soup spoon and followed her lead to eat, giving her time to bolster her courage to tell him her latest idea.

They both continued eating without conversation. Matt had never seen Diane this way before. He decided to take the bull by the horns.

"Diane, do you want to tell me that you have changed your mind about marrying me?"

"No," Diane said nothing more she just kept eating.

"Is it Lily and the adoption?" Matt asked with some fear.

"No." She was running out of salad. *What now?*

"Diane, help me here."

"I . . . I must tell you I was apprehensive about working with you in the beginning, so I made up my special diet." She stopped. *Will he think I am crazy?*

That can't be it. Unless Diane accepted his proposal because she had lied to him. No, a special diet isn't a reason to take a man in matrimony.

"Diane, a special diet confession isn't serious enough to drink the way you have. It must be more serious. I am not a mind reader. Help me here."

"You are doing fine," said Diane absurdly. Her avocado salad was gone. She picked up her wine again.

"Diane, stop right now. This has gone on long enough. Why did you invite me for lunch? Which is turning out to be a drinking lunch for you."

She dropped her hand to the table and spilled her wine."

"Oh dear!" She got up, grabbing her purse, and ran out of the restaurant. Matt threw some bills on the table and followed her out. Memory serving him, she had done this once before. He looked around, and she was gone. He went to the parking lot to pick up his car. He drove to her office. Matt had never been there before. But he knew where it was.

When Matt asked the receptionist, "is Miss Mackenzie in?"

The girl replied, "Miss Mackenzie is out of the office at a luncheon. Could Laura Anderson help you? She is Miss Mackenzie's partner."

"No. Please give Miss Mackenzie the message. I will see her tonight." Colleen looked at him with interest. This man must be Diane's fiancée.

"Yes, I will pass that on to Miss Mackenzie as soon as she returns."

Diane breezed in, looking at some mail she had picked up at the post office on her way back from her dreadful lunch. She sailed by without looking up, commenting, "Colleen, hold all my calls. I don't wish to be disturbed."

"Miss Mackenzie," Colleen gushed, "this gentleman wishes to see you."

The fact that Colleen had called her Miss Mackenzie, Diane knew without looking back who the gentleman was. Diane stopped dead in her tracks. Then picked up the pace heading for her office. Matt was in hot pursuit. He put his foot in the doorway as Diane tried to close it. Colleen strained to see what was happening.

"Diane, you had better let me in unless you want a scene out here." Diane let go of the door. Matt pushed his way inside. She headed for the window, putting the desk between them. Matt circled the desk and drew her around to face him.

"Diane, you had better tell me what is going on."

She looked at him rebelliously, crossing her arms in front of her to stop him.

"Diane, I am not going to beg anymore." He pulled her forward with a jerk, causing her to uncross her arms and her hands landed against his shoulders to balance herself. Matt dipped his head to kiss her, only to deepen the kiss as her hand encircled his neck. Drowning in their embrace and each other, Matt gradually released her lips, wanting more. His lips pressed hers once again, kissing her ecstatically until she was like putty in his arms.

He finally released her. But he had to grab her again as she swayed light-headedly.

"Diane, I didn't mean to do that. I mean, I am glad I did."

Her eyes flew open as she remembered her dilemma. "Matt, I . . . I want a divorce."

"Diane, we aren't married." Now he started to laugh as Diane's hand covered her mouth as though she was trying to stuff the words back in.

"I know that," trying to muster some dignity. Diane pulled away from him, drawing out her chair and plunked down to put some space between them.

"Diane, I am not leaving this office until you tell me what's the matter, even if it takes all night."

"You wouldn't." Diane looked cornered.

"Yes, I think I would enjoy a night with you," he said wickedly.

"But you promised in name only if we got married," she squeaked out.

"That may change if you don't tell me what's going on."

"Matt, I've changed my mind."

Matt's heart fell.

"I can't tell you why I wanted to see you," she finished. Matt's heart started pumping again.

"Answer two questions, and I'll leave you alone. Do you intend to marry me? Are we still adopting Lily?"

"Yes, I promise to marry you. Yes, we are still adopting Lily. But I refuse to say anything more."

Matt was so relieved that his two questions were still yes. He dropped a kiss on her forehead and headed out the door, closing it behind him.

Laura and Colleen were standing outside the door and quickly parted to let him by.

"Good afternoon, ladies," he said with a pleasant air and sailed out of the office. Diane and Lily were still his, thank goodness.

Then he lost his smug look as he remembered his meeting this afternoon with Danny. He didn't have time to worry about Diane's odd behavior. He had to see Danny and convince him Diane was keen to marry him.

He pulled up in front of the Church of the Ascension. A young lad was awaiting his arrival. Danny must have given him a description of Matt as he addressed him as Mr. Hadden and turned in the direction of Father O'Malley's office. Danny was making sure that he got there as Matt had canceled the Sunday meeting.

"Come in, Matt. Have a seat."

Matt looked worried. He noted Danny was crossing himself as he invited him in. This visit would not bode well for him. Matt was sure.

"Hello, Father O'Malley," Matt said formally.

"Matt, how could you mislead Mother Anthony? What did you do to Diane to make her go along with your wishes?" Father O'Malley wasn't beating around the bush. He was going for the kill.

"Danny, I never meant this to happen." He paused.

"Father O'Malley, to you, only special friends call me Danny," he said pointedly.

"All right, Father O'Malley, I never meant to lie to Mother Anthony. It just happened. It just slipped out somehow when I heard you were showing Lily to a couple from your congregation. I figured you were taking her out of my reach because you knew I wanted to adopt Lily."

"That was not my intention. I had already spoken to the couple before your request to adopt. The couple had just decided to see Lily simultaneously that you made your feelings known. It was strictly coincidental, that's all. I didn't have time to let you know. Matt, I thought I was your friend. Do you think I would ever treat my friends vindictively?" Danny said with some hurt in his voice at Matt's insinuation.

"Father O'Malley, I am deeply sorry. But I lost my head when I found Lily missing from the orphanage." Matt's voice was remorseful.

"I'll accept that. But what did you do to get Diane to agree? I know you were not seeing her. You told me yourself when I asked recently." He stopped waiting.

"I went to see her after leaving Mother Anthony's office. She agreed to come to see Lily. I mean to meet Lily."

"Did you tell her about the adoption?" he asked sternly. He knew from the look on Matt's face what his answer would be. But he still waited.

"No. I wanted to, but I thought it best to see how Diane reacted to Lily first."

"And how did she respond?"

"Better than I had hoped," Matt said with a grin.

"What happened then?" Father O'Malley wasn't about to let Matt off the hook. He was still working him.

"Sister Ruth said Mother Anthony wanted to see us. So, I thought she wanted to meet Diane. I didn't know she had already started filling out the papers."

"You could have told Mother Anthony the truth."

"I know, but I didn't want to embarrass Diane. And then, Diane seemed to be going along with the interview answering the questions asked of her. Then I began to hope. Honest, Danny, I didn't know Mother Anthony intended filling out the papers when Sister Ruth gave me the message that Mother Anthony wanted to see us."

"But Diane didn't know at this point that she was supposed to be your wife-to-be, did she?"

"Well, no. But when I proposed, Diane answered yes," said Matt hopefully.

"But the truth of the matter was that Mother Anthony believed you were asking Diane to change the date from one year to three months. When in fact, that was when you asked her to marry you." Father O'Malley wanted all the facts out in the open.

"Well, yes."

"Why in the world did she say yes to your marriage proposal? It wasn't really a marriage proposal, was it?" asked Danny in amazement.

"You're right. It wasn't a proper proposal. But I had to say something because of Mother Anthony's question of when the marriage was to occur. I have asked Diane a few times since, and she still keeps saying she wants to marry me. I gave her an out," said Matt defensively.

"You gave her an out. That's mighty big of you, considering that she now knows about Lily and the adoption. She would feel bad for the child if she refused."

Matt clammed up. He was digging too deep a hole to get out of easily.

Father O'Malley sat there, shaking his head. Matt figured that meant he intended to block the adoption. But his following words surprised him.

"Matt, how did you get that girl to agree to your proposal more than once?"

Matt blurted out, "she said yes with provisions."

"Provisions! What are they?" inquired Danny curiously.

Matt had not intended to tell Danny this part. It just slipped out.

"The marriage would be in name only, and she didn't have to give up her career completely."

Danny started to laugh. Matt watched as Danny laughed hilariously. He wasn't sure he liked that. Danny was still laughing uproariously with visions of Matt being in close proximity to Diane without touching her.

"Danny, it isn't that funny," said Matt indignantly.

"Buddy, it certainly is." Danny wiped his eyes of tears as he had laughed so hard.

"Next question. What about Lily if Diane doesn't intend to give up her career?"

"We compromised. If Diane has business commitments, I would be home with Lily. Otherwise, she would work more in her home office on her computer, and I will spell her when she wants to spend some time in the office."

Father O'Malley said, "that might work."

"Does that mean you won't block the adoption?"

"No, it just means I intend to give it more thought instead of the definite NO I had intended before you arrived here today."

Matt perked up. He hadn't said he was against the adoption entirely. There was still hope.

The two men sat, staring at each other. Their relationship had changed. But was it for the better?

Chapter Fourteen

When Matt got home, he called Diane. On the way to dinner Sunday, Matt had told her that he had delayed meeting with Danny until today.

"Hello, Matt, how did things go with Father O'Malley?"

"Well, let's put it this way, he didn't say no to the adoption, but he didn't say yes either."

"What do you mean?" Diane was curious now.

"He said he is giving it more thought after our talk before he gives me a definite answer."

"Matt, you do realize the marriage is off if he says no to the adoption." Why had she said that? She still wanted to marry him. But not in three months, maybe a year.

"Diane, you can't do that. How can I ever convince Father O'Malley if you back out?"

"But Matt, if he says no. There is no need to get married."

"But if we were married, then I may have a chance of changing his mind," said Matt logically.

Diane knew that Matt had a point. But she also knew that if there was no Lily, what purpose would there be to their marriage? She remembered the sensual kisses in her office that day, although there was no love between them. They had been on fire and definitely beyond a friendly peck. It had been out and out passion. At least on her part, she amended.

"Diane, are you still there?" She had been so silent. He didn't know what she was thinking. Did it have anything to do with whatever was bothering her at lunch?

"Yes, I'm still here. Matt, I'm afraid to say yes or no right now. So, I think we will just leave it at no Lily, no marriage."

Matt's heart sank. Couldn't she tell how much he needed her in his life by his kisses? Kisses that had started in anger but soon changed to out and out love for this girl. He had told her he loved her the day he proposed. But he knew that was overshadowed by his conniving ways in front of Mother Anthony.

He had to accept her answer. After all, he had tricked her into the proposal, and now he would have to pay the price. She would never believe him if he declared his love now.

"Diane, I wish you would believe me. I fully intended to tell you ahead of time. I planned to give you a choice after you met Lily. It was taken out of my hands by Mother Anthony having the papers already prepared."

"Matt, I believe you. But that doesn't change the fact that you didn't search me out until you were turned down as a single parent for the adoption. That I surmised from Father O'Malley's conversation."

"I know, Diane. But I had intended to get in touch with you sometime soon anyway. I wanted you to know the truth about Norma. However, I was caught up with the activities at the orphanage. The time never seemed to arise. Diane, I really want you in my life." Matt finished seriously.

"Matt, it still stands no Lily, no marriage. Goodbye, Matt." Diane put the phone down sadly. She couldn't see past the fact that he hadn't come seeking her out until after Lily's adoption was refused initially.

Diane put her head down on the arm of the sofa and cried. She wanted to marry Matt, and now it wasn't meant to be.

Matt was sitting beside the phone with a dead receiver in his hand. When a voice crackled from the phone, "please redial your number." Matt hung up.

Why had he not approached her sooner? He had definitely wanted to. The blond Adonis had put him off. Seeing her with that man in his car had thrown him for a loop.

Their meetings in the woods always turned out to be disasters. No, not really. Just two lovesick dogs were trying to direct their owners in the same direction. That is what he should've done, taken the woods path walking Suzette, and met with her again. But it was too late now. If he lost Lily, he would lose Diane also. He sure had bungled his life.

*****

Tuesday, he arrived in the afternoon as usual at the orphanage. Lily was waiting on the veranda. But the rest of the children must've been with Mike.

Lily was hiding until he reached the bottom step. Out came her hand before his. He put a finger in her palm, and she grasped it tightly and said, "Daddy." Matt's heart lurched. Lily knew. How did she know?

She walked towards him, throwing herself in his arms. "My Daddy." She gave him a smacking kiss. Matt kissed her on the cheek but didn't speak. He looked up when he heard the door open. Sister Ruth stood there anxiously.

"Yes, Lily knows. Renee told her that she overheard Mother Anthony and me talking. We were unaware that she was around. The approval hasn't come through from the church yet." Sister Ruth told Matt, knowing how concerned he was.

Matt held onto Lily tighter, wanting to protect her from the hurt if the adoption was refused. He finally said, "thank you, Sister." He had a feeling that Sister Ruth knew about Diane's on the spot proposal. He didn't know how, but he did believe she knew.

Matt's hole was becoming a gully with no way out. Lily was happy in Matt's protective arms, not knowing how her fate was still in the hands of Father O'Malley. His decision could tip either way. But he felt right now that it would go against him. What had he done? Poor Lily would be devasted.

Matt and the children played their games with enthusiasm. But anyone who knew him would know that his heart wasn't into sports today.

After the afternoon activities, a whoop went up from the children. They ran helter-skelter for the door as Father O'Malley had arrived. The children expressed their usual abundance of joy.

Besides the usual Benito and Martin holding his sister, the only two that hung back were Lily and Running Deer. These two stayed at Matt's side.

Father O'Malley was walking towards Matt. He yelled a greeting to Mike. Mike, along with two older children, Ken and Donna, were putting the equipment away.

Matt stood waiting, trying to read Father O'Malley's expression. But his face was quite deadpan, although it changed to a smile when he looked at Lily and Running Deer.

"Run along, children. I want to speak to Matt." Lily climbed into her cart. Running Deer held onto the back of the seat, running beside Lily to the school doorway where her cart plugged in under a portico.

"Hello, Matt," holding out his hand, Father O'Malley greeted him.

Matt grasped his hand warmly. But didn't return the greeting. Danny held Lily's life in his hands, not to mention for him Diane's too. He waited to see what Danny had to say. No matter what, Father O'Malley would always be Danny to him.

"I have come to tell you that I haven't arrived at a decision. The Board and Mother Anthony have approved the adoption. But then, we know they don't have the full story. So, their approval is academic."

"What can I do to make you understand I love Diane? I realize now that I have loved her for quite a while."

"But you weren't even seeing her until after I told you that I wouldn't approve Lily's adoption to a single male parent. Isn't that true?"

Matt agreed.

"So, why don't you believe that I find it hard to understand Diane and your relationship? I am surprised that Diane accepted your proposal. That is why I am here today. I want to have Diane come and see me in my office alone. Can you arrange that for me?" Father O'Malley was looking very serious. So, Matt was not pleased about the 'alone.' He wanted to be with her. To cushion her against any questions that might embarrass her about accepting Matt's unethical proposal in front of Mother Anthony.

"Yes, I can arrange it. When do you want to see Diane?" Matt's voice was less than enthusiastic.

"Do you think she can come tomorrow afternoon? If that doesn't work for her, give Diane my number and have her call for an alternate appointment. Otherwise, I will expect her Wednesday at two." He smiled this time.

"Matt, I just want to query her feelings on the matter and get to know her a little better. It may help me make my decision, that is all." Danny put his arm around Matt's shoulder. "Come, my friend. Shall we go in? I have to say goodbye to the others. I have to go to another meeting."

Despite his deep-seated worries, Matt felt reassured with Danny's arm around his shoulders like old times.

*****

That night he went over to Diane's house, taking Suzette with him this time.

"Do you want to take the dogs for a walk?" Suzette and Handsome were barking up a storm. Their tails were wagging, and their tongues were meeting in love kisses.

Looking down at the dogs, Diane said, "I guess we had better." She went to get the dog leash and her runners while Matt kept the dogs in check. Not that it was essential.

Diane arrived back, grabbing a light jacket on the way. She had her runners in her hand as well as the lead. She sat down on the bench to put the running shoes on while Matt put Handsome's leash on. When they were ready, the two dogs led the way, with Matt following. Diane stopped to lock the door.

They strolled to the woods in small talk while the dogs were romping. Handsome and Suzette were so happy to be together. You could see it in every step.

Matt wanted to hold Diane's hand but thought she might misconstrue his reason. Especially when she found out, Father O'Malley wished to see her.

The walk through the woods was going well. The dogs decided to behave, which Diane was thankful for, though she slightly missed their tying antics with Matt and her.

Suddenly the thought entered her mind that Matt was acting differently today. More reserved somehow. Diane wondered when Matt would start to speak?

"Diane, how is your schedule for tomorrow? Do you have some free time between, say, 1:30 and 3:30 in the afternoon?"

She knew this was it. She stopped, but Handsome kept moving and pulled her into walking again.

"I think I can be free. Any particular reason?" There was puzzlement in her voice.

"Father O'Malley would like to meet you in his church office at 2:00 pm. It is the Church of the Ascension. Do you think you could make it?"

"Are you going to be there?" Diane queried with interest.

"No. Father O'Malley just wants to meet with you. We already had our meeting, which I told you about."

This time Diane did stop and pulled Handsome to a stop too. "Alone?" looking at Matt in dread. "Matt, you know he knows about your proposal in Mother Anthony's office was impromptu. What can I say? I can't go alone."

"Diane, Father O'Malley only wants what is best for you and Lily. He is not out to catch you in some crime or falsehood. He thinks I have pressured you into this unfairly. He knows it is me that is in the wrong, not you."

"But, Matt, he knows I went along with the charade. What will he think of me?"

"Father O'Malley is a caring man. His children come first and foremost. So, he wants to make sure that he makes the right decision. If talking to you will help him, then please go talk to him."

"Matt, what about our stipulations?"

He wished he didn't have to answer that. But honesty was necessary at this moment. She would soon find out at the meeting that Danny already knew.

"Diane, I told him already when I spoke to him. I had no choice." Her look of horror was hard to look at. He started walking, hoping she would follow, and she did.

"Diane, I had to tell 'him. I want Lily, and I want you in my life." he pleaded.

"Everything! You told him everything that I said that was part of the provision."

"Yes, Diane, everything." There was dead silence. Matt didn't look at her. He wanted to give her time to digest this latest information.

The two joggers came running by. Jogger #1 asked, "not tied up?"

Jogger #2 replied, "no, they probably got hitched."

Jogger #1 grinningly said, "you mean tied the knot?" Both broke into gales of laughter, slapping their legs in hilarity. They jogged off, their laughter trailing behind them. Matt winced. Their comments were not conducive to helping matters at that particular moment.

Thankfully, she didn't react to the two joggers. He knew that Father O'Malley was uppermost in her mind.

"Matt, I can't believe you told him. That was personal between you and me. Why would you tell him?"

"Because I want you and Lily in my life. Danny is my friend, so I had to be honest."

Diane's expression still held disbelief. She was shocked to learn that he had revealed their secret. "Matt, I can't face him, not now."

"But, Diane, if you don't go, then we don't get Lily for sure."

The rest of the walk through the woods passed in silence. Both deep in thought.

When they got back to Diane's place, she invited him in. Matt asked if she had any wine? Diane went to the fridge to get the bottle she always stored in case someone dropped in.

Matt was still in the living room pacing. Diane put some cheese, crackers, and green grapes on a plate. Then she carried the tray bearing the dishes and wine glasses into the living room.

Handsome and Suzette were lying together before the fireplace, watching Matt pace. He appeared to be muttering to himself.

Diane set the tray down and picked up the two glasses, carrying one to Matt. He took the wine glass and stood in front of her. He raised his glass in salute.

"To you, Diane, the woman I want most in my life even if I don't adopt Lily. Please believe me in this?" he raised his wine glass to his lips and drank. Then leaned forward and kissed her lips fleetingly. Then he stepped back for her reaction.

"Matt, I want to believe you but . . ."

Matt set down his glass. Then he picked up her left hand, placing the engagement ring on her finger. The ring was twinkling up at her. It was the same ring he had given her before.

"I put this ring on your finger in mockery, which I regret. I bought this for you with high hopes. Please accept this ring along with my heart."

Diane looked at the ring, sparkling up at her. She had once worn this with pride. How did she feel now?

At Diane's lack of comment, Matt added, "if you would like to pick out another ring, that is fine with me. I know how you must feel about this one," he offered.

"No, Matt, it is lovely. You have me spellbound with your proposal for me to accept the ring." She looked down at the ring. Her heart expanded, and she decided to accept the ring and wear it with pride again. Diane reached up on her toes to seal her acceptance with a kiss. Matt removed the glass from her hand and pulled her into his arms. The kiss was a true pronouncement of their feelings at the moment. Matt was head over heels in love. The kiss went on into a fiery infernal. When they finally came up for air, Diane was so lightheaded she leaned against Matt in contentment. He held onto her, gratified.

Diane's head cleared and zoomed back to her dilemma. "Matt, what about Father O'Malley?"

"Diane, if I could do this for you, I would. If I could go in with you, I would. But he stressed alone."

"I wish now that I had never told you my provisions until after we found out whether we would get Lily or not."

"Diane, I surprised you with my proposal. So, the provision was a natural reaction. I'm sure Father O'Malley will think it is apropos under the circumstances. So, don't even think about it. Besides, he will not embarrass you. The stipulations will probably never come into your conversation."

"But, Matt, he knows. Now I know he knows." There was still horror in her voice.

"Would you feel better if I drove you and waited outside?" Matt asked encouragingly.

"Yes, maybe that would help." Her finger felt good with the ring back where it belonged. At least, she believed at the moment that the ring did belong there.

Matt stayed for another hour. They ate the crackers and cheese and drank their wine while covering several topics of interest and the orphanage children and their sports program.

He talked about getting Diane involved if she was interested. She agreed to do that as her compassion went out to the children.

When Matt left, he kissed her lovingly. But with a little less passion. He felt he had better control his ardor until after Diane's appointment with Father O'Malley.

Chapter Fifteen

Wednesday dawned with clouds and rain. Diane felt her anxiety clutch her stomach. This day would be forever until 3:00 pm, and the interview would be over.

After she dressed, she noticed her clothes were as gloomy as the day. She went into her closet and picked out her brightest outfit, which happened to be fuchsia—something she had bought on a dare.

Diane changed her clothes but didn't look in the mirror. She was glad she had already applied her cosmetics. While she was putting the finishing touches to her makeup, she noticed her drab appearance.

Diane went out the door, letting her bright appearance take over to brighten her spirit.

Colleen's mouth fell open. Diane sailed by with a cheery 'good morning.'

"Good . . . Good morning to you too." Something was definitely up for Diane to come in dressed like that. She buzzed Laura.

"Yes?"

"Laura, wouldn't you like to discuss something with Diane? Why don't I tell her you want to speak to her?"

"Okay, Colleen, what's up?"

"You'll find out as soon as Diane walks into your office." Colleen rang off and then dialed Diane.

"Diane, Laura would like to see you in her office."

"Okay, thanks." Diane got up from her desk and trooped down the hall. She tapped lightly on Laura's closed door. Laura preferred it closed the better to concentrate.

Laura said, "enter." She pushed back from her desk and crossed her arms in waiting mode, not knowing what to expect.

Diane stood framed in the doorway.

"Good, God. What is that you have on?"

"It is a crepe dress. What do you think?"

"Well, I am speechless, that is for sure. What is this in aid of?" waving her hand to indicate Diane's outfit. Laura tried to keep a straight face until she heard Diane's explanation. Then maybe she would let go.

"I have an appointment with Father O'Malley. I didn't want to look gloomy."

"Well, you certainly succeeded there. There is certainly nothing gloomy about that outfit." Laura started laughing. "Diane, what do you hope to accomplish with that getup? Father O'Malley's eyeballs will burn up from the shock. Besides, why are you going to see Father O'Malley?"

Diane came in and sat down.

"It is about Lily's adoption. He has the final say as to whether we get accepted or not."

"Well, you certainly will get his attention. No, shy wilting female here. Don't you think you overdid it a bit?"

"Do you think so?" Diane looked down at her dress. "It is kind of bright."

"Bright, that's too mild a word."

Diane's face fell.

Laura felt mean, so she cooled her comments down. "You're right, Diane. You must feel like you can tackle the world in that dress. Father O'Malley will be aware immediately of your sparkling personality." Under her breath, she added, *and your shocking exterior.* Laura smiled winningly at her. It was then that she spotted the diamond ring on Diane's finger.

"That gorgeous ring is back. You're officially engaged this time, are you?" Laura got up and came around to hug Diane, wanting to inspect the ring closer. It was a big diamond with two guarding stones on each side. The two side diamonds were big enough, but the center diamond was a knockout. Laura kissed Diane. "Congratulations, soon to be a wife and mother. Does that mean I have to look for a new partner?"

"No, Matt and I have agreed that we would share Lily's care. I will spend some time in my home office on my computer. But I will come in occasionally, and anytime business requires my presence, Matt will be there for Lily."

"Diane, I'm glad to hear you aren't quitting altogether. It sounds like an okay arrangement. But we will miss seeing you every day. Matt sounds like a caring man, agreeing to your continuing."

"He is understanding. He did offer a Nanny, but I want to be there for Lily."

"Diane, tell me if it is none of my business, but isn't this rather a sudden relationship?"

"Laura, I love him. If the only way I can have him is because of Lily, I want to grab the chance."

"Diane, I hope you are doing the right thing." She switched ideas. "Think positive. Matt will love you the way I do. He won't be able to help that." Laura changed from doubt to the need to reassure her friend. This relationship has to work out for Diane. She is too sweet a person to go unloved. Matt better be good to Diane, or he will have to answer to me. "When is the wedding?"

Diane did not know what to say. "We sort of agreed on three months. But nothing is definite yet." *Maybe never if the adoption doesn't go ahead. After all, that was her stipulation.*

One thirty arrived along with Matt. Diane had been too excited to eat lunch. She hoped her stomach wouldn't gurgle. Colleen and Laura wanted to see Matt's reaction to

Diane's dress. So instead of sending him in like she usually would have. Colleen asked him to wait while she let Diane know he was here.

Laura was pretending to study files at Colleen's desk. She smiled at Matt. "How are things going for you?"

Matt made some reassuring remarks and fell silent. He spotted Diane walking towards him, and he gave her a big smile but hid his amazement at her choice of attire. Much to the disappointment of Laura and Colleen. This guy had to love her to respond in this way. He covered up his astonishment well.

"Hi, Diane. Are you ready to go?" He nodded to Laura and Colleen, taking Diane's arm, leading her towards the corridor.

Diane hadn't said anything. *Did he think her dress was too much?*

"Diane, try not to be nervous. Father O'Malley is a nice guy. Don't forget, I have known him for a very long time."

"I wish you were coming in with me. If only Father O'Malley didn't know about my 'in name only' condition.

"I agree. I had no idea that Father O'Malley would want to see you personally." Matt pulled the car out into traffic. The trip didn't take long before pulling up at the church as traffic had been light.

"We are early. Should I go in?"

"Maybe, he will see you sooner. Then it will be over earlier." Matt got out of the car to open her door. He took her hand and helped her out. He gave her a light kiss and squeezed her hand, hoping to boost her confidence.

With stiff and unyielding legs, Diane managed the stairs. She looked back at Matt, encouraging her with a smile before Diane slipped inside the door. She walked down the aisle, observing the ornate altar and pulpit.

A voice to her left called her name. Father O'Malley stood in a doorway near the confession boxes, so Diane walked to the front of the pews. Then she turned in his direction.

"Hello, Diane. I am pleased that you could make it today."

"Hello, Father O'Malley."

He took her hand with both of his, holding them warmly, which gave her a bit of confidence. "Come into my office. Mrs. Kinsley will bring us tea now that you are here. You do drink tea, don't you? It is herbal." He continued walking before she could murmur her assent.

They went into his office. He pulled out a chair at a table off to the side of the room near the window. He looked out and observed Matt was sitting in his car in the parking lot. It seems he did care about this woman. He sat down, looking at Diane with interest.

Diane felt better. The conversion wasn't going to be formal with him sitting behind his desk.

"How has your day been?" Father O'Malley had been taken aback by her colorful dress but kept a bland face. Why had she worn that particular dress? Was there a statement here he was missing? He felt sure Diane did not dress this way regularly.

"My day was fine," answered Diane shyly. Why had she worn this dress? He must be horrified but too polite to mention it. It will probably give him the wrong impression of me.

"Diane, I have asked you here today to discuss the adoption and Matt. How long have you known him?"

"About six months. We worked on a business project together. Although, I did see Matt occasionally other than for business."

"You probably know that I knew there was no engagement before that moment in Mother Anthony's office when he asked you to be his wife? Mother Anthony, of course, thought you were answering her question as to when the wedding would take place."

Diane blushed. "I know, and I didn't elaborate."

"I am not going to ask you why not. But I do feel you may have felt pressured into it. Is that right?"

"No, I wasn't pressured. I just felt it was the right response at the time."

"I also know that you have stipulated that it is to be in name only. Can you explain why?"

"That was in response to Matt's not discussing it with me in advance. When I realized that he tried to adopt Lily without me, which was denied, then he approached me to meet Lily. I responded with two provisions, which includes remaining with my career on a lighter scale."

"So, you intend to pursue your career?"

"I will be working from home, mostly. If I have a necessary business appointment, Matt has promised to be with Lily," Diane stated honestly.

"Why do you feel you still need your career? If you marry Matt, he can well afford to support you and Lily both?"

"I worked long and hard to obtain my standing in the business world. I have a partnership with my best friend, Laura. Matt was agreeable to my desire to continue to work, particularly from home."

"The fact that you intend to work mostly from home makes a difference, I agree. Do you want children of your own, Diane?"

"Someday, I will probably be ready." Diane blushed, knowing that he knew Matt wouldn't be sharing her bed.

"Diane, I want you to think carefully about my next question before you answer, all right?"

She nodded.

"The church is all about family and love. As a result, children come from a loving family component. Now, do you think you will be ready to accept Matt in your bed to consummate the marriage in three months, six months, or a year?"

Father O'Malley opened the door to Mrs. Kinsley and the tea trolley. There was a teapot, 2 cups and saucers with shamrocks on them, and a plate of fancy sandwiches.

Mrs. Kinsley poured while Father O'Malley placed the tea on the table in front of Diane. Mrs. Kinsley put the plate of sandwiches in the space between them, leaving the teapot handy on the trolley cart. She left the room with Father O'Malley's thank you.

"Do you take anything in your tea, Diane?"

"No, Father O'Malley."

"Let's cut that down to Father, I think, for the duration of our conversation."

"Yes, Father."

"Help yourself to the sandwiches. I intend to indulge myself, and I hate to eat alone." He smiled winningly at her. Diane reached for a sandwich, nibbling on it. They both sipped their tea, which had an apple spice flavor.

Diane was trying to decide how best to answer his question. Because of Matt and her short time back together again, she felt that the marriage should be in name only. How could she back down now?

"Diane, are you ready to answer my question?"

"Yes, three months."

"Good. Now, if I decide to refuse you and Matt adopting Lily, will you still marry him?"

"No. Matt only wanted to marry me for Lily."

"Then you don't believe he loves you?"

"I don't know."

"Well, we'll leave that for now. What do you think of Lily?"

"She is adorable. One can't help but love her."

"You do realize she will need extra care with her legs the way they are?"

"Yes, I understand, and I look forward to giving her that care."

"Were you raised as a Catholic?"

"Yes, Father, but I must confess I have devoted so much of my time to my career I sort of dropped out of the church. But we will attend church with Lily."

"Now, is there anything you would like to ask me?"

"Yes, Father."

"What would that be?"

"Running Deer is very attached to Matt. Don't you think he will be deeply hurt if we choose Lily?"

"Yes, I have noticed Running Deer's devotion to Matt. You are quite right. It could be a problem." His brow creased, then he continued. "Do you have a suggestion, or why would you bring it up?"

"Well, Father, if we take Lily and leave Running Deer behind, he will be quite devastated. So, I am suggesting adopting both of them." She colored at her presumption of thinking that he would approve not just one but two adoptions.

"Do you realize the magnitude of that decision? What if Matt only wants Lily?"

"Two children can't be that much more work than one. Matt wants Lily. He can't see beyond that possibility of only one. But if he knew he could adopt two children, Running Deer would be his second choice."

Father O'Malley sat contemplating this idea, taking another sandwich and drinking more tea. He was silent so long, Diane figured that he was dreading telling her that he couldn't approve Lily's adoption because of Diane and Matt's irregular marriage agreement. When in fact, he was contemplating saying yes to Running Deer too.

She was starting to squirm when Father O'Malley finally came out of his reverie.

"Diane, I know Matt is waiting for you. I saw him through the window. I want you to convey my decision to him. I won't keep him waiting any longer." He stopped, took a breath. Then congratulated her on her perfect family of Lily and Running Deer.

The tears shone in her eyes like diamonds. She put up her hand to brush them away when Father O'Malley spied her ring.

"Congratulations. I see you are officially engaged." He pulled her hand into his, inspecting the ring. "Matt chose a nice setting, I see." He felt this indicated devotion on Matt's part.

"Thank you, Father O'Malley. I want to tell Matt right away." She smiled happily.

"Go, my child, with my blessing. Do I get to perform the marriage?"

"Of course, who else would be more fitting?" Diane laughed now that it was all over. "Oh, and, Father. Please excuse the dress, but I didn't want to feel gloomy. No matter the outcome of the interview."

"That is all right. It sure brightened my day. Now go in peace." He did the sign of the cross on her forehead. Then he reached forward and kissed her cheek. "Matt is waiting for you. Say hi to him for me. I won't come out. You will want to be together at this point when you tell him the good news.

Diane said goodbye and thanked him for approving the adoption of both children. She was anxious to get to Matt with the news.

Chapter Sixteen

Diane walked sedately but swiftly on winged feet until she passed the door of the church. Then she ran to the parking lot. Matt saw her coming and got out of the car.

Diane was running fast toward him. Her face wreathed in smiles. Matt opened his arms for her to run into. He kissed her lovingly. Matt was so happy to see her smile. Then he remembered that he was in a church parking lot and ended the kiss.

"Tell me, did everything go well?"

"Yes! Oh yes! Matt, we are the proud parents of Lily and Running Deer." Diane's tears of joy clouded her eyes, and she smiled happily at the same time.

"Lily and Running Deer?" Matt was amazed, petrified, and elated, all at the same time.

"Yes, I told Father O'Malley that Running Deer would be devastated if we took Lily and not him. He worships you, Matt." She was talking so fast in her excitement. "You do want Running Deer too, don't you?"

"Diane, I would never have dreamed of asking for two. But of course, I want Running Deer. You dear sweet girl." Matt kissed her again.

Father O'Malley stood at the window watching, knowing in his heart that he had made the right decision. Those two would make the perfect loving parents for his orphans. He smiled at his success in placing two of his children. Introducing Matt to Saint Andrews Orphanage had been his idea, so he unequivocally took the credit for its outcome.

Diane said, "Father O'Malley says hi. Father saw you through the window." Matt quickly looked up, and there was his friend looking down on them. Matt still had his arms around Diane. He lifted one hand and gave Danny a thumbs-up sign in gratitude.

Father O'Malley gave the thumbs-up sign back with a 'way to go' cheer.

Matt ushered Diane into the car. They headed to Saint Andrews Orphanage to see their children.

"Diane, how did we come to get Running Deer too?"

"Matt, remember the day I asked you to lunch? But I didn't follow through with what I wanted to say. Well, that was what I wanted to ask you."

"What do you mean?"

"I was talking to Laura about the children at the orphanage. I was describing Lily, but in my mind, I envisioned you with Lily on one side and Running Deer on the other side. The two children are always around you. So, I was going to suggest that we adopt them both. But I felt so unsure of myself that I chickened out."

Matt swerved to the side of the road and stopped the car.

Diane looked around. "Why are we stopping here?"

"Because, my darling, I want to thank you properly for being a generous person. So willing to adopt these children for me." His arms drew her in to show his gratitude, love, and commitment to her with one loving kiss.

The sounds of twitters broke them apart. They had collected an audience of two elderly ladies and a gentleman. The man tipped his hat in salute, causing Diane and Matt to laugh. Matt started the car, and they continued their journey to their children.

When they arrived, two children were on the veranda, Running Deer with Lily hiding behind the post with one hand exposed.

Father O'Malley must have phoned Mother Anthony. They quickly exited the car and walked to the veranda. He reached out his hand to Lily, pulling her firmly towards him. Lily said, "my Daddy." He lifted her into his arms and kissed her.

"Yes, my darling, you are my daughter." Lily laughed and gave him a smacking kiss. Matt passed Lily to Diane. "This is your Mommy." Lily went willingly into Diane's arms. They shared a kiss.

Matt turned to Running Deer. His face was a study of a sad child. Although, he was bravely holding back his tears. Matt put out his hand towards him. "You are my son." Running Deer leaped into Matt's arms, kissing him and kissing him. He was strangling Matt with his arms. "Yes, son, and this is your mother." Matt turned to Diane and circled her shoulders with his arm. Running Deer leaned close to kiss her too, and Diane embraced him.

Sister Ruth must have been watching because the door soon opened to view the perfect picture of a happy family before her.

"Congratulations, you happy parents of two." She came forward to embrace the four of them. She knew these two would not like to be separated from their children quite yet, nor from each other.

The two children were chanting, "My Daddy and My Mommy," Matt was chanting back. "You are our son and daughter."

Sister Ruth stood back, so pleased that this loving couple wanted both children.

"Mother Anthony is waiting for you both. I guess there is no point in saying leave the children here with me while you go in to see her."

"You are right. I'm afraid we can't let these darlings go quite yet." Matt and Diane walked to Mother Anthony's office with their children held tightly in their arms.

Mother Anthony stood at the door, watching them with their faces wreathed in smiles. This was the family picture she would always hold in her mind.

"Congratulations. I see you have two children."

"Yes, we have two. Thank you for your approval," Matt said thankfully.

"No, thank you for being a determined young man and you, sweet lady, for your generous heart. Now come in. We have more papers to sign."

They sat down with a child on each lap. The children stared in wonder at the number of forms they were signing, which made their family unit complete.

"When are you two getting married so that you can have the children?"

Matt looked at Diane. "Next week, I think. We can't wait any longer than that," he said honestly.

Diane nodded her head. "Father O'Malley wants to perform the marriage ceremony."

Matt exclaimed, "Tuesday afternoon instead of their usual sports. We are going to celebrate a wedding. All the children are invited as well as the nuns, and you, of course, Mother Anthony." Diane was nodding determinedly with a huge smile. They embraced the children.

Matt's heart was cheered. "I think we had better go back and call on Father O'Malley again." Matt laughed at his enjoyment of his new perfect life.

The children indicated that they wanted down. Then they changed places, holding up their arms to be lifted. Their new parents lifted them onto their laps for another embrace. Mother Anthony looked on approvingly, and there was no doubt that these children would both be well-loved. It is a shame that the children would be unable to go home with them today.

Matt spoke to Lily and Running Deer. "Your soon-to-be parents would have to get married before you both can come home with us. We will spend the time getting your rooms ready. We will come on Saturday, as usual, to be with all the children. Then on Sunday, we will come to take both of you out for the afternoon."

Matt looked up at Mother Anthony. "Are those arrangements all right with you, Mother Anthony?"

"Yes, of course. I see no problem with that."

Sister Ruth entered and came towards them.

"Sister Ruth, accept our invitation for the nuns and all the children to come to the church to witness our wedding vows on Tuesday. Lily, you can be a flower girl. Running Deer, you can be a ring bearer."

"Mother Anthony, if I provide the tents and the caterers for the food. Can we have the reception here at the orphanage on the sports field after the church service?"

"Yes, I think that would be a perfectly acceptable arrangement." Mother Anthony was so thankful that this happy couple wanted to share this momentous time in their lives with everyone from the orphanage.

Matt explained, "I will provide bus transportation to the church for everyone. We will also be taking Lily and Running Deer with us after the reception. Hopefully, the paperwork will be finalized by then. Then we will never be separated again. How's that?" looking at Lily and Running Deer.

Lily clapped her hands in approval, and Running Deer joined in. The two children had wide grins on their faces. Then Lily gave Matt another smacking kiss.

Running Deer followed suit with a kiss for Diane. Matt thanked Mother Anthony once again, and they left. Mother Anthony and Sister Ruth followed them down the hall, both beaming for the happy family picture portrayed in front of them.

As they came to the door, Matt's arms engulfed the two children explaining, "you are staying for a short time while we get ready for the wedding and set up your rooms."

The children gave Diane and him kisses on the veranda as they were leaving. Mother Anthony and Sister Ruth stood with the kids to wave them off.

Matt inquired, "before we get to the church, I want to ask you something. Diane, we have never discussed religion. I haven't exactly been a perfect Catholic, not attending church the way I should. How about you? What is your faith?"

"I, too, have not been much of a churchgoer due to my career priorities. But I assured Father O'Malley we would bring the children to church as I am Catholic too."

"Good, I am glad to hear that. I so want to marry you, and the sooner, the better, so let's get to the church to arrange the wedding." He squeezed her hand gently with a big grin.

Matt directed the car back to the church to see Father O'Malley.

Father O'Malley was surprised to see them back so soon. He was pleased that they were proceeding with their marriage immediately. It confirmed that he had made the right decision. Matt explained that everyone from the orphanage would attend. Lily will be the flower girl, and Running Deer will be the ring bearer.

"The wedding will be at 11:30 am on Tuesday and the reception at 12:30 pm at Saint Andrews Orphanage. Is that all right with you, Danny?"

"It will be a great privilege to perform your wedding ceremony. I am pleased you had the forethought to invite Saint Andrews Orphanage's residents to witness your vows."

He took Diane's hand, and Matt's hand linked them and then placed his hand over theirs.

"Bless you, may you always be happy and fulfill your dreams. I am confident that Lily and Running Deer are in safe, loving hands."

"Thank you, Father O'Malley, for your final approval for both children. We went to the orphanage to sign the adoption papers for Running Deer. The children were happy with the news that we are their parents. We told them that we would have to leave them both until we are married. They accepted that readily enough. Now, we will have to go home and make more plans." Diane exclaimed happily. Matt was nodding his head in agreement as she spoke.

"Bless you both. I am quite honored that I will be able to oversee your wedding and that I was instrumental in placing two of my children in your loving hands. Bless you, both. Goodbye until Tuesday morning." He shook hands with them. Father O'Malley and Matt linked hands in special friendship and trust.

Once they were away from the church, Diane inquired, "we haven't talked about any details as of yet. Where are we to live? Who are we inviting to the wedding? Are you making all the arrangements, or am I?"

"Temporarily, we will live in your house until I sell my condo. Then eventually, we will get a larger home. You can invite as many as you wish. Just let me know how many so I can arrange the details with the caterers. I will take care of all the arrangements. Are you getting a wedding gown?"

"I was going to get a nice outfit on our way home."

"I would like to see you in a proper wedding dress. Perhaps you and I should go shopping for the dress and the things for the children's rooms on Friday. So, they can be delivered Saturday or Monday."

"You are not buying my wedding dress. However, Laura will help me." She laughed joyously in her excitement.

Matt grinned at her laughter, but he wanted to get his point across. So, seriously he said, "Diane, I want this to be a proper wedding even though it is rushed." *In name only for you because to me, this is for real. I will convince you of that. If only you were ready to hear I love you, Diane.*

"Matt, I promise you won't be disappointed. I will take care of Lily's and my dress. You can arrange for yourself and Running Deer."

"Fair enough. Now for the children's rooms. Let's go shopping. I don't want to wait any longer."

"I thought we were going on Friday."

Instead, they went home to Diane's to make up the guest list, consisting of both business and personal friends. It was understood that because it was so hurried and on a weekday that many might not attend. Miss Canning's job was to let their prospective guests know the reason for the speedy marriage was because of the readymade family that doesn't want to be apart any longer.

*****

Thursday, Laura and Diane closed the office early. They stopped by Saint Andrews Orphanage to pick up Lily. While there, Diane introduced Laura and Colleen to Running Deer and Sister Ruth. Lily wasn't hiding this time as the three women greeted her.

Benito, his usual distant self, caught Colleen's attention. She took a fancy to him. Colleen and her husband had never been blessed with children. But she felt sure this was about to change. Here was a boy that needed a loving couple to change his defiance to life that Diane had mentioned. Colleen thought she and her cop husband would be perfect as parents for this abandoned boy.

Diane was amazed at Colleen's fascination with Benito. She had never inquired why Colleen had no children. Instead, she had assumed that it was because of her husband's job dealing with unsavory characters, making his occupation sometimes unsafe.

Benito's gruff attitude appealed to Colleen's heart. She would speak to Trevor when she got home.

Diane took Lily's hand to install her in the car safely. Then the three women and Lily headed off for the exclusive wedding shop that Laura suggested where her friend should get her wedding creation. Laura took time choosing three wedding gowns while Diane and Colleen selected Lily's dress. Lily was wide-eyed and speechless at the prettiness of the dresses. The one they finally chose was to the floor and hid her braces. It was pale green and brought out her sparkling green eyes and her auburn hair. Laura supported their decision.

Laura, Colleen, and Lily sat in a conversational grouping of chairs to await Diane's arrival in her dress. The stylist realized the choices Laura had made were perfect for Diane. She had an eye for the eloquent. The fitter aided Diane in her fittings.

Diane started with her least choice for viewing. She had already made her choice as soon as she saw the three dresses. But to please Laura, she would try on all three.

Lily was excited at Diane's white angel-like appearance. Then Diane returned to the dressing room for the next creation, and she walked serenely in front of her friends. She told them to hold their opinions until she had tried on all three.

Diane knew as soon as the third dress settled down around her body that this was the dress that she wanted for Matt. It was a simple dress but had an intricate lacy pattern on the bodice and sleeves. It came down in a straight line to her knees, then flared out in an ultra-becoming way.

The stylist stood back, appraising her. "This dress, my dear, was designed with someone exactly like you in mind. Now go out and show your waiting audience to see if they agree."

Diane walked serenely before the awestruck three. Her body seemed to float with the filmy swirl of cloth flowing around her like a cloud.

Laura jumped up. "Diane, you are beautiful in that." She whipped a veil and flower tiara off a nearby stand, placing it on Diane's head. It came to her waist but so filmy, giving her a demure maiden look, and the stylist approved of Laura's choice. This was the perfect wedding ensemble for Diane.

Lily sat wide-eyed with a big 'o' on her lips but with no sound. Diane was awe-inspiring to the little girl, such splendor in her simple orphan life.

Minor alterations were necessary, so all the arrangements were made for the delivery. Laura was to be her maid of honor. Her dress was chosen with the stylist's aid, zeroing in on a similar dress in a deeper green than Lily's.

The foursome went for afternoon tea to give Lily a treat at a specialty tea shop. They had stopped at a florist on the way to pick out the flowers for the wedding and reception.

Lily was impressed with everything she saw. The three women enjoyed Diane's new daughter in return. Diane's heart was overflowing with her wise decision to accept Matt's unusual proposal that day in Mother Anthony's office. That gave her this enchanting, unspoiled, and awestruck child.

That night, Matt came over to hear the news of her day's excursion with Lily. He related his outing with Running Deer. Matt's male bonding with his new son during the task of picking out their wedding garb pleased him. They would be wearing tuxedos in gray with the cummerbunds in an auburn shade similar to Lily's hair. Running Deer was so pleased with his new shiny shoes. Matt let him wear them instead of his regular brogues. Running Deer carried the bag with his old shoes grasped in his hand. He kept stopping to admire his new shoes. The excited look on his face caused the people passing by to grin in response.

Matt took him to an ice cream parlor. They did the boy thing by having banana splits. They talked of their soon-to-be family life, their sports days, and Diane as well as Lily. Matt explained to Running Deer that it would be their job to look after and protect these two females coming into their lives. His response was more than Matt could have hoped for. Matt was so glad Diane had asked Father O'Malley for both children.

Diane and Matt excitedly continued talking about their shopping trip set for tomorrow, which Matt was anxious to do. That night, when he left Diane, he kissed her good night. Not with the usual quick kiss, he had been giving her, but with a more passionate one. When they finally broke apart, Diane was so weak and wanting more. She felt like liquid that could flow away. Matt grasped her shoulders tightly and put distance between them. He bowed his head. *How long could he be platonic with this woman? To be in the same house and not share her bed.* When they got married, he was to sleep in the study on a pullout bed. But he hoped that would change before long.

"Diane, I had better be leaving. Tomorrow is shopping for the children's rooms. So, I will be back to pick you up at ten. Do you want to do the dog walk together first? Say at eight is that too early?"

"No, it will be fine. Handsome likes an early walk." Diane was glad that Matt had broken the embrace when he did. Otherwise, she wouldn't be able to keep her resolve to retain the stipulation of separate bedrooms.

They parted, and Diane took Handsome out to the backyard. She sat under the stars thinking about her whirlwind days since Mother Anthony's office first visit and Matt's proposal. Handsome tired of sniffing around, came over to Diane and put his paw on her lap to bring her out of her contemplations

Chapter Seventeen

*F*riday, Matt whisked Diane off to the shopping area that Miss Canning assured him was the best place. They were like two children let loose in a toy shop. Their purchases piled up, furniture, clothes, toys, books, and bedroom frills. Each bedroom was to have a different theme. Lily's bedroom was very feminine, and Running Deer was to have his traditional native motif.

Diane liked the Friday shopping. The clothes they had bought mainly were basic things such as pajamas and outdoor playthings. She still wanted dress-up clothes for them both.

The more they shopped, the more they laughed. Matt felt he was getting to know the genuine Diane. He liked, no, he loved this wonderful girl unveiling herself before his eyes. She expressed her thoughts, wishes, and hopes for the children, which gave him a clear picture of her.

Matt was amazed at how much her thoughts were identical to his. He was getting more excited about the prospect of his marriage to Diane.

Matt was also thinking forward to looking for a new house. But he would hold off until the sleeping arrangements altered into one master bedroom for the two of them. That would be his priority once they were married, showing her that she wanted a valid marriage rather than in name only. He knew he would need lots of cold showers in the first weeks. But he hoped that didn't become months.

"Matt, I want to get the children some clothes from a specialty shop that is quite near here. I saw some pretty children's clothes when looking for a gift for a friend who had just had twin boys. The shop impressed me."

"Diane, if that is what you want to do, I am all for it. Let's do it before we go to dinner."

She was amazed at how in tune she and Matt were in taste and thoughts for the children. In the process of choosing dresses, pants, and tops, they were both happy with their choices. On passing a toy store, they looked at each other. Grinned, then dived in happily choosing many toys until Diane had to remind him. "Matt, the size of the rooms we are outfitting are not huge." Matt laughed, putting back an overstuffed colossal bear.

Their purchases were stowed in the trunk and back seat. They looked happily at each other for a job well done.

"Diane, are we ready for dinner now?" holding out his hand. She put her hand in his. They walked to the restaurant he had in mind for their dinner. "Mike should be here soon."

The dinner's purpose was to meet with his best man, which was to be Mike because Craig was away in Europe on business and wouldn't be home in time. Matt asked Mike as his second choice amongst his friends. Mainly because of his connection with Saint Andrews Orphanage.

While they waited for Mike and his girlfriend to arrive, they sat discussing various subjects that flipped from the wedding to the children coming into their lives. These two were converting their lives into a relationship of harmonious destiny.

"Hi, Matt. I hope we are not late." Mike Snyder and his girlfriend approached the table.

Matt stood up to greet Mike. Diane liked this young man already. The way he handled himself with the children at the orphanage. The girl he had with him was a brunette. She looked like a career girl.

"I would like you to meet Tara. Tara, this is Matt and Diane." They all exchanged greetings.

Matt encouraged, "shall we look at the menu? I will order a bottle of wine. Do you have a preference, Mike?"

Mike replied, "we are both easy, so you go ahead and order the wine."

While they waited for the meal to arrive, they discussed the wedding and the reception. Then the conversation floated into the activities at the orphanage. Mike made an effort to include Tara in the conversation. So, she didn't feel left out when she knew little about Saint Andrews Orphanage, having never been there. But Tara had taken in the niceties from Mike's conversations with her, so she did absorb some things mentioned.

Diane soon understood what Mike was trying to do. She revealed to Tara her viewing of the sports with the orphanage children.

"Would you like to come on Saturday when I intend to show up with some T-shirts that one of my staff designed for the girls and boys with slogans? I wonder what the shirts will say?"

They were having fun batting around ideas trying to think of what Laura had come up with for T-shirts. They came up with things like:

Baseball Achiever   Soccer
Fulfiller   Fulfilled and Having Fun
Achiever and Gratified   Achiever and Succeeded

The evening passed. Matt was thrilled at the outcome. The men even let the women take the floor and that they did. Tara offered to help outfit the children in the T-shirts. Tara tried to guess the children's sizes, which set them all laughing.

Then Diane and Tara came up with the brilliant idea of a tournament. They would referee a baseball game of Matt's team against Mike's team to have a fun day for a change on Saturday. Mike ended the evening, saying, "thank you for the evening. I think I had better get home and rest up for the next day's baseball tourney."

Matt laughed. "I guess I better get home and get some rest too. See you both tomorrow for the great baseball event." Diane and Tara added their goodnights.

Diane and Matt liked Tara and Mike, expressing that the evening was an enjoyable break from the wedding prearrangement pressures.

Matt dropped Diane off but did not go in. Diane was tired, so she didn't dissuade him.

The next day Matt and Diane walked the happy dogs that behaved without incident. Then he arranged to come at 9:30 to go to the orphanage. He arrived back to pick her up, and Diane was ready. Matt was thrilled at the idea of having her in his life. The more he saw of her, the happier he was.

She slipped into the car, leaning over to give him a quick kiss on the cheek. After which, she settled back on her side, putting some distance between them. He wanted her to stay glued to his side.

They arrived at the orphanage. Running Deer leaped off the veranda and ran towards them. Matt swept him up, then Diane leaned over to kiss Running Deer. Matt placed the boy down, then they both took his hands and walked towards the veranda. Lily was standing, openly waiting. She came forward to walk off into Matt's arms as he quickly dropped Running Deer's hand. The family was complete.

Matt carried Lily towards her cart. Running Deer ran ahead to pull the cart out, ready for Lily to get in. Matt and Diane noticed how protective of Lily he was. They went to greet Tara and Mike. They were getting the children sorted out as to size. All were anxious to try the T-shirts on, not wanting to wait for the fitting. The sizes were solved, and all had donned a T-shirt. The T-shirts read -- Sports Days Are Fun.

Matt and Mike chose their teammates. The younger children settled on the ground to root for their favorites along with Father O'Malley. Tara was teaching them cheers and chants.

First, Mike's team did well. Then Matt's team crept up to their score. It went a couple of innings with no runs completed. Then Mike surged ahead only to have Matt's team tie them. As the game neared the ninth inning, Matt stole a base when the ball went to the outfield. He ran past first to second base. Diane noticed that he hadn't touched the first base before heading to second. She whispered to the opposing team to tag him out for not touching first base. Diane declared him out. That made three out for Matt's side.

Matt threatened Diane with unfair refereeing tactics, chasing her around the field to the running children's delight. Tara gave him a tackle from behind. Matt fell on top of Diane. Then it was arms and legs everywhere and more laughter from the children.

Then Tara declared them both out, and she went into the game for the last inning as Matt's replacement. Mike was up to bat. Tara stood waiting in front of first base, prepared in case he bunted. Mike hit the ball. Tara caught the ball then dropped it. Mike continued running, but Tara retrieved the ball and touched him out. Mike picked her up and kept running to first base. The children were all yelling and screaming.

Diane was yelling, "unfair tactics."

Matt was yelling, "that's not legal."

Benito was next up to bat. Mike still held Tara over his shoulder, head down. Benito hit the ball. Tara caught the ball and tagged out Mike, who had started to run, making a double play. Diane declared it legal.

Everyone's antics brought the ball game to an end with a tie score. Father O'Malley declared the referee the winner to everyone's cheers because Diane had avoided the ball Martin hit directly at her.

A truck arriving on the field caught the children's attention. It was an ice cream truck with a clown inside. Everyone ran to choose their favorite flavors.

While everyone was licking ice cream cones, Diane declared the game officially ended. Mike and Matt shook hands, both claiming to be the victors. The clown came out to amuse the children and became the star of the show.

Diane had an ice cream cone for Lily. She walked over and knelt beside Lily, saying, "to you, Lily, with love." Lily accepted her cone and Diane's love with a kiss. Matt plunked down beside them and pulled Diane on his lap, directing Diane's eyes to watch Tara. Tara was putting the finishing touches on a giant ice cream cone she was building for Mike now that the clown was busy entertaining.

Mike and Tara licked the giant ice cream cone, laughing, accusing each other of unfair licks. All in all, they were being silly to amuse the children. They succeeded.

The afternoon ended on a happy note, with no team winner but all winners of the clown's special attention and his ice cream treats.

Sunday, Matt took Lily, Running Deer, and Diane on a picnic. The children enjoyed their first picnic and ended up rolling around on the grass giggling as Diane and Matt tried to pick them up.

After which they visited the zoo. Lily was in her cart with Running Deer running beside her, holding onto the back of the seat. Matt and Diane were proudly bursting their buttons over, Running Deer's protective way with his sister. The zoo visit's highlight was when a deer came over to Lily for a pat. The deer kept butted her hand for more pats.

Matt took pictures of his new family so they could start an album. Lily and Running Deer became photo stars, striking funny poses together. Then Diane got a priceless photo of Running Deer on Matt's shoulders, patting an elephant. Simultaneously, Lily was trying to climb Matt's leg like a monkey. Their family officially started that day, as far as Matt was concerned.

They had an early dinner. Then their new parents took the children back to the orphanage. Soon this trip wouldn't be necessary.

When they returned to Saint Andrews, it was to find out that the children had come up with another song.

We are the children of Saint Andrews
We love you, Matt and Diane too
We will miss you both
We love Lily and Running Deer
We will miss them both too
We wish the best for you
And your new family too

Diane and Matt were so pleased that they would sing this memorable song for them as they stood with Lily and Running Deer linked between them.

Matt said, "we will still be coming to see you, and we will bring Lily and Running Deer. You certainly will never be forgotten by any of us."

Sister Ruth released the children to go out to play. Sister Juanita and Sister Anne were awaiting the children in the yard.

Sister Ruth came forward to talk to Matt and Diane and their soon-to-be children.

"Did you have a good picnic?"

The two children shook their heads excitedly. Then Running Deer blurted, "I patted an elephant at the zoo. Daddy helped me." Lily, not to be undone, spouted, "I wished I had patted the elephant, but I couldn't reach. But I did pat a deer, and it wanted more." Matt and Diane were smiling down at them in pride.

Sister Ruth conversed, "we have another child being placed in a good home, thanks to you, Diane. Your friend

Colleen and her husband are taking Benito. She took quite a shine to him that day she came with you to pick up Lily. It must've been his standoffish nature, his armor for the hurt his mother has caused leaving him. Fortunately, Colleen and her husband, Trevor, didn't care when I explained."

Diane responded, "that is good. Colleen's husband is a cop. He works undercover a lot, and Colleen could use the company. But Trevor is extremely nice. I know it will work out."

Sister Ruth thanked Matt for his first adoption request and the resulting additional adoptions. Matt passed it off with a nod.

Diane and Matt bent down to say goodbye to their children. "You will be coming home with us the next time we are together because we will be married." The two children hugged and kissed their new parents. Running Deer led Lily away to play with the other children at Sister Ruth's direction.

Sister Ruth watched Diane and Matt's expressions. A new family that would prosper in their love for each other.

Matt affirmed, "all the tents, tables and chairs, etcetera will be arriving shortly after nine Tuesday morning. The caterers will be arriving at noon. There shouldn't be anything for you to do, except, of course, to attend the wedding. The bus will arrive at eleven in the morning to take everyone to the church. We will leave now. Happily, the next time we meet will be at the wedding."

Sister Ruth smiled. "Bless you both. I'm looking forward to the wedding on Tuesday." Matt finally took Diane's hand and said goodbye to Sister Ruth. Diane smiled her goodbye too.

In the car, Matt mentioned that he had arranged for Diane to have a pampered day at a health spa to relax her on Monday. Then an evening out with the girls. He, of course, was being roasted by his buddies. They would not see each other again until the wedding.

"The furniture will arrive early on Monday. So, I arranged for Miss Canning to go over Monday morning to handle the children's furniture setup and placement by the delivery men. Miss Canning was more than pleased to be included in our plans before the wedding while you are out. Thank you for the spare key."

Matt was to move some of his things over to her house since he had the key. Diane was getting butterflies in her stomach at the latest arrangements. It was all happening so fast.

Secretly, Matt had been looking for a larger home but had not found the right one yet. Besides, when he moves there, he wanted Diane to be with him in the master bedroom as his loving wife.

Diane didn't know what was going on in Matt's mind. He seemed preoccupied, and she hoped that it was not with second thoughts. She was enjoying having him around.

The next day, Diane went for her spa treatment, which entailed going from room to room, pampering her body from head to toe. The massage relaxed her so much. She must have fallen asleep. After eating a light lunch, she had a beauty treatment, her fingers and toenails, and a facial. The last was to be a distinctive hair styling for the wedding.

Who should she see during the facial, but Norma? Norma, in her usual vindictive manner, started relating stories. She was telling the lady doing her facial in a loud voice what Matt was like in bed. Knowing full well that Diane couldn't help but recognize the male she referred to.

Diane must've flinched at Norma's explicit details because the girl working on Diane's facial apologized for the disturbance. Their facials happened to end at the same time. Norma breezed by her, pretending not to see Diane, then turned around with a look of shock, which Diane was sure was fake.

"You're Diane Mackenzie, aren't you? I didn't realize that you were here. Congratulations. Via the grapevine, I hear you are marrying Matt. It came as a surprise. I always thought your engagement was fake. Did Matt feel obligated to marry you because you wouldn't give him back his ring? The last time I saw Matt, he said he was trying to ditch you. Oh well, you're welcome to him. He has become a has-been lover anyway. He is losing his power to satisfy me. Power meaning rather limp, if you know what I mean." Norma turned around and flounced out.

Diane wanted to sink into the floor in embarrassment. Florence, the girl working on her, said. "don't take any notice of her. She is a pathological liar. I heard that from another patron while she was mouthing off to you."

Diane thanked her for her kind words, wending her way to her wedding hairdo. Florence made it a point to arrange a private session with their best hairdresser so that Diane wouldn't run into Norma again. Florence felt guilty that she hadn't stopped Norma. But she had been so taken aback by Norma's crude outburst only to let her client become mortified.

Diane was humiliated but thought of Norma's past performance at that fated lunch and Matt's later assurance that Norma told lies. She decided to take the same attitude to this latest episode.

On her way to her hair appointment, an attendant directed her to a side room. She found that she was to have a private hairdo, thanks to Florence, the attendant said.

Norma was miffed when Diane did not appear in the coiffure room. She fully intended to continue her spiteful dialogue, but Florence thwarted her, although Norma didn't know that. She assumed Diane had left in embarrassment. Norma wore a self-satisfied look.

Florence looked in to see if Norma was spouting off any more and saw her expression of pleasure at Diane's no-show. Florence was pleased that she had managed an alternate service for Diane. She went back to her facial room, satisfied that she had upset Norma's open slurs.

That night Diane met with Laurie and Colleen, who had gotten in touch with Diane's bistro friends. They met at a bistro downtown famous for its seafood delights. A casual but intimate setting where friends could gather in groups or couples.

Diane knew the owner, Andy, because his wife worked in the advertising field as she did. They had collaborated on occasion to the betterment of both, which was unusual as most career women were only out for themselves.

Andy had decorated the place with Diane, Matt, Lily, and Running Deer printed on plaques, streamers, and napkins. There was a heart on each table's center with their names on it.

The evening went merrily with many glasses raised in praise of Diane's bravery of not only taking on a husband but two children as well. They wished her well but said a eulogy to the dying breed of bistro people that would miss her.

They all pulled out their little black books and tore out her name, lamenting it wouldn't be any use to them anymore, handing the page to Diane in a mournful way only for Diane to laugh because each page contained a poem of good wishes.

Laura and Colleen got up to sing a song wishing the best hopes and dreams for Diane in her new adventure. Diane was in tears at the joy of having these good friends. Then Andy's wife Greta gave her a gift certificate for two, entitling her to two evenings of fun at the bistro over the next two years so Diane wouldn't forget them.

Matt was being roasted royally by his fellow bachelors for his abandonment of their worthy cause. The married men were roasting him jovially for the life he would lead when Matt joined their club of the harried husbands and breadwinners supporting the wife and kiddies and becoming workaholics to make ends meet.

Matt laughed at both sides of their grievances. He was more confident than ever that he was doing the right thing. He just hoped none of these guys found out about the separate bed stipulation.

Father O'Malley dropped in to jokingly say a prayer of lament for the bachelor group. Then a prayer for the married group depicting their fulfilling life. Then ended up with a wish for Matt, the reverse of both prayers. Then Danny gave some antidotes of Matt's university exploits, which had the guys in stitches.

He related one particular incident. "Matt on a dare wore a professor's vestments with a wig that the professor inherited from his stately uncle from Oxford. The professor was so proud of it that he had it sealed in a glass case in his office. Matt had gone in and picked the lock, showing up in class in the outfit, sat through the lecture. Then he returned the suit before the professor could catch him."

Matt's defense in the matter was the vestments were under lock and key, so how could he have worn them? The professor later was quoted as saying that it hadn't happened. It was an illusion, to which later Matt had the vestments laid on the professor's desk for his next lecture. Matt won an award for the most convincing lawyer as a result by his fellow scholars."

"Then there was the time that we went to town for our girl night. We went to a bar, and Matt didn't want to cooperate by acknowledging a beautiful redhead because he said he didn't care for redheads. So, I helped her by bringing her over to our table. She brought her friend, who was a cute blonde. As the evening progressed, the redhead came onto Matt, which he politely tried to ignore. As the evening ended, I was going to take the blonde home. So, being the gentleman, Matt offered to take the redhead home. Just then, this burly guy shows up, and the redhead pretends that she didn't know the husky man, putting her arm around Matt. You guessed it. Matt showed up for class the next day with two black eyes and a cut lip. He commented that he ran into a two-fisted doorman because a redhead was holding onto him, so he was unable to defend himself."

Matt joined in the laughter and chicanery. But his mind was on his wedding tomorrow. He did little drinking so he would enjoy every moment of his wedding day.

Chapter Eighteen

The day of the wedding was bright and sunny. Laura came over to help Diane dress. She had picked up Lily and Running Deer on the way.

Lily looked like a little princess and Running Deer, a handsome prince in their outfits. It was decided that instead of a ring bearer, Running Deer would hold the basket, and Lily would throw the petals as they wanted to walk down the aisle together in front of Diane.

Mike had the rings. It was to be a double wedding ring ceremony, which Laura knew, but Diane didn't. Matt was sincerely looking forward to sharing their vows and the rings.

When Diane donned her wedding apparel, the photographer took pictures. Even Handsome was in some of the photos.

The chauffeur informed Laura that it was time to go. Matt had arranged the limousine to pick them up. A unique gift was awaiting her, a wreath of flowers to go on the tent entrance with their names entwined. The chauffeur had it displayed on the limousine.

The children came out hand in hand, then Laura and Diane. The chauffeur must've had a lot of practice with wedding parties. He quickly assisted them into the limousine after they exclaimed their joy over the wreath. He particularly paid extra attention to their elaborate dresses. The children were giggling excitedly.

They arrived at the church to the sound of the bells chiming in the steeple. Father O'Malley was heralding his friend, Matt, and his marriage to Diane and their adopted children.

The guests were more than they expected, along with Mother Anthony, Sister Ruth, the nuns, and the children from Saint Andrews Orphanage filling the church.

When it was time to go down the aisle, Laura went first. The two children held hands, using their other hand to grip the basket and throw the petals, and Diane followed.

Diane's gaze went to the alter to Matt, proudly watching the children and Diane come down the aisle. She was so proud of her children. There were murmurs from the congregation of the cuteness of Lily and Running Deer. Lily's gait was not noticeable when she slowly strolled as they did. The children turned to smile at Diane. She blew them a kiss.

Matt was so happy he was bursting with joy. His family was coming toward him. He couldn't believe that he had been so lucky. When the children had turned to smile at Diane, he wanted to go to them and hug them all.

When they arrived at the altar, Father O'Malley asked, "who gives this woman in holy matrimony?" Lily and Running Deer both said clearly, "we do." Lily and Running Deer were standing in front of Diane and Matt. Matt had a hold of Diane's hand, ready to accept her in his life forever.

Father O'Malley performed the wedding vows, asking Diane, "do you, Diane MacKenzie, take this man, Matt Hadden in Holy Matrimony to love and cherish in sickness and health, forever?"

Diane smiled at Matt. "I do."

Father O'Malley turned to Matt, asking, "do you, Matt Hadden, take Diane Mackenzie in Holy Matrimony, to love and cherish in sickness and health, forever?"

Father O'Malley barely got the words out when Matt enthusiastically said, "I do, and the children too." Laughter rang out amongst the guest.

The rings were exchanged, with Diane and Matt staring profoundly into each other's eyes. Father O'Malley pronounced them husband and wife and told Matt to kiss his bride.

Matt kissed Diane endearingly. The children were pulling on his pant legs, turning he picked up the children. Diane and Matt and the children shared wedding kisses before Matt put them down.

Diane put her arm through Matt's, and Running Deer stepped forward and took Diane's hand. Lily took Matt's hand.

Then Father O'Malley introduced them to the congregation. "I wished to present Matt and Diane Hadden as husband and wife and proud parents of Lily and Running Deer, their children. The guests all clapped as they walked down the aisle. The photographer captured the family on film.

When they got outside, the children of Saint Andrews Orphanage stood as an honor guard on each side of the walk to the limousine awaiting them. The wedding party was waving in thanks to the honor guard.

The guests spilled out of the church, observing the honor bestowed on the wedding couple and their children, flashing their cameras at the scene. The wedding party dipped their heads as they were escorted into the limousine heading for the Orphanage reception. They stopped at a nearby picturesque park to take pictures.

The wedding party arrived at the Orphanage with great expectation.

Sister Ruth exclaimed, "Congratulations." She ushered Matt, Diane and the children to the playfield. Under a tent canopy were tables and chairs for the reception. It was such a lovely sunny day. The wreath of flowers with their names entwined had been placed above the entrance. Matt stopped under the wreath to give Diane a loving kiss, to which Running Deer and Lily clapped. Matt picked up Running Deer, and Diane picked up Lily. They all kissed while the guests' cameras snapped.

When everyone was seated after the reception line was over, the two children sat between their parents at the head table with Laura, Mike, Father O'Malley, and Mother Anthony. Father O'Malley called everyone's attention to the back door of the Orphanage. The children came from the orphanage singing. They were all wearing T-shirts in red and white. The boys displayed as 'Matt and Diane,' the girls as 'Lily and Running Deer.' Laura's contribution to the children for their song.

Matt and Diane today did wed
forever to be a couple
Lily and Running Deer today did join
forever to be with this couple

Father O'Malley, Mother Anthony,
Sister Ruth and we do too
Wish you much happiness and love
in marriage and as parents too

Then the children all blew Matt and Diane and their children a kiss. This tribute was one of the highlights of the wedding reception.

Without a doubt, this couple was meant for each other. The way they exchanged glances.

It was difficult for them to kiss with the two children between them. However, the guest did try with the ringing of their glasses with their spoons. Finally, Matt got up and pulled Diane up to give her a special loving kiss while many cameras caught the spontaneity.

The speeches were accolades of happiness for this new family and their future together. Matt rose to make a speech too.

"To my wife, Diane, my beautiful bride, I give you my heart. To my children, Lily and Running Deer, I give myself and my wife as loving parents. To Father O'Malley and

Mother Anthony, I give my thanks for believing in me enough to place these two little ones in my care. Without your faith in me, this day would never have happened." He raised his glass in salute, and everyone raised their glass in response. Then he leaned over to kiss Diane, Lily, and Running Deer.

Matt knew he had tears in his eyes, but he didn't care who saw them.

Father O'Malley had the children give a rousing cheer to the wedded couple and family.

A musical trio arrived that got them all up dancing to the music.

The first dance was for Matt and Diane, switching shortly with Diane with Running Deer and Matt with Lily. Then Matt encouraged all the children to join in. Later in due course, the others followed. Father O'Malley danced with Sister Ruth, and everyone was enjoying themselves. Colleen danced with the smiling Benito while her husband looked on happily.

The time passed swiftly. It was time to go. There was quite a parade of children taking the suitcases for Lily and Running Deer to the limo. Lily's electric cart was part of the procession. The sister and brother stood by the limo, receiving these accolades from their orphanage brothers and sisters. Lily and Running Deer shook hands with them, including Father O'Malley, Mother Anthony, and Sister Ruth. Matt and Diane joined in the handshaking.

The two children sat between their parents waving, and the guests waved back as the limousine slowly pulled away.

When they arrived at Diane's place, Mike, Tara, and Laura were there with the two dogs to greet them and threw rose petals all over them.

Matt, Diane, and the others laughed at the dog's antics. The dogs circled Matt and Diane and tied them up with their leashes. Then both dogs sat down contentedly. Laura, Tara, and Mike waved goodbye, leaving them tied together. The children were delighted as they tried to untangle themselves as the dogs kept circling them in their efforts.

Matt and Diane gave up, kissing each other while the dogs unwound themselves. It was as though the kiss was what the dogs awaited. Then they all laughed when they broke the loving kiss. They all went into the house, a happy bride and groom and happy mother and father of their little ones.

Matt and Diane took delight in showing Lily and Running Deer their new rooms. The children were so excited. Matt stood with his arm around Diane's waist and watched as Lily showed Running Deer her room, touching its beauty in awe. Upon seeing the second bedroom, Running Deer came over to his new parents, thanking them, and held up his sparrow-like mouth for a kiss. Matt and Diane bent over to receive his offering. Lily was quickly there for her kiss too.

Then Matt lifted Lily. They were going down to the family room to see the dogs.

As they passed Diane's room, there was a sign on the door. To the happy bride and groom. They looked in. Laura, Tara, and Mike had decorated the room like a lover's nest with heart-shaped pillows. Hearts spread on the quilt with Champagne and chocolate-covered strawberries on the bedside table. There was a pink light shining down on the bed, which would have given them a glow had they been lying there.

Diane looked with horror at the room, then at Matt. He had a dreamy look of anticipation. His desire surfaced, noticed by Diane. But it wasn't going to happen, not with their name only provision.

Running Deer and Lily loved the room's decorations even though they didn't understand. Matt looked at Diane with an inquiring look. The shake of her head was no in return.

"No harm in trying." Matt smiled in defeat.

To make sure that there was no misunderstanding, Diane went over and picked up the champagne along with the bucket. She indicated for Running Deer to bring the strawberries.

They all trooped downstairs to the family room. The dogs were waiting for them, lying happily together. The children went over to the dogs, kneeling to pat them. Suzette and Handsome gave Running Deer and Lily their acceptance of being part of the family with tongue licks to the chin.

Matt had picked up the bottle of champagne. He began to open the bottle, but he wasn't sure whether it was in celebration or disappointment. But he called the children's attention as the cork was released, sending the cork like a projectile to the ceiling, then the wall. The kids laughed in glee. The dogs joined in barking then chased after the cork.

Diane went to get some pop for the children and glasses for Matt and her. They all enjoyed the celebration as a family at last

The happy couple sat watching their children eating the strawberries. The perfect end to a perfect day as the dogs looked on blissfully.

Chapter Nineteen

After a week, the new family had fallen into a routine. Lily and Running Deer played with the dogs and each other. While Diane did her day's work and Matt went to his office. Diane went out on certain days, and daddy stayed to keep an eye on them. But either way, Running Deer and Lily felt secure in their new family life, sharing in their parent's love.

On Saturday, it was off to Saint Andrews for sports day with the orphanage children. A practice Matt intended to keep. Colleen and Trevor had officially adopted Benito, so Martin was the top dog now but not as happy. He missed Benito's rivalry, and it finally sunk in that his mother wasn't coming back for them. Glenda had become more independent of him. Martin's best days were playing sports, and he was now helping Mike organize the games.

Matt and Diane always let Running Deer and Lily mix in with the others, as if they still lived there. The children seem to like that a great deal too. Diane spent more time with the older girls talking about clothes, makeup, and hairstyles with Sister Ruth's approval. Something they could look forward to in their future. Diane had brought some magazines so the girls could see the latest fashions. That way, the boys could have a sports event without the girls. The boys enjoyed the opportunity of rivalry, a happy situation for both.

Matt still worked mainly with the little ones. He was so proud of Running Deer for always looking after Lily, running beside her cart, holding onto the seat except when playing baseball.

Matt had caught Mother Anthony watching them out her window. He was sure she was pleased with her adoption decision and reassured with their continued attention to the children.

After spending the day with their friends at the orphanage, they came home tired but pleasantly so and content with their continued involvement in Saint Andrews.

However, Matt was getting more frustrated as the days went by. Diane was loving with the children and Matt during the day, sharing affection easily. But each night, Diane would change as the evening progressed. Matt knew then that it was another night without her in his arms.

Nighttime had become a happy ritual of bathing and bedtime stories after romping with the dogs. The dogs were also allowed in the bedrooms until it was lights out. Matt and Diane took turns with the stories, switching with each child each night as they did with the dogs. Then it was prayers and kisses and lights out.

Along with the dogs, Matt and Diane would head for the family room. The nights spent talking about their childhood days, hopes, dreams, and business dealings. They enjoyed each other abundantly. But when bedtime came, it was a light kiss, and they departed for their separate nighttime arrangement.

Diane was sorry about making the name-only clause. She would go up the stairs so forlorn—neither taking the step to end the ridiculous provision.

After one of their intimate evenings of talking, Matt had hoped that she would show that she wanted to end the nightly separation. He never made any overtures, knowing that there would be no stopping once he started. So, each night it was a stalemate and separate beds. Matt was finding it harder and harder to get to sleep.

*****

One day Matt stopped in to see Danny, to express his wishes to have Danny find another school to start competitive sports outside the orphanage. After Danny arranged the other school, he asked Matt about his new family's home life. It had been six weeks since the wedding.

Matt's forlorn look must have said it all. Although he quickly said, "it is wonderful with the children and Diane." He even related some happy incidents of their family life.

Then Danny started to chuckle. "She isn't letting you in her bed yet, is she?"

Matt grunted his dissatisfaction, then a begrudging. "No."

Father O'Malley consoled him. "Patience, my friend, it will happen," with a smirk in his voice.

"That's fine for you to say. But I'm the one going to bed alone each night, thinking about her in her bed. I want and need more to this marriage. That darn provision."

"Maybe it is time for a visit from me. I think I will drop in to see Diane one day real soon." Danny was still chuckling to himself when they parted. Diane had stuck to her plan, poor Matt.

The following week Father O'Malley showed up at the house. The two children gave him a rousing welcome. Diane served tea in the garden so he could see the children at play with the dogs. Father O'Malley could see that the dogs loved the children. He watched Diane watching them. The love was spilling out of her with her look of complete contentment. But again, he thought, poor Matt.

"Diane, I came to see you today to ask if you were happy with Matt. I can see the children are settling in well. How about you and Matt?" Diane gave him a startled look. *Had Matt told him that we were still sleeping separately?*

"Matt and I are getting along fine. We spend a lot of time just talking."

"And?" Father O'Malley prompted.

"And the relationship is progressing nicely."

"But?" Father O'Malley was persistent. Diane's answer was a surprise.

"But he never gets personal. He hardly kisses me in the evening. The trip upstairs each night gets lonelier and lonelier."

"What do you want to do about it?" he asked quietly, giving her a chance to make her wishes known.

"I made that stupid restriction, and now he is living up to my wishes. I find I am the one who wants to break it. He seems to be distancing himself from me. And yet, he is affectionate in front of the children, or I would doubt he loved me."

"Why don't you tell him that?"

"I just couldn't. I made the stupid stipulation, so I will have to live with it. I couldn't possibly recant now."

Father O'Malley realized her dilemma. He knew that Diane wouldn't make any overtures to change the situation. Father O'Malley knew that Matt would have to bide his time until she was ready. So, he left after speaking to the children and wishing Diane well.

A week later, a thunderstorm crashed overhead, causing the house to shake. Lily woke up crying. Diane went into her, and it wasn't long before Running Deer was in there with them. Diane was moving them to her bed for comfort when Matt appeared on the staircase. "What's happening here? Is the thunder disturbing everyone's sleep?"

Lily was in Diane's arms because Lily had her braces off. Lily put her arms out to Matt when another loud boom sounded. Matt couldn't help noticing the baby doll pajamas Diane was wearing but tried to ignore them.

When they got to Diane's room, everyone climbed under the covers, including Matt. Matt and Diane leaned against the headboard, each with a child in their lap. Matt put his arm around Diane, pulling her closer to his side. He talked about the storms in his youth that he had witnessed and reassured the children that it could be fun watching a storm from the veranda.

Matt's leg stretched out along Diane's bare leg was becoming excruciatingly warm, so talking became a chore. His hand on Diane's shoulder slipped down, settling against her breast, which tightened in response. But she didn't move away. The thunder had moved off. Lily had fallen asleep, and Running Deer was closing his eyes too.

"Diane?" Matt's voice was a whisper of hope. His hand cupped her breast more fully. She didn't move away but too shy to tell him she didn't want him to leave. Endearingly, Matt moved his hand carefully not to awaken Running Deer, who was asleep against her other breast. They looked at each other, questions in their eyes. Their feelings could not be ignored any longer. Matt kissed Diane passionately. He moved his head, and his warm breath drifted into her ear, causing goosebumps along her arms. She snuggled closer to him.

They both knew their wedding night had arrived, not wanting to deny it any longer. They carried the children back to their bedrooms. They met again in the hall and melded their bodies together, devouring each other's lips. Matt picked her up and carried her back to her bed, knowing he would never sleep alone again.

They shed their clothes and their confines, reaching for each other, seeping into their emotional ecstasy. That night became their heaven and the morning their peace.

Running Deer had managed to help Lily with her braces. They arrived at Diane's bedside only to note that Matt was embracing Diane in their sleep. Running Deer and Lily's giggling woke them up.

Diane was thankful that they had donned their discarded clothes before going to sleep. Matt dragged the two little ones onto the bed. They climbed over them like monkeys, happy little scalawags in their parents' bed.

Matt gave his wife a substantial kiss good morning. The children were kissing them too, thinking this was a new game. Matt laughed in complete happiness. It was time at last to seriously find that perfect house.

Breakfast filled with laughter as Matt was unable to pass anywhere near Diane without showing his newfound open expression of love. The more they kissed, the more the children got into the action too. Anyone happening on that family scene would know that this home contained true love in every aspect. The children liked this new game and were happy to participate, bringing Diane and Matt together for more kisses.

Matt did not want to leave for work. However, his commitment dictated otherwise. So, they all shared one last kiss.

As soon as Diane was alone, she went to the phone to call Father O'Malley. He was surprised to hear from her. He wanted to know if anything was wrong.

Diane exclaimed, "definitely not. I am calling you to let you know that Matt loves me."

Father O'Malley laughed. "So, you two have discovered each other at last. I knew all along how in love you both were. But I couldn't say anything. You had to work it out for yourselves. Bless you, my child, and much happiness for you both in your special love."

"Father O'Malley, when did Matt first pronounce his love for me?"

"Matt said he loved you when he first proposed to you in Mother Anthony's office. That was what he expressed to me also at my interview with him shortly after. I admit that I was a bit skeptical at the time, but now I am not so sure."

"Thank you, Father O'Malley. Unfortunately, I had to share my newfound love with someone. The children think our kissing is a game, and they like to participate fully. So, our breakfast was fun-filled with the children's antics.

Father O'Malley, with some amusement, pictured the breakfast scene Diane described. The freely shared kisses and the happiness in this blissful marriage. He chuckled to himself as though involved in promoting their unusual love affair, putting down the phone with a feeling of accomplishment. That was an excellent way to start the day with a success story.

Chapter Twenty

*I*n the late afternoon a few days later, Matt got a call from his realtor. The realtor proudly said, "I found the house you are seeking." Matt arranged to view it immediately. It was in a part of the city where there were stately homes and properties. This house had been passed down through several generations. The woman who owned it had never married and was now residing in a nearby nursing home.

As soon as Matt saw it, he knew that this was the home he wanted for Diane. The house radiated grace and grandeur, a place for love to grow. The updated house met current standards, but the ancient home's ambiance was retained in every room except in the modern kitchen. The terrace and the gardens were opulent and homey at the same time. He could picture the children and the dogs romping there.

The house radiated a warmth that he felt right at home instantly. On entering the master bedroom, he noted that it overlooked the garden and the sea's blue water in the distance. The furnishings completed the room's ambiance.

Matt asked, "is any of the furniture for sale?"

The realtor replied, "yes, the furniture is going out for auction."

Matt was predominantly interested in the master bedroom furnishings as he wanted the setting to stay this way for Diane. He had never given Diane a wedding gift. Now, his offering to her was this home and any furniture she wished to keep.

As soon as Matt got back to the office, he called Diane to tell her how much he loved her and to show his love, he wanted to take her to dinner.

"What about the children?"

"They can come too," he said enthusiastically. He recalled the children's bedrooms. A couple of decorated bedrooms showed that they had once belonged to a boy and a girl. There were two guest rooms, as well. The thought crept into his mind that these rooms might be used for some orphanage children to visit, especially Glenda. Lily would like that. Matt's mind was tumbling a mile a minute.

He arranged to pick the family up at 5:30. They whizzed off for their dinner in a joyful mood of expectation. Diane did not know how to dress. So, she outfitted herself and the children for an opulent restaurant, figuring that was Matt's intent. She knew from his voice something unusual was in the offing.

When Matt steered the car towards the older part of the city, she couldn't imagine any restaurant there. All she was aware of were stately homes. Matt had a silly grin as he pulled up in front of one of them. The spacious grounds were well kept, and inviting with a majestic home residing upon a knoll, showing it off to its best advantage.

Matt opened his door to get out. Diane watched his pride of step as he rounded the front of the car to her door, which he opened with a flourish.

"Madame," holding out his hand to her.

She laughed nervously. Who were these people that they were visiting?

Matt helped the children out too. They were staring bug-eyed at the house. Their little mouths formed into O's of wonder.

He guided them to the house, handing Diane the key. She opened the door, instantly knowing as she crossed the doorstep that this was for her. Looking back at Matt, his nod indicated 'yes.' Diane came into his arms. Their kiss sealed the gift as a perfect one in every way. Lost in each other, their kiss deepening naturally until the children's laughter brought them back to earth.

The house tour began with Matt and Diane walking hand in hand. They entered a spacious living room with a wide window view and to the side French doors inviting them into an elaborate dining room. The next room had shelves and so many books, more like a library rather than a study. Diane knew that this would be her office, which Matt could share as it was so big. There was a breakfast room overlooking the back terrace and garden. Beside that, a family rumpus room with a fireplace.

They headed upstairs. Running Deer helping Lily up the grand oak stairway, the majestic carpet stifling the sound of her braces. Back home, the braces clicked on the stairs.

The children quickly found their bedrooms. They were touching the trophies, the dolls and toy soldiers poised for war, along with plush animals from yesteryears. Matt told them that these might not come with the house as his understanding was that only the furniture was for sale.

"But I will inquire about your wishes. There are some furnishings I intend to request."

Then they entered the master bedroom. Diane stopped in wonder. "If it was my choice, I would keep this the way it is now." She turned around in a circle, drinking in her fill. "Matt, could this stay this way in its grand ambiance?"

"Yes, darling, this room is a must this way for you." Diane went into his arms to thank him the only way her bursting heart knew how. Matt drew her over to the window and its view of the garden and the sea in the distance. This home was beyond Diane's wildest dreams.

Next was the ensuite bathroom with its opulent tub and fixtures and a separate shower room, and a walk-in closet and dressing room completed the master suite. The children were running around happily, showing their glee in their new home.

Could Matt afford to give her this house? They had never discussed finances. She knew he was well off and was successful in the business world. But he had never put on airs of being wealthy.

He must have realized what concerned her because Matt elaborated, "this house is not as expensive as it looks. It is well within my budget. We will even be able to afford a gardener for the grounds."

He had saved the kitchen for last. They went into the kitchen, where there was a large counter in the middle with high chairs around it. It was set for a meal. Matt went to the fridge and started extracting trays of food, which he had placed there before picking up Diane and the children. When he finished setting the food around, he stood back, giving a slight bow.

"Dinner is served, madame." Diane laughed. The food was to be a perfect meal with an atmosphere beyond anything she could imagine. Matt helped Lily and Running Deer onto the high bar stools.

The dinner conversation included planning the furniture they would keep and the changes they would make, which were few. Diane still felt she was dreaming. When she had left home, she had no idea what was in store for them.

After dinner, Matt gave her a glass of cognac with dessert and a card. Enclosed was a picture of the house and a key. The message read:

> With all my love, I give you my heart and
> this home too.
>
> Love forever,
> Matt

Diane had tears in her eyes. She went into his loving arms, and the kiss they shared was as tender as the message on the card. When they broke apart, Matt said in a joking manner.

"Do you want to christen the bed in the master bedroom?" he gave her a sly look. Diane laughed but wished she could follow him there this instant. With a tinkling laugh, Lily said, "Mommy and Daddy, it is too early to go to bed." Running Deer laughed, agreeing with his sister.

The move to the house went smoothly. Life flowed forward in a perfect pattern. Matt was captivated by his wife, and his happiness was evident with spontaneous grins.

The children had settled in and were very happy and loved to play in the spacious backyard with the dogs.

Matt was delighted as his dreams had come true. The spare bedrooms had occasional visitors from the children of Saint Andrews. Glenda came more often because he knew Diane had felt bad not adopting her too. Lily and Running Deer learned to be the perfect hosts.

It was challenging to choose which children should come first. Matt told the children to be patient. They would all get a turn, and the days would be sunny and bright.

The days started with the usual joy of sharing breakfast with a loving family. Matt always delayed leaving the house until the last minute. Their abundant goodbyes traveled with him during his day.

It was midweek. Matt was planning a baseball game Saturday with a local catholic school team. Saint Andrews Orphanage was making a name for themselves in sports. Their team was undefeated after four games, with one of the games a tie. There were two schools involved, along with Saint Andrews. Father O'Malley was happy that Matt was still taking an interest in his pet project. He thanked him profusely as he left.

Matt arrived at the office, expecting to toil there for the rest of the day. He thought of taking Diane out for dinner when a call came on the intercom.

Miss Canning said, "Mrs. Hadden is on line one."

Diane's voice was hardly recognizable. "Matt, come home immediately. The dogs have fought off a cougar. Lily was outside playing with the dogs. Running Deer was helping me with some chores. The cougar attacked Lily. I imagine Lily approached the cougar, thinking that it was a big friendly cat. The dogs stopped the cougar, but Lily is . . ."

Matt yelled, "I'll be right there."

He ran out of the office, yelling, "I'm leaving for the day." He broke more traffic rules on the way but still made it home safely.

A neighbor was waiting for him in the driveway. He ran up to Matt's car.

"Your wife and family have gone to the hospital. You are to go there too."

"Where is the cougar?" Matt was looking around.

"The cougar took off, and the police are tracking it."

"Do you know if the dogs are okay?"

"One dog was hurt, and a neighbor took it to the vet because your wife had to help your little girl. The other one is in the house howling."

Matt thanked the neighbor. He quickly backed the car out of the driveway. *Not his Lily, God, please look after her,* was Matt's silent plea.

He raced to the hospital. He parked his car near the door as possible and ran into the hospital. He saw his wife and son as soon as he got into Emergency. Diane was crying into Running Deer's shoulder. He had his arms around her neck.

Matt walked quickly to her. He sat down beside them, pulling them both into his arms. He had to get her calmed down so he could get some coherent information out of her. His supporting arms must have given her the strength she needed. She pulled back from him enough to look into his face. Matt was shocked to see the change in his wife since this morning. This tragedy had almost aged her. Her face, wracked with sorrow and horror.

"Matt, our little girl, is hurt. The cougar was mauling her and biting her. The dogs stopped him, except Handsome got hurt too. A neighbor took him to the vet for us." Diane let out two sobs and continued. "Oh, Matt, she was blood everywhere. I don't know how badly she is hurt." Her voice failed her. She began to sob against his chest. Running Deer stood between Matt's legs, his arms encircling Matt's knees and looking up into their faces. Tears were running down his son's face unchecked.

Matt wanted to hug and comfort him, but Diane needed him more at the moment. A nurse arrived with tea and apple juice.

Matt thanked her as she put it on the table nearby.

"Diane, we may have a long wait. I want you to drink the tea. You have cried so much you need to replenish your fluids." He eased her away from his chest. The tears were still streaming down her cheeks, but the loud sobs had quietened. Matt reached for the tea, wrapping her hands around it for its warmth and control. He helped her hands bring the cup to her lips. She sipped some tea. Her mind was too numb to notice the drink's sweetness, which she usually took sugarless. Matt helped her until she was able to control it herself.

He then pulled Running Deer onto his lap. Running Deer burrowed into Matt's chest the way Diane had. He consoled his son while he watched Diane drink her tea. He was thankful she was passive now.

Matt's mind was going a mile a minute. What were Lily's injuries? Will she die? Will her pretty little face be disfigured? No matter the damage, he would get her the best plastic surgeon in the country.

The three seemed to huddle together in their grief. The sadness and worry were evident. It had been three hours, and still, no word had come. The nurse offered food. Matt accepted a sandwich for Running Deer. He knew that he and Diane didn't want any food with their worry.

How could a few minutes in time have changed their lives so rapidly? Matt wished now that he had stayed home today. Would Lily still have been mauled by the cougar? Where had the cougar come from? He intended to look into that with the local police. There was no area around their home that cougars roamed. How could this have happened?

It was then that the doctor came to see them.

"Lily is going to live. We managed to save her left arm, but she may have limited use of it. The chest wounds were deep, but fortunately, they didn't affect any organs. However, I feel some skin grafts may be necessary, depending on how the damages heal with the stitches. No leg injuries, I believe her braces saved her there. There was a head wound, as well. That is where most of the blood came from, but that should heal quite nicely."

"All in all, she has about fifty-eight stitches on various parts of her body. She was lucky she had the dogs to intervene to protect her, or she wouldn't have lived, I'm afraid." He paused, knowing that this was heartbreaking news for them.

"Lily will recover once the arm heals. If she gets into physiotherapy immediately, she may recover all of her arm movement if she is willing to work hard at moving it. Lily will need constant attention for the first little while. She is liable to have serious nightmares. You might consider therapy for that."

Matt inquired, "when can we see her?"

"You can go in to see her, but we have her heavily sedated. She won't be awake for a while. The longer she sleeps, the better. The nurse will show you to her room." The doctor felt sorry for this family and their sad days ahead. The recovery of their child would take a while.

They thanked the doctor. The nurse gave them directions to Lily's room. Matt and Diane walked with

Running Deer holding on between them. They passed down the hall in silence, trying to digest what the doctor had expressed.

When they entered Lily's room, Diane uttered, "oh, Matt. She looks so tiny and vulnerable." Her arm was bandaged from wrist to shoulder. There was a bandage on her head, and there was evidence of missing hair. The cover was up high so that they couldn't see any other injuries. Her other arm was under the cover, but there was no indication that the blanket covered any bandages. Lily was lying there still as death. Diane's sob broke the silence.

"Matt, look at our baby. She looks so battered." The IV needle was protruding out of her little hand. Diane was puzzled why they hadn't put it on her other hand as this was the arm that was severely damaged.

Matt wanted to gather Lily up into his arms to rock her, to tell her that he would never let this happen again. But could he have stopped it from happening had he been home? Matt bent down and kissed her. He then picked up Running Deer and let him bend over to kiss his sister. Then Running Deer patted his sister's face.

"Lily, I am sorry I didn't save you," he said in a tearful voice.

When Diane bent over to kiss Lily, her tears fell on Lily's face. Matt wiped them away with his fingers.

The nurse suggested they leave and come back later when Lily was awake. They didn't want to leave. But they knew it was for the best. Diane was now in a state of shock, and her sobbing had ended as numbness had set in. Her tears fell silently. Matt put his arm around her giving her support, as they left the room.

Matt drove them home. It was as though their happiness had been turned off like a light. When they got to the house, Father O'Malley was there.

Diane went into his arms, crying on his shoulder while Matt looked on helplessly. He picked up Running Deer for his own comfort. Father O'Malley looked at Matt. Matt shook his head, indicating things were not good.

Gradually Diane's tears started to recede. She pulled back, giving Father a sick smile. She invited him into the house.

They assembled in the living room, sitting sort of hopeless. Father O'Malley was saying words of sympathy when a knock came on the front door. Laura stepped inside. Diane saw her friend and broke down again, running to her. Laura held her friend in her arms tightly. Laura said, "it was on the news but not in much detail or the extent of Lily's injuries." Her voice trailed off.

Matt came out into the hall to welcome Laura. He gently pulled Diane away from her and into his arms. Laura muttered something about making tea, not knowing how else to comfort them.

Matt took Diane back into the living room, sending Running Deer into the kitchen to help Laura.

Father O'Malley started to talk in a gentle voice. "The world is not perfect. Sometimes, things happen, and we say why? God hasn't made this happen. But God is there for you to give you the strength to endure. Put your faith in God, and he will heal Lily. He is with you both if you don't turn away from him at this time. Let him into your hearts, and let his powers heal Lily. She is like a candle. She has flickered, but she hasn't gone out." Diane had stopped crying, bolstered by his words.

Matt held Diane while deep in thought. Yes, Lily has survived. She was still with them, which was the best way to look at it. Her tiny life had not been snuffed out.

Father O'Malley continued with a prayer. His words were penetrating.

Diane knew in her heart that she was weakening herself by letting the horror takeover. She would have to put that part behind her and be strong for Lily's recovery. Matt felt Diane's body change from the pathetic crying woman to a person who seemed to be drawing from the prayer's declarations.

Father O'Malley's prayer was comforting to them both. At his amen, Laura arrived with the tea tray, and Running Deer carried a plate of cookies.

He offered the cookies to everyone. Then he put the plate down on the table. Not that anyone was interested in cookies, but they took one as a formality.

Laura said, "I have brought some aspirin, Diane. It would be best that you take some." Matt reached out for the glass of water and the aspirin bottle wanting to help his wife in the only way he could. He was glad her body was straighter and that she was more in command of herself. They would need to be strong to face the trips to the hospital. To visit their little girl and give her the strength to fight back against this unforeseen tragedy.

Diane took the aspirin and reached for the tea. Then she looked to everyone to see they were comfortable. But there was nothing she could do as Laura had taken care of everyone.

Diane started to talk. "Matt, the dogs were so brave. I was looking out the window to see why the dogs were barking so wildly. Lily was under the tree in the backyard, calling to something amongst the hillside's shrubs and rockery. I couldn't make out what was there. But as I turned towards the door, I caught sight of the cougar leaping upon Lily. I ran out the door, telling Running Deer to stay inside."

"My feet covered the space in seconds. I had nothing to fight it with, so my only hope was to draw its attention away from Lily lying there. The dogs were on it, biting the animal. That is what distracted the cougar from Lily. Then the cougar attacked Handsome. I picked up a massive rock, and I found the strength to throw it directly at the cougar. He slunk away."

Diane's voice held no inflection of emotion. She only made a statement of fact. She knew the story had to come out for Matt's sake. Matt looked at Father O'Malley. His look was indicating that it could've been much worse. The cougar could have attacked Diane too, instead of slinking away. Both men were relieved that this had not happened.

Matt got up, saying, "I'm going to phone the vet to see how Handsome is doing. I wonder where Suzette is?"

Diane realized Suzette hadn't come to greet them. She quickly got up, excusing herself and followed Matt out of the room. The two dogs spent most of their time on mats in front of the fireplace in the family room. Diane headed that way. Running Deer scooted past her with the same direction in mind.

At the door, he stopped, looking back at Diane. "Suzette is here." They both looked in.

Both dogs had their own mat. Suzette had scrunched up Handsome's mat on top of hers, lying on both in complete sadness. She was almost lifeless, to the extent that she hardly acknowledged their presence, which was so strange for her. Suzette usually ran to them as soon as they entered the room. This time she just lifted her head then put it back down on Handsome's mat. There was some dried blood on her white fur. Matt continued to the phone.

Running Deer fell on his knees beside Suzette, patting her. Diane was just about to do the same when Matt came in.

"Handsome is okay, but he will have scars from now on. But he can wear them proudly. I am so thankful to him for saving Lily. Diane and Matt knelt beside Running Deer so they would be near Suzette. Matt said, "yes, Suzette, we miss Handsome too. Thank you for helping save Lily." Suzette responded by lifting her head, looking at them sadly. Then she put her head back down on Handsome's mat.

Matt said, "we better get back to Father O'Malley and Laura," helping Diane to her feet.

Father O'Malley was standing when they returned. "I am sorry, I have to go. I have a meeting. But I will call in to see Lily on my way."

They thanked him for coming. Father O'Malley took their hands, bonding them together. "You will give each other the strength to get through this. Your love will see you through." He could see already that there was acceptance, melding together in their distress. These two would be strong enough to see this terrible tragedy through. To have the courage to help Lily and to make the necessary adjustments in their lives to mend their child's fragile body.

Laura had cleared away the tea-things and worked quietly in the kitchen, making some light food to tide them over until the shock had passed.

Diane looked at Matt. "Matt, I am going up to Lily's room to get some things for her. Then I want to go back to the hospital. I want to be there in case she wakes up."

"Alright, I'll see that Running Deer gets something to eat and gets ready for bed. Then Laura can put him to bed when she thinks he is ready. She will stay, won't she?"

"Of course, I am sure she will. But you better check and make sure."

Diane went upstairs to Lily's room. She stood looking around, picturing Lily playing in the room with her animals and dolls. Lily had her animals displayed in sociability groups, or so it seemed. She loved her animals, so it was natural for her to be unafraid of the cougar. She was probably treating it as if it was an oversized cat. Diane noted the cougar and tiger were with the cats in their consortiums.

She reached out and extracted a dog that was one of Lily's favorites to take to the hospital. The dog was not the same as Handsome. But Lily had called it Handsome Two.

Diane went to the closet. The case she pulled out was the one Lily had brought from Saint Andrews. She put some nighties and a housecoat inside, along with Lily's slippers and favorite doll. Matt had purchased the doll that looked similar to Lily and arranged for it to have braces on her legs, which he named Lily Doll.

She went to the washroom to pick up Lily's toothbrush and toothpaste. It was then that Diane remembered that her left arm was so severely injured. Luckily it wasn't her right arm. She closed the suitcase, carrying it and the stuffed dog. She headed to her room to change her bloodstained clothes and tidy her hair.

Matt came upstairs. They met halfway. He took her into his arms, hugging and comforting her. When they drew apart, Matt said, "give me a minute. I want to change too."

Diane continued down the stairs. The voices in the kitchen drew her in. Running Deer and Laura were eating and talking about Lily. Laura looked up to see Diane standing listening.

"Diane, Matt said you are going back to the hospital. Have some soup and a sandwich first. You need something to eat as it may be a while before you eat again." Laura got up and walked to the stove to get the hot soup.

Diane sat down, not wanting the food but knowing she should eat as it would probably be a long night. She reached over and ran her hand over her son's hair, needing the contact to comfort her. He smiled lovingly at his mother in response.

Laura brought the poured soup over to the table. Picking up a spoon, Diane began to eat. She politely refused the sandwich.

"Thank you, Laura, for staying. It may be a long night as I intend to stay until Lily awakens."

Matt arrived showered and dressed casually. Diane's heart turned over, looking at his masculinity. Then her eyes rose to his tormented face, which stared back at her with lines of worry etched there. He came over and put his hand comfortingly on Running Deer's shoulder. "It is best that you stay here with Laura. Have a good night, and say a prayer for Lily when you go to bed."

Diane ate as much as she could. Matt reached for a sandwich. Laura handed him a bag, saying, "eat these on the way. Give my love to Lily. Tell her we will be rooting for her."

Diane hugged and kissed her son. She thanked Laura again for staying. Laura hugged her and said, "give my blessing to Lily."

Chapter Twenty-One

When they reached the hospital, they asked the nurse if Lily had awakened yet? The nurse replied, "no, but now you are here, she might."

Diane and Matt wanted to be there when Lily opened her eyes. The room was silent when they entered. Lily was lost in the big bed like a little doll with her right arm lying on the covers. There was no bandage, thank goodness. Diane worried about all her injuries remembering all the blood.

Diane and Matt separated to stand on both sides of the bed, watching Lily. They hoped that she would open her eyes. As if their prayers were answered, Lily's eyelids moved, fluttering. Then opening wide, her eyes moved quickly back and forth between her parents. Then she gave a beatific smile embracing them both. The pain must have seeped into her mind. Her face suddenly turned into a hurt expression.

Matt wanted to lift her into his arms to take away the pain. "Lily, we're going to be with you as long as you need us." Tears crept out of her eyes and ran down the sides of her face.

"Daddy, I hurt. I hurt a lot. Why did the big cat hurt me?" she asked in a timid voice.

Diane let go of a sob then quickly stopped herself. Her baby was going to be hurting for a while. Diane placed her fingers on Lily's cheeks, wiping away the tears.

"Lily, Mommy loves you so much, and so does Daddy." Diane bent over and kissed her forehead. She was thankful that the cougar had left her pretty face unscathed, at least.

Matt bent over from the other side and kissed her, giving him time to clear his voice. "Daddy knows it hurts, baby. Daddy would love to take the hurt away. But I can't."

"Daddy, why did the big cat hurt me?"

"Because, darling, he doesn't know you. So, he didn't know how friendly you were." Matt didn't want to paint the cougar evil or dangerous in the hopes it would stop Lily from having nightmares.

A nurse came in to hang two little bags, attaching them into the bigger IV bag on a pole. "These bags are an antibiotic and a painkiller." The nurse took Lily's pulse and her temperature to record it on the chart. While she performed her duties, the nurse talked soothingly to Lily. Lily's eyes followed every movement.

Lily seemed to accept the IV and the bandages as part of the hurting. When the nurse left, Matt and Diane sat close to the bed, making it easier for Lily to see them. Each had one of Lily's hands. Matt held the hand with the IV needle. So, he handled it cautiously.

"Daddy, can Running Deer come to see me? Can Handsome and Suzette come too?"

"Yes, we will bring Running Deer. It may take special permission, but I will get it. However, Handsome is at the vet's, hurt by the cougar when he helped you. Suzette is sad alone at home on Handsome's mat. The dogs can't come into the hospital. You will just have to get better quickly."

"Daddy, the dogs were biting that mean cat."

"I know. The dogs were protecting you the only way they knew how. They love you so much. Handsome should be home sometime tomorrow."

"Can I come home too?"

"No, darling, not yet. You have to wait a little longer." Matt noticed Lily's eyes would close then flutter open. The medicine was taking effect. "Sleep, my wee darling. Daddy and Mommy will be waiting here when you wake up."

Her eyes closed, and she fell into a drugged sleep. Diane kissed her, and Lily's lips smiled a tiny bit.

The night vigil had started—the worried parents wanted Lily to sleep away her pain and heal her body. But at the same time, they wanted to talk to her. Needing her voice to help with the relief that she was still alive.

She woke up once more during the night. Diane was asleep with her head on Lily's pillow. Lily reached up and ran her fingers over Diane's face very gently like a feather. Diane's eyes opened, but she didn't move. Instead, she just let Lily touch her, enjoying the feel of her fairy touch. Lily was whispering, "Mommy, I love you."

Matt sat transfixed, watching the two who meant so much to him. His heart burst with love for them both, his beautiful little angel and his lovely wife. He was such a lucky man to have them and Running Deer too.

How could he have thought that he had a fulfilling life being a bachelor? Sharing love, sharing each other that was real life. Matt couldn't help but put out his hand to cover the little hand that feathered over Diane's cheeks.

Lily watched that big hand, knowing it was her Daddy that had joined hers, softly touching her Mommy.

The nurse walked in. Diane straightened up. Lily turned to her father, using one word that pierced his heart. "Daddy."

That word was all he ever wanted since the first day he saw her on the veranda when one little finger had touched the palm of his hand. It was like a connection to life, awakening him to the feeling of wanting to get close to someone forever. That moment had changed him.

Diane and Matt moved away so the nurse could attend to Lily. Matt knew that the pain was back because her tears had started again. The nurse attached the magic liquid into the IV pouch before taking her temperature and pulse.

Matt put his arm around Diane and kissed her forehead. In response, Diane leaned into him.

The nurse finished. Turning to the parents, she asked if she could get them a coffee or tea.

Matt replied, "no, thank you, once Lily goes back to sleep, we will leave for a while." The parents went back to their daughter, each taking a hand. The nurse stood watching. When she first entered the room, she had hated interrupting that scene of love enacted between the three. It made her wish that she had a husband and child. But, so far in life, she concentrated on her career, not having found a man to sweep her off her feet.

It was not long before Lily went into her drugged sleep, which was good to know before leaving. Their little girl was without pain at the moment.

Matt took his wife home. They went to check on Suzette. The dog was still lying on Handsome's scrunched-up mat on top of her own. Suzette made noises of sadness. Then put her head back down and closed her eyes. Matt knew Suzette would stay there until Handsome returned to her.

They went to bed after looking in on Running Deer and kissing him.

Matt and Diane made love that night as if it was their first time. They were so gentle in their love that it was like a ballet of passion. Their fulfillment was ecstasy.

Diane curled into her loving husband's arms, going into an exhausted sleep taking Matt with her. They both had not mentioned the tragedy since leaving Lily, wanting only to hold onto the love they shared in that hospital room. Temporarily closing out the hurt, relegating it to the back of their minds.

Matt was first to awaken. They were still lying in the same loving embrace. Dawn was over, and the sun was peeping in the window.

A new day was here. He wished the last 24 hours had not happened. But it had, and they would have to deal with that as best they could. This morning they would go pick up Handsome after seeing Lily at the hospital.

Matt knew he wanted some answers from the police today. Where had the cougar come from? Who had brought it into their peaceful neighborhood? Had it been caught yet? He was seething inside with anger at whoever had released that cougar in the vicinity of his family. In his rage, he must've tightened his hold because Diane jolted and opened her eyes. The tragedy of yesterday was back with her.

"Matt?"

"I'm sorry, darling. I was thinking about the cougar and who could have brought it into our neighborhood. I was angry at them. I intend to get some answers from the police today."

"I can't believe how fast life can change because of one moment in time. But I guess we have to be thankful that Lily survived the attack. Matt, there is no reason for the cougar to be here. But it was, and now we will have to deal with Lily. We have to make her feel better. Anger isn't the emotion we need right now," Diane said wisely. "But I do think you should inquire to see if the cougar is in captivity so that it won't maul anyone else."

Running Deer burst into the bedroom. "Mommy, Daddy, you're home." He took a running leap, ending up on the bed. Matt grabbed him, pulling him against his chest saving Diane from their son's energetic body.

"Well, young man, how are you this morning? Besides, being glad your Mommy and Daddy are here."

"Daddy, how is Lily? I miss her."

"I know, so do we. But Lily is not in pain when she is sleeping. So, that is the way they are keeping her right now."

"Will I be able to see her?"

"Yes, she asked for you to come." Matt plunked him down between them so Diane could put her arm around him too.

"I think we will go to the hospital this morning. Then Running Deer and I will pick up Handsome at the vet. Suzette wants him home, and so do I."

Matt continued. "I'll keep Running Deer with me today so Laura can leave. But maybe she could come back tonight again. I intend to ask her that."

Diane sat up, ready to leave the bed. "Yes, I want to go to the hospital and be with Lily. I hope Handsome will be okay."

"I'm sure he will when he is back with his Suzette again. He is going to get a special treat for saving Lily," Matt stated firmly. He put Running Deer down on the floor.

"Scat, young man, we want to get dressed. You should get dressed too if you want to see Lily." Running Deer, living up to his name, raced out of the room after a big 'yes.'

Lily was awake when they got to the hospital. She was happy to see them, particularly Running Deer. But you could see her face etched in pain. Matt was upset for Lily, wanting the discomfort to go away from his special little girl.

Running Deer climbed up on the bed, patting his sister. "I love you, Lily. I need you to get well and come home to me. The house is empty without you."

In a small voice, Lily said, "Running Deer, I love you too. I want to go home to be with you. But the pain will not go away. So, I can't come home."

Diane noticed that her face seemed somewhat flushed. Then she felt her forehead to find it burning.

"Matt, I think that Lily needs a nurse."

Matt pressed the button. Diane kissed Lily, and Running Deer did too. Lily's face screwed up, and she started to cry. "Please make the pain go away. I want to come home." Diane caught a sob before it could escape, looking sadly at Matt.

The nurse bustled in, wreathed in a smile. "How's, my little darling, this morning?" She took Lily's vital signs. "We do feel under the weather, don't we?" Lily was crying in earnest now.

The nurse looked at the unhappy child. "I think maybe we should have a doctor come to see if he can make you better." She quickly left the room.

Matt talked soothingly to Lily while his heart broke in slow motion as her tears continued to fall rapidly.

It was then a stretcher arrived, pushed by a nurse and an orderly. "We are going for a little ride, princess," the orderly said as they lifted her gently onto the waiting stretcher.

Matt had whisked Running Deer off the bed as the stretcher arrived. He was crying into his Daddy's neck, knowing his sister was hurting a lot because of her tears. He wanted his Lily better. Her parents looked at each other, knowing something was wrong.

The nurse that had taken her vital signs came in as the stretcher was wheeled away down the corridor. "Dr. Emerson is going to have a look at Lily. Her high temperature indicates there must be an infection somewhere. She is on her way to the operating room. If you would like to wait in the waiting room down the hall, I will direct Dr. Emerson there when he finishes locating the problem."

Diane followed her out the door. Matt and Running Deer trailed behind her, going to the room the nurse indicated. When they were inside, Matt sat down and pulled Diane against his shoulder. Running Deer climbed into his lap. They both started to cry. Unwelcome fear was upon them. What had gone wrong?

It was an hour later before Dr. Emerson put in an appearance.

"Mr. and Mrs. Hadden, Lily has developed an infection in her left arm. I am rather worried about that. We hoped the antibiotics would have alleviated this. So, I have changed her medication. But I am now afraid that she might lose her arm if we can't stop the infection from spreading. We won't know for sure for another twelve to sixteen hours. I have cleaned the wound as best I can. To do this, I had to open her arm up again to put in a draining tube. The best I can suggest is that it will be a waiting game. But I will be here monitoring her progress." He paused to let that sink in.

Matt cleared his throat, but no words came out. Diane's tears were silently rolling down her cheeks. Running Deer was openly crying into Matt's neck. He loved his sister a lot and wanted her home again.

"I would suggest you leave for a while. Lily will be sleeping for at least three to four hours as she is under heavy sedation. Are there any questions that I can help you with?"

"How bad is it really, in your honest opinion?" Matt was so worried about his child.

Dr. Emerson looked at him for a minute, weighing this man, then he said, "honest opinion? I don't hold much hope in saving the arm." Diane gave out a strangled cry of anguish. Her tears were no longer silent. She could not contain herself any longer.

The doctor looked at them sadly. Then left the room and the young couple to their sorrow. He hated this part of his job. When he had looked at that tiny little angel's arm when she first arrived in the OR, he had been sick at the sight of her mangled limb. But he had worked diligently repairing it with the skill required. He had thought he had won. Now today, he wasn't so sure that his ability had been sufficient for the task.

Huddling together, the three sat back down to absorb the news. The possibility of Lily losing her arm was torture to them. Lily's braced legs were enough to handle in her life. Matt was in the process of seeking a possible operation with a specialist from the States for her legs. The arrangement was to take Lily there in three weeks, and now a delay would be necessary.

Finally, he said, "Diane, we have to go and pick up Handsome. Will you come with us?"

Diane wanted to stay, but she knew that the waiting would be unbearable alone. Unhappily she said, "yes."

They arose as Matt put Running Deer down to walk between them.

Handsome was so glad to see them. He had one bandage tied around his middle and one around his back leg. He was gingerly walking as though it was painful. Running Deer dropped to his knees, hugging him while Handsome tried smothering him with kisses. Running Deer was laughing. The first time since the cougar's devastating visit.

Matt paid the bill, thanking the vet, and agreed to bring him back in five days to check the stitches.

"Come, Handsome, we have Suzette at home pining for you." Matt gave the leash to his son. At the sound of the name Suzette, Handsome's body became excited to leave the vets.

When they arrived home, Suzette was at the door to greet them. She must've heard Handsome's bark as he got out of the car, announcing that he was glad to be home.

Suzette kept nuzzling Handsome and kissing him, her tail wagging madly. This was her soul mate. She wanted to nurture him better. They soon disappeared to their mats in the family room. Matt looked in, Handsome laid on his mat, with Suzette's head draped over his neck. Matt had a feeling that there would be no romping for a while. They just wanted to lie together. He believed that they would be okay to leave alone as Diane was anxious to return to the hospital.

Matt had talked her into tea and some food for each of them before leaving.

A hospital plays out its dramas every day. The tragedies are basically the same, but the scenarios are different, as are the victims and their grievers. Nevertheless, the heartbreaking stories of bullet wounds, heart attacks, and car accidents were all there.

The hospital was its usual bustling self, with emergency sirens and people sitting around awaiting attention. Some were dazed and distressed at their plight that this could happen. People cried in grief or were sadly waiting to hear if their loved ones would live or die or maybe a cripple for life.

Hospitals have their happy stories too. The birth of a baby, which is so rewarding that it puts a fresh perspective on life. The success stories, the miracles were all there too.

Diane and Matt were both praying for a miracle as they entered the hospital to see their daughter. The nurse offered, "she is back in her room." But she did not provide anything more.

Matt let Diane go in first. She looked into the room. Her glance was drawn quickly to the bed. Lily was lying as pale as a ghost, except for red spots on her cheeks indicating the fever was still with her. She was so tiny that her body hardly made a bump in the bed. Why had this little girl been exposed to this tragic event? She was so frail.

Diane bent over to kiss Lily on her forehead, noting her arm contained a fresh bandage. However, Lily neither moved nor opened her eyes. Diane started praying for a miracle to save her little girl and her arm. Diane became weak with fright and sunk into the chair, holding her daughter's hand. The IV had left behind a considerable bruise on her left hand. She gently switched to her right hand with the IV.

Her gown had slipped off her shoulder, and there were faint teeth marks on the side of her left shoulder as though the cougar was stopped from full penetration by the dogs, which Diane had not noticed yesterday. Diane's breath caught, seeing them. They brought back the horror of seeing Lily with the cougar's mouth and teeth trying to devour her little girl. Her mind had blocked it out until this moment. Then, all her fear came rushing back, and she broke down and cried. Diane must've given off a loud wail because Matt quickly entered the room and pulled Diane into his arms. Running Deer stood helplessly beside them.

"Matt . . . the teeth marks on her . . . shoulder brought back the memory my mind had blocked out. Matt, it was so horrible, and Lily was like a rag doll. That cougar was tossing her around and shaking its head and making vicious noises. The dogs were barking and jumping on it, biting him. Lily fell to the ground. They were trying to distract the cougar away from her with angry growls and bites."

Matt had tears in his eyes, vividly picturing his wife's horrid scene in the garden yesterday. He wished Diane had kept the horror suppressed. His eyes went to the offending teeth marks on Lily's shoulder. His breath caught in his throat.

Running Deer was whimpering too. Matt knew Running Deer had watched the cougar attack through the kitchen window. What does a man say to take away the horror from their minds? Only time and God could heal them.

It was then that they heard a little voice. "Daddy, it hurts so much." Then silence. Three heads swiveled to the little girl. Her eyes were still closed. She hadn't moved, but the words spoken in almost a whisper had penetrated the room and its occupants. No more sound came from the bed as all eyes waited in anticipation.

Chapter Twenty-Two

Dr. Emerson entered the room. The stance of the three-standing immobile struck him. As though they were waiting for something to release them into action. His soft plastic covered shoes made no noise. So, he got to the bed before they realized he was there. He had just come from the OR, so his attire was that of the operating room.

Matt realized that the doctor was there. "Lily has just spoken. She said, 'Daddy, it hurts so much.' But she doesn't appear to be awake."

Dr. Emerson commented, "she must sense that you are here and cried out her pain. Although she is probably still asleep." The doctor went to the other side of the bed, bending over the child as he was a very tall man. He gently pulled back Lily's eyelids to check her eyes. Gently he untied the gown behind Lily's back and pulled it down, exposing her chest. He put the stainless-steel end of the stethoscope on her chest, listening. Although most people reacted to the cold stethoscope with skin contact, Lily didn't acknowledge it.

With her gown pulled down, Diane and Matt could see the bandages and more teeth marks. Their poor baby was lucky to be alive. The doctor lifted the bandage's edge, checking the left arm wound. He appeared to be satisfied with the drip. Then he covered her again and tied the tie.

A nurse entered the room, covering the space quickly to the bed. "I am sorry, Dr. Emerson, I wasn't able to be here when you needed me." Dr. Emerson acknowledged her statement with a shake of his head in acceptance. He pulled the covers over the little girl and took her pulse. Then he suggested, "perhaps you could take her temperature for me."

Matt and Diane had eased away from the bedside but had not left the room.

Dr. Emerson said to Running Deer, "hi, little man, I guess you are worried about your sister? She needs your love right now."

Running Deer was craning his neck to look up at the tall doctor as he murmured, "I love, Lily."

With the temperature and the pulse reading recorded, the doctor turned to her parents, indicating that he wanted to talk to them. They followed him out of the room. Dr. Emerson took ten giant steps with his long legs, then stopped to wait for them.

"Lily's fever is still soaring. That means the infection is still there to a significant extent. I had hoped it would have decreased slightly by now, indicating the new antibiotics' effectiveness in the infection's containment. But apparently, this isn't the case." His voice drifted off like he had said something they were supposed to know.

Matt knew that he was thinking of the removal of Lily's infected arm, knowing that was Dr. Emerson's silent message. Diane was quiet now, as though dazed, and the doctor's unsaid words hadn't penetrated her mind. Matt hoped to keep it that way until it was a fact.

Diane was deep in guilt. She hadn't protected Lily from the attack. *How can any mother protect her child from unforeseen hazards that they are unaware of? Where did that cougar come from?*

Dr. Emerson quietly spoke about his concerns. "The next four to six hours will tell the tale. Either the fever will continue to rage, or the antibiotics will work against the infection."

"Thank you, Doctor." Matt was dreading the outcome.

Matt led Diane back into the room with their son following. Lily wasn't aware that they were there. But they kept up a conversation with Lily as though she could hear them.

Laura showed up at four, offering to take Running Deer home and attend to the dogs for them. She could see that Lily didn't look well and that Diane and Matt would not want to leave their vigil here.

Running Deer gushed the doctor's conversation to Laura. Her head swung to Matt, noting his shaking head indicated don't ask.

Laura nodded her head in understanding, and she took Running Deer home. They immediately looked in on the dogs.

Handsome and Suzette were excited to see them. They indicated that they wanted to go out into the backyard.

Laura was afraid to let them out in case the cougar was still around. So, she called the police, "Is the cougar still loose?"

They specified, "no, the cougar is contained."

When she explained who she was, the police inquired about Lily and the dog's condition. Laura told them the dog was okay, but the little girl, Lily, isn't doing well since she had developed an infection.

They extended their condolences and their hopes for Lily's recovery.

Assured by the phone call that the cougar wasn't around, Laura played outside with Running Deer and the dogs for an hour. Unfortunately, handsome was still not his usual self.

Back at the hospital, Matt and Diane took a break, going down to the cafeteria for a drink, but not staying long. When they arrived back in the room, Dr. Emerson was there. He was looking at Lily very seriously.

Matt feared the worst. But when he asked, Dr. Emerson replied, "there doesn't appear to be any change yet." Then he added, "she looks like a Dresden doll. Such a little girl for all this hurt. I wish I could have made her the way she was before the cougar attack."

He turned to Diane. "How are you feeling, Mrs. Hadden?"

"Me? I am okay. I'm just worried about Lily. My poor wee girl."

The doctor looked back at Lily, wishing that the fever would break. Lily began to whimper. He put his hand on her head. Was it getting less, or was that wishful thinking?

The nurse entered, and the doctor was grateful. The nurse took Lily's vital signs. The doctor waited, wanting to know if there was any change. After recording the results and showing them to Dr. Emerson, she stepped out of the room. Indeed, Lily's temperature was down a tiny fraction, the doctor noted.

He looked at the anxious parents. "Her fever is down a small fraction. That is a hopeful sign at this point. I've changed the bandage. The wound doesn't look good. But the reduction in her temperature indicates that the new antibiotics may be working at last. This is a hopeful sign at this time."

The parents sighed in relief.

"We just have to hope for the best. Well, I have other patients to see." The doctor headed for the door.

Diane and Matt murmured their thanks. They still were not daring to hope too much. Lily was not out of the woods yet.

Their vigil began, one on each side of the bed with hope in their hearts.

Matt began to talk. "Lily, sweetheart, you are my special little girl. Daddy loves you so much. Please let the medicine help you. I want my little angel to get better.

His voice faded out. He knew he was asking God rather than Lily for help. He swallowed once and started talking.

"I remember the first time I beheld your little face, looking up at me with those beautiful big green eyes. Your little finger that first entered my hand touched me right to my heart. I was yours from that moment, my darling Lily. You are in my heart forever. So, please get better. So, you can come home to me. Come home to your Mommy and Running Deer. They need you too."

Matt had been holding her hand. Now, he raised it to his lips. Then he moved his head until his forehead rested against her hand.

The minutes passed as time ticked away. Matt finally raised his head and looked at the silently crying Diane. Tears ran down unattended, filled with guilt for her failure to protect her daughter.

The nurse hesitated at the door watching the two adults devouring each other with their sad eyes, communicating their deep sorrow silently.

The nurse came in to check the IV. She hung more antibiotics. Silently she put out a prayer. *Please antibiotics, do what we expect of you, and help this little girl.*

She asked if she could get them something to drink?

Matt thanked her, saying, "no, thank you. We will take a break in a little while."

When she had gone, Diane uttered. "Matt, what will we do if she doesn't get better?"

"We will do whatever is necessary to make her life comfortable if her arm removal is necessary." Diane gave a flinch. Matt recoiled in his bluntness but went on. "Then I will find the best technology for an artificial arm or whatever it takes. I just want our Lily back home with us."

"Matt, you have such a positive attitude. I wish I were more like you. I, too, want Lily to get through this and come home." Her voice broke, and she couldn't go on.

Matt started talking, "Diane, you are a good mother. I am so proud of the way you have taken to the children. Both children love you very much. I have watched them when you are together. You are exactly the kind of mother they need in their life."

He reached for her hand and brought it to his lips. "Diane, I am so glad you accepted my unusual proposal and made this all happen. If you had not said yes, the story would be quite different. Without you, Father O'Malley and Mother Anthony fully intended to refuse me. I just wish that I had told you how I felt before you walked out on me at the restaurant. I am sorry that I didn't make an effort to tell you that when we met in your backyard before that day at the orphanage. I had every intention of telling you before the adoption came into play." He kissed her palm.

"Even this situation with the cougar doesn't change the love we all share in our home. It just makes our love stronger. I am sure Running Deer would say the same if he were here."

A movement by the door drew both their heads in that direction.

Father O'Malley came into the room with a kind smile for each of them. Matt stood up to greet him, walking over to shake his hand. Father O'Malley went over to Diane. He put his hand on her shoulder. When she looked up into his face, he bent over and kissed her on the cheek in greeting. "Bless you, Diane."

His eyes flipped over onto Lily. "How is she?"

Matt relieved Diane from answering. "Lily still has a high fever. They are giving her a new antibiotic in the hopes of conquering the infection. If that is not successful and doesn't do the job, they will have to amputate her arm. But they are holding off as long as possible."

"Oh, dear, that doesn't sound too good. Will you join me in prayer?" Father O'Malley bowed his head, continuing to touch Diane's shoulder. "Dear Lord, we ask that you take Lily unto your bosom. Hug her and give her the healing she needs to fight the fever and infection. Lily is one of your children that needs a little more compassion. But I know you will be there for her. Lily is a child that has had burdens already in her young life. Help her to overcome this latest affliction. Bring her back to this loving couple to share their lives and to spread their love around her. Thank you, Lord. Amen."

"Diane and Matt, I feel in my heart that things will improve. Lily will keep her arm. Put your trust in the Lord, and he will come to you and Lily, giving his blessings and grace."

The loving parents gazed at each other in encouragement while Father O'Malley talked to them, wanting to believe that all would be well.

Lily's eyes moved under her lids, trying to come back from the deep blackness. Lily heard Father O'Malley; her mind was crying out. *I am here. Talk to me.* But she couldn't use her voice, nor could she see him.

His soothing droning voice continued talking to her Mommy and Daddy, reassuring them in their faith. Then she heard him talk to her.

"Lily, we're here for you. Please come back to us. We are waiting. Running Deer is waiting and all your friends at Saint Andrews Orphanage. Mother Anthony and Sister Ruth continually pray for you to get better. Everyone wants to be with you again. The orphanage children tell me each time I go there how much they miss their Lily. Lily, get well. Your Mommy and Daddy are waiting here for you."

I am here, and I want to talk to you. But the blackness is still around me. I can't see you, and I want to come back. Lily's eyes continued to move under her closed eyelids.

Father O'Malley asked Matt to go to the elevator with him. Then he said goodbye to Diane. He did the sign of the cross with his fingers on Lily's forehead. Then he turned to leave. Matt and Father O'Malley strolled down the hall.

"Matt, don't lose your faith. Believe that she will pull through because she will. Lily has such a fighting spirit. I know she will fight this, and the infection will disappear, and her arm will heal. Then you will have your Lily back.

Diane is taking this very hard. However, she is not saying so. Diane blames herself for the cougar attack. She needs your reassurance now more than ever. Be there for her as well as Lily."

He paused. "Have they found the cougar?"

"Yes, apparently, someone was transporting him through a nearby area in a cage on the back of a pickup truck. He claims that some punk teenager jumped on the back of the truck and opened the cage door while he stopped at a red light. The cougar took the opportunity to escape. But by the time the driver could get out of the truck, it was already too late. The cougar had taken off for parts unknown, and the teenager had disappeared. The cougar was free for three hours before he arrived at our place. So, he had traveled quite a distance. Probably chased at some point or more. The police said they were deeply sorry, as they regretfully had to shoot the cougar, as they didn't have a tranquilizer gun."

"Well, that's too bad. It wasn't the cougar's fault that he was let loose in a residential area." Matt agreed with him.

They reached the elevator as the doors opened. A lady and a child stepped out.

Father O'Malley said a quick goodbye to Matt. "Take care of the family. A lot of people are praying for Lily." The doors closed as his voice trailed off.

Matt walked back to his wife. He didn't know what he would do if he ever lost Diane and Lily. They were such a part of him now. He could not imagine life without them and Running Deer.

"Diane, are you all right?" She was sitting, staring at Lily, not moving at all. He had stood in the doorway, watching her. She hadn't noticed him. Usually, you can sense someone nearby, but she was too absorbed in her thoughts.

She jerked around. "Yes, I am okay, Matt. Why was that cougar in the backyard? Did you ever find out? You said you were going to call the police."

"I did call them. It was transported through town in a cage on the back of a truck when some imbecile kid set it free. We were unlucky enough to be in the cougar's path."

"Matt, I couldn't save our little girl. Handsome managed to save her. If it wasn't for Handsome, I don't know what would have happened." Her voice broke at the last comment. "Matt, I am so sorry. I let our little girl get hurt. I could see Lily seemed to be talking to the shrubs. Not realizing that it was the cougar hidden there. She probably thought it was a big friendly cat. The cougar leaped on her. I was so shocked as I ran to her." Tears were streaming down her cheeks.

Matt pulled her into his arms, holding her tightly.

"Diane, what happened was not your fault. You couldn't see the cougar amongst the shrubs. Lily probably didn't realize the danger she was in, coaxing it to her. Maybe the dogs' barking attracted the cougar. You just don't know, but it wasn't you. You never caused it to happen. You did your best to try and save her, throwing the large rock. Thank heavens, Handsome, and you succeeded." Matt pulled back to look into Diane's face. "Darling, I love you very much. No matter what happens in our life together, I will always love you."

Matt kissed his wife lovingly. Once he started, the kiss took over, profoundly kissing her, overpowering his senses and hers amongst their grief. Diane was moaning in response when a little voice broke the spell.

Chapter Twenty-Three

"Daddy, you are kissing, Mommy."

They both whipped around and leaned over the bed.

"Lily. Lily, you are awake."

"Yes, Daddy."

"How do you feel?"

"Thirsty."

Matt reached for the jug on the bedside table and the cup, pouring water for her and holding it to her lips. She took a couple of tiny sips. Then she settled against the pillow.

"Mommy, I knew you were here. I could hear you talking. I heard Father O'Malley too. But I couldn't find my way out of the darkness."

"You did fine, Lily. Matt, do you think you should let the nurse know that she is awake?"

Matt left the room while Diane continued to talk to Lily.

"Mommy, the hurt doesn't go away. I asked for it to go away. But it is still there. Why did the big cat hurt me?"

"Lily, the big cat, didn't mean to hurt you. The dogs must have scared it with their barking. That big cat was a cougar, and he doesn't live in our area. So, he was probably scared because he was alone and away from his home."

"Mommy, the hurt is really bad now. Can I cry if it hurts?"

Diane's heart lurched. "Yes, darling, you can cry. When things hurt that bad, you are allowed to cry." Diane looked to the door as Matt came in, followed shortly by the nurse with a new bag of painkillers and antibiotics.

"So, Puppet, you are awake, at last?" the nurse picked up Lily's hand, taking her pulse. "Now, we will take your temperature." The nurse waited until the indicator went off. "Good," checking the reading, "your fever is dropping. That is a good sign. I think the antibiotics are working, at last," she said with a huge sigh of relief. "I will let Dr. Emerson know. He was worried about you. You, my dear, are a lucky girl." Tweaking Lily on her cheek. The nurse left the room as quickly as she came.

"What did she mean I was a lucky girl, Daddy?"

"Well, Muppet, you were very sick, and now you are getting better. Your mommy and daddy are so pleased. In fact, we are very happy." Matt leaned over, kissing Lily.

"Daddy, can I come home now? I don't like it here. I want to be with you and mommy and Running Deer at home."

"I know, sweetheart, we want you to come home too. But I need to know you are truly well. The hospital is the best place for you. They have the medicines to help you get completely better so you can come home. Now, you talk to mommy while I phone Running Deer and Laura to give them the good news. I will also call Father O'Malley. He is quite worried about you."

"Daddy, I wanted to talk to Father O'Malley, but the blackness wouldn't let me go. I heard him. But I couldn't talk to him. Please tell him I wanted to talk to him and see him." Matt's heart went out to his daughter. "I will, darling. Now, I'll go make those calls while you and Mommy have a visit, okay?"

"Yes, Daddy. I love you, and I love you, Mommy, and I love Running Deer too. I love Handsome and Suzette too."

"I love you too, Lily. Everyone loves you." Matt happily kissed both of his girls before he left the room.

"Mommy, why did daddy have tears in his eyes?"

"Your father loves you very much. He doesn't like to see you sick or hurting. So, he was thrilled you are getting better. Those were tears of joy. Just like mommy gets."

Lily gave her mother her right hand. Although it still held the IV needle. "Mommy, I want to be just like you when I grow up. Do you think I can?"

Diane took her daughter's hand gently. "Yes, Lily, if you want to be like me when you grow up, that would be an honor for me."

"Mommy, does Running Deer want to see me if I can't go home?"

"Yes, darling, now that you are getting better, he can come. Now, I want you to go back to sleep. Let the medicine help you. You need to sleep to get better." Diane could see the pain invading Lily's face. It wasn't over yet. She kissed Lily's eyes to help her close them.

"But, Mommy, daddy's coming back, and I want to kiss him." Lily's voice was fading as she said this. Diane kissed Lily again. "That is from daddy, and I'll collect the kiss from him." But she knew Lily was already asleep. Diane was thankful the nurse had hung a new bag of painkillers on Lily's pole so she could escape the pain.

Dr. Emerson arrived. "I hear she was awake and quite bright." His broad smile was immensely beatific. He was so happy that her temperature had dropped. He studied the chart noting it was a bit above normal still.

"Oh, yes, doctor. Lily was bright and wants to go home. That is a good sign, isn't it? I know she is still in pain."

"Yes, that is a good sign, asking to go home. But Lily isn't out of the woods yet. We need that fever completely gone and the antibiotics to completely fight the infection. But it seems the latest antibiotics are being successful." Dr. Emerson looked up and noticed Matt had returned to the room.

"Well, Mr. Hadden, it looks like our little girl is on the mend. But we still have to keep her here for a while yet. However, the fact that her temperature is falling is an encouragement. I needed this good news of your daughter's recovery to lift my spirits after a bad day." He smiled reassuringly. "Do you know how happy I am that she is recovering because I certainly was not looking forward to removing her arm?" His smile was now from ear to ear with relief. "Well, I must be going. Congratulations on your brave daughter's recovery." Dr. Emerson quickly left the room.

Matt and Diane grinned at each other.

Diane intended to stay. "I am not going to leave here until Lily can stay awake for at least three hours. I want to see more improvement. Matt, you will have to go home and be with Running Deer until I can come home."

"Well, I think you should come home with me. So, we can be with Running Deer together and have a celebration. Lily needs her rest. She knows we have to go home sometime. Please, Diane, we need a break from here."

"But, Matt, I want to be here every time she wakes up."

"I know, Diane. But it would help if you had a break right now. I want us to be together when we tell our son and Laura about Lily's latest update from Dr. Emerson."

"All right, but I am coming back after we celebrate."

Matt bent over and kissed Lily. Then, he took Diane's arm, leaving the room to go home.

When they arrived home, Running Deer greeted them at the door.

"How is Lily? Can I go see her?"

Matt leaned over and hugged him. "Lily is going to be okay, and we are going to celebrate. So, go tell Laura to get the champagne out of the fridge. You can have sparkling water so that you can have bubbles too."

After Matt released Running Deer, he took off down the hall at a run yelling at the top of his voice. "Laura. Laura, Lily is going to be okay."

Diane laughed, and Matt hugged her.

"Diane, after we celebrate with Laura and Running Deer, can we have a private celebration?" Matt whispered to Diane, placing feathery kisses on her ear, chin, and neck.

Matt's kiss was so tender and loving as his lips claimed hers. At that moment, Diane knew she truly loved this man.

Running Deer broke them apart, running to Diane to capture her legs with his arms. "Mommy, I love you like daddy does. Right, Daddy."

Matt eased back from Diane, looking directly into her eyes.

"Yes, son, I love your mommy so very much."

"I love you, Running Deer, as daddy does." Diane squeezed him closer.

Matt leaned forward. He placed a tender kiss on her lips, his seal of love.

Diane could only look up with loving eyes as he pulled back.

Then she whispered reverently, "I love you too, Matt. I have always known in my heart that you were what I wanted. Now, at last, I can tell you."

"Hey, darling, you are stealing my lines."

"No, darling, those were my thoughts that came to me with your kiss. I will soon have good news to share, I think."

Matt's eyes widened. "You mean a baby?"

"I haven't had it confirmed as of yet. But I think so."

Running Deer piped up, "are you going to adopt a baby?

Matt and Diane laughed. Chuckling, Matt said, "no, this baby is mommy and daddy's baby."

"How do you have babies if you don't adopt them?" This was something that Running Deer had never heard before.

Matt started wondering how do I explain babies to Running Deer?

"Saved," he breathed when Laura sailed into the room with the drinks tray. "The celebration is about to begin," pouring the glasses with champagne for Laura and him. "Diane, we better make yours sparkling water." Laura was surprised at this comment but didn't twig to the reason.

"Running Deer, do you want to make the toast?" Matt happily asked.

"Raise your glasses to my sister, Lily. May she come home soon. Also, drink to my new brother or sister, mommy and daddy's new baby."

Laura spouted, "Baby? Diane, are you having a baby?"

"It isn't confirmed yet, but I am happy to say I think so."

"To Lily and Baby," said the voices as they sipped their drinks.

"Now, can we go to the hospital to see Lily?" yelled Running Deer. They all laughed.

"Of course. We should all go celebrate with Lily."

Sadly, Laura said, "sorry, I better get to the office. Work is piling up. Sorry, I can't come with you. I will drop in later to see Lily."

"Thank you for all your help through this, Laura," Diane hugged her.

"Thank you, Laura. You are special, giving up your time to be with us. It was such a big help." Matt added with a hug. "Now, come on, we have to go see Lily."

Everyone scurried around, getting ready.

When they arrived back at the hospital, they quickly went to Lily's room. Quietly, Running Deer tiptoed over to the bed. Lily was sleeping. He picked up her hand and kissed it lovingly.

Lily's eyes popped open. "Running Deer, you are here."

"Yes, I am here. I wanted to see you very much. I broke up the celebration for you that you're getting better because I miss you so much. I had to see you right away."

Matt came up behind him, lifting him onto the bed.

"Be careful with her."

"Yes, Daddy, but can I kiss her cheek?"

Lily smiled at her brother. "I want a kiss."

Running Deer leaned over to kiss her on the cheek. As he started to draw away, Lily turned her head, kissing him on the lips in return.

"Lily, mommy and daddy are going to get a new baby. We will soon have a baby brother or sister. Won't that be exciting?"

Lily's eyes flew to her parents. "Really?"

Quickly, Running Deer replied with a big grin, "yes really.'"

Matt and Diane were smiling proudly. Soon they could take Lily home to be with her family, along with Handsome and Suzette, and the expectation of the arrival of a new baby.

Epilogue

Chapter Twenty-Four

Lily was on the lawn with Running Deer trying to teach the dogs new tricks that they had seen performed on television. The dogs were taking turns trying them out. But mostly, they enjoyed the treats the children enticed them to do the tricks with more.

Suddenly Lily took off running across the lawn. The dogs followed her barking, loudly. Running Deer was laughing, trying to catch up. He was ecstatic that his sister could run freely with him now.

Diane sat under the umbrella on the terrace, with fourteen-month-old baby Sara sitting on her knee, clapping her hands in glee, watching the children and their lawn activities. It was such a pleasure to see Lily enjoying life to the fullest.

Matt stood at the barbeque, supervising the almost ready dinner. The table was set and laden with salads and drinks. The sun was brightly shining, and the day was warm for their outside dinner.

Their house was full of laughter and happiness with this loving family.

Lily and Running Deer were six years old now. Their parents were so proud of them.

Over time, Lily had two operations by specialists. Due to the doctors' tremendous skill, Lily was a whole person now living without braces, and most of the scars had disappeared with the help of plastic surgery. Her left arm was almost as good as new. It had been a sad and hurtful journey for Lily and her family, but the successful healing was over now.

Lily was happy that her life had changed and she could keep up with her brother and the dogs. They spent a lot of time running and jumping together.

The most amazing entity is that Lily suffered a cougar attack and miraculously suffered no lasting trauma that usually accompanies such a disturbing event. She even talks about the sad cougar that was lost. Now her cat collection is spearheaded by the cougar.

Lily was a new person with a bright future with her past life obstacles overturned by God's grace and skillful doctors. The painful journey was eased a bit by her loving parents and Running Deer always at her side. Their love and support saw her through the pain.

Matt called out, "dinner is ready." He gave Diane a grin and Sara a wink. Sara giggled. The proud parents watched their laughing children run up the stairs, trailed by two happy barking dogs.

*****

*Thanks for reading Misfits Anonymous.
You can find my other works on my
website. www.dorothycollins.ca*